MORE MYSTERIES FROM THE
BERKLEY PUBLISHING GROUP . . .

FORREST EVERS MYSTERIES: A former race-car driver solves the high-speed crimes of world-class racing . . . "A Dick Francis on wheels!"
—Jackie Stewart

by Bob Judd

BURN

CURVE

SPIN

FRED VICKERY MYSTERIES: Senior sleuth Fred Vickery has been around long enough to know where the bodies are buried in the small town of Cutler, Colorado . . .

by Sherry Lewis

NO PLACE FOR SECRETS

NO PLACE FOR DEATH

NO PLACE FOR SIN

NO PLACE LIKE HOME

NO PLACE FOR TEARS

INSPECTOR BANKS MYSTERIES: Award-winning British detective fiction at its finest . . . "Robinson's novels are habit-forming!" —*West Coast Review of Books*

by Peter Robinson

THE HANGING VALLEY

WEDNESDAY'S CHILD

GALLOWS VIEW

PAST REASON HATED

FINAL ACCOUNT

INNOCENT GRAVES

JACK McMORROW MYSTERIES: The highly acclaimed series set in a Maine mill town and starring a newspaperman with a knack for crime solving . . . "Gerry Boyle is the genuine article." —Robert B. Parker

by Gerry Boyle

DEADLINE

LIFELINE

BORDERLINE

BLOODLINE

POTSHOT

SCOTLAND YARD MYSTERIES: Featuring Detective Superintendent Duncan Kincaid and his partner, Sergeant Gemma James . . . "Charming!" —*New York Times Book Review*

by Deborah Crombie

A SHARE IN DEATH

LEAVE THE GRAVE GREEN

ALL SHALL BE WELL

MOURN NOT YOUR DEAD

LENNY SCHNEIDER MYSTERIES: "Cross a New York City private detective with a former stand-up comedian, and you get Lenny Schneider." —*Walterville Sunday Sentinel*, [ME].

by Ed Goldberg

SERVED COLD

DEAD AIR

DEAD AIR

Ed Goldberg

BERKLEY PRIME CRIME, NEW YORK

DEAD AIR

A Berkley Prime Crime Book / published by arrangement with the author

PRINTING HISTORY
Berkley Prime Crime edition / May 1998

All rights reserved.
Copyright © 1998 by Ed Goldberg.
This book may not be reproduced in whole or in part,
by mimeograph or any other means, without permission.
For information address: The Berkley Publishing Group,
a member of Penguin Putnam Inc.,
200 Madison Avenue, New York, NY 10016.

The Penguin Putnam Inc. World Wide Web site address is
http://www.penguinputnam.com

ISBN: 0-425-16297-4

Berkley Prime Crime Books are published
by The Berkley Publishing Group,
a member of Penguin Putnam Inc.,
200 Madison Avenue, New York, NY 10016.
The name BERKLEY PRIME CRIME and the BERKLEY PRIME CRIME
design are trademarks belonging to Berkley Publishing Corporation.

PRINTED IN THE UNITED STATES OF AMERICA

10 9 8 7 6 5 4 3 2 1

This book is dedicated to the memory of
Gordon DeMarco—labor organizer,
historian, detective novelist, friend.
Read his books!

Acknowledgments

I would like to thank the following for invaluable assistance in the writing of this book. Thanks to Judith Bieberle, who told me how a real Portland P.I. works; to Julie Vader, former sports and crime writer for *The Oregonian*, who told me how a Portland reporter really works; to Phil Wikelund, John Henley, and everyone else at Great Northwest Bookstore for their unfailing support; to Powell's City of Books, the single best research facility in Portland; to David Keller for his advice on the manuscript; to Patty Vincent, supervisor of the Hollywood Branch Library, who helped me find my murder weapon; to Paul Krassner, from whom I stole a joke; and, of course, to Adele.

one

MANY A TALE'S BEEN TOLD of the men who moil for gold in the land of the midnight sun. But I'm a private investigator; the only buried gold I see is in people's teeth, and where I come from, a "moil" is a guy who does circumcisions.

Last Monday night, I sat cold and uncomfortable, scrunched in the front seat of Bruno's black Buick Riviera. ("Official Staff Car of La Cosa Nostra," he would say, with a piranha grin.) Bruno occupied most of the seat. The springs twanged like out-of-tune guitar strings as he slowly shifted his vast body to a less anguished position. We were just out of range of the cone of light projected by a streetlamp, and his movement in the murky dark reminded me of H. P. Lovecraft's tales of nameless horrors from the bowels of the galaxy slouching through the New England night.

It was the first really cold night of the autumn, and the windows in the big car were steamed. We could have been two teenagers doing underwear inspection for all anyone outside the car knew. Bruno cleaned off a slim area of the windshield every couple of minutes to peer through.

Bruno's large hands clenched and unclenched on the steering wheel. I wondered if he could crush the wheel to polymer dust with a quick squeeze. Not three hours before I had heard him caressing, and there is no better word, Thelonious Monk's "Ruby, My Dear" from the keyboard of a Yamaha grand piano. His long, tapered fingers moved on the keys like ghostly spiders, as the gorgeous love song's melody rode on a string of legato phrases. I remember thinking how these hands looked like they had never done a lick of work. And, in any conventional sense of the words, they had not.

He was capable of lifting grown men with one of these hands, and extinguishing them with rattlesnake suddenness. Yet I would trust him with my life, or any life precious to me.

We were doing a job for a friend for short bread. Just a few bucks for beer and maybe some mussels marinara at Luna's. But it probably wouldn't take more than a night, two at most. And the guy was an old pal, one Weezil Furnham.

Weezil was my homeboy. He himself was capable of wreaking serious harm on another human being, having been a Green Beret in 'Nam, and a mercenary for a few years thereafter. His letters from exotic places had brightened my life, as he fought and screwed his way around the world. It was only recently that he returned to The Apple to inform his friends that he was gay, HIV-positive, and was devoting the time he had remaining to teaching dance with his lover, a Cambodian named Lam. It was then that I realized that Weezil's letters had never been gender-specific about those with whom he danced the horizontal mambo. My straight-male gestalt had done that.

Weezil told me that a couple of gang wanna-bes were hanging around outside a bar, the Eagle's Den, in the east thirties, and hassling, annoying, and lately hitting men entering or leaving the premises. No, not hitting *on* them.

The vermin apparently believed that bashing a few queers would establish their bona fides with their social betters. Weezil himself had renounced violence in renouncing his old life, and asked me if I could help. When he offered me money, I opted for the food and beer. I called in Bruno as my consultant, and we devised a simple but elegant plan. Hence our vigil in the frigid Buick, staking out the aforementioned.

Around about midnight, three burly young men sidled to within a few yards of the entrance to the bar. Like a half-sleeping crocodile, Bruno opened one eye to survey the scene. The rag squeaked on the frosty windshield as he cleared a spot. Groups like this had hovered around and entered the bar on several occasions, but Bruno's preternaturally tweaked instincts caused him to take more than casual notice. He raised a small pair of binoculars to his eyes, and then gently touched my sleeve.

"Lenny, you awake?" he whispered.

"Yo. Whaddaya got?"

"Dose t'ree dudes off to the left. Got shaved heads under dem baseball caps."

"Yeah? So?"

He shifted forward slightly and squinted through the glasses.

"Big one in the back got a gang tattoo on his neck. You can just see it over his collar."

I stretched and yawned, at least partially from nerves.

"Ready?" I asked.

He nodded, and slowly opened the driver's side door after flipping off the overhead light. Making as little noise or movement as possible, we exited the car, staying outside the area lit by the streetlight.

Bruno touched my shoulder. I looked over at his vastness, draped in black like some King Kong ninja. He made a gesture with his head, and a small motion with his hand. I nodded. Then, he was gone, as though 6'5" of bone, sinew, and muscle had suddenly been transformed into vapor and risen silently into the gloomy sky. I hunched my shoulders and began walking toward the bar.

I crossed the street and headed for the bar entrance. One of the toughs said in a quiet voice, "Hey, you a faggot?"

I stopped, and turned toward them. They were in shadow, and it was difficult to distinguish who was speaking.

"Why? You need a date for the prom?" New Yorkers like to answer questions with other questions.

Snickers from one of them. The voice said, "You a fuckin' wise guy?"

I said, "You sure ask a lot of stupid questions."

They began to move toward me. I backed up a step or two, and they spread out across the sidewalk, still moving toward me. I reached into my pocket for my French blackjack, a gift from Weezil. It was a bag of lead buckshot attached to a spring-steel handle, and all covered in chic black leather. Very snazzy. I continued to back up slowly.

Meanwhile, they were arraying themselves in dog-pack formation, with two closing in on my flanks, while the top dog hung back for the kill. The galoots on either side of me began to reach for me, a kind of stupid blood lust visible on their faces even in the dim light. The guy in the middle gave me a little smile and hummed a tuneless dirge.

I short-circuited their strategy by rushing the middle guy and performing rhinoplasty on him with the sap. He howled in surprise and pain, and raised his hands to his nose, which was running rills of blood. With his hands up to his face, I was free to gut-punch him.

His buddies froze in place, like in a game of Statues, but recovered themselves and were about to step in, when the one on the left suddenly seemed to be doing a dive. Actually, Bruno had grabbed him by the ankles from behind and flipped him over on his face, which made a sickening crunch on the sidewalk. Bruno then stepped over the prostrate lug toward the last guy, to my right, who by this time had gone chalk-white, and pissed in his camouflage pants.

When my victim saw Bruno perform, he forgot his smashed hooter and took off down the street, screaming like a goosed banshee. Bruno grabbed the remaining kid and threw him against the corner of the brick building the bar was in. The brick's sharp edge opened the back of the lug's head, and blood began trickling down his neck.

I stepped over to him. "Listen, scumwad, one of your friends is trying to set a land speed record for the Jersey swamps, and this one here," I gestured at the unmoving form on the sidewalk, "is gonna look like a Pekingese the rest of his life. I don't know what your problem is, and I don't give a shit. Stay away from this bar, and every other bar like it. If I catch you fag-bashing once more, I'll turn you over to my friend here to be his sex slave."

Bruno leered, licked his lips, and cracked his enormous knuckles. The kid's eyes rolled back in his head. I thought he was going to faint. I grabbed his lapel and brandished the blackjack.

"Now get this garbage off the street and get outta here! *Capice?*"

He hesitated for an instant. "Bruno," I said, "maybe he's like one of those eight balls, and you gotta turn him upside down to get an answer."

Bruno lunged forward. The punk shrieked. He picked up his buddy and tried to run, half-dragging and half-carrying him, until they were out of sight. There was blood and pieces of several teeth on the sidewalk where his buddy's face used to be.

"Hey, Bruno, wanna get a beer?"

We walked inside, and the whole bar, maybe a hundred guys and a few women, gave us a standing ovation.

Weezil walked up.

"You were great! We got the whole thing on video."

Bruno smiled slightly and drawled, "I hope youse got my good side." He threw us a profile.

The bar closed officially at two A.M. At about three-thirty, the Official Barbara Bush Drag Contest commenced: nine or ten middle-aged men wearing white fright wigs and pearls, sashaying across the floor in their Sophie Tucker-sized evening gowns, and doing variations on the "rhymes-with-witch" theme. One of them even had a passable stand-in for Millie. A male, natch. The music was "Don't Worry—Be Happy."

We were there until about seven-thirty that morning, drinking, singing songs, and sampling bizarre chemicals and herbs smuggled in from foreign jungles. I haven't had so much fun since I was a hippie. Bruno and I considered the job paid in full.

Good old Bruno. Once only a sometime presence in my life, he had become an unofficial associate and as much a friend as he was capable of. He's the one that clued me in on the vulnerability of the nose in dealing with an opponent who wishes to do you harm. Every trick he ever showed me has worked in a hairy situation.

This doesn't have much to do with what comes next. Well, a little. But it was fun, and I hadn't been having much lately. It was the early autumn of my discontent, made glorious summer, however briefly, by this son of New York. Which is why my week is worth talking about.

Quite a week it was. Seismic rumblings in my personal life, and my love life; a visit from a living baseball card with a heartbreaking story; and death in the Northwest. As usual, I'm getting ahead of myself.

Suffice it to say that a few days after the incident at the Eagle's Den bar, I was on a plane for Portland, Oregon, and trying to sort it all out. Don't forget the Dramamine.

two

So, here I was on a plane waiting to take off for Portland. Flying is not one of my favorite things to do, but I don't mind it for vacations, or if I'm getting paid to do it. This was on the clock, trying to locate . . .

I'm getting ahead of myself again. The week has been like this. It's a metaphor for my life: periods of stasis punctuated by spasms of too much activity. But airplanes do this to me, make me think about anything but that I'm in a metal tube which can not fly in any real universe. The flight attendant has just announced that we're next in the takeoff queue, meaning that we have fifteen minutes to all night to wait.

So, since I can't order a drink, I'll ruminate.

The plane began to taxi, and my gut began to do the hokeypokey. Once we're in the air, flying is no different from a bus ride. Takeoffs and landings scare the hell out of me, causing me to break cold sweat and suffer light-headedness. I tightened the seat belt to tourniquet-snug and gripped the armrests until my fingertips got numb.

If we didn't take off soon, I would pass out just from my precautions. The guy next to me was already taking out his calculator and analysis pad, although he darted a surreptitious look at me when he could. He acted as if it didn't matter that we could suddenly be singed off the mortal coil in an extravagance of flaming jet fuel. My shirt collar was damp, and things were getting dim.

The engines screamed in a hysterical attempt to lift off the metal monster, and the pilot pulled back on the stick. Within a second of the engines failing and hurtling us into a fatal inferno, we left the ground, the plane began to climb effortlessly, and my hands began to cramp, indicating that I had returned to a "normal" state. I never really relax on airplanes.

Over the intercom, a female voice told us that we were on our way to Portland, would achieve an altitude of 36,000 feet, and probably be right on time. Beverage service would begin shortly, dinner would be served in a couple of hours, and we would have a movie.

I was calming down sufficiently to loosen my seat belt a bit. Going over the last week, I realized that I was entering my winter doldrums, anyway. The first really dank November day was Tuesday, the day after the bar incident, and the day it all began.

I remembered hauling my sorry butt up the stairs of the Union Square subway station that morning, having had no sleep, and noting with displeasure the unmistakable signs that winter was breaking and entering. The streets were damp with a slow, freezing rain that became deadly slick on any metal surface.

I hate winter. It's too damn cold, so you have to wear too many clothes, and the precipitation is always a drag. Don't tell me how beautiful snow is. It's beautiful for about half an hour, until it turns into filthy slush and hangs around the streets getting dirtier until it melts, or gets covered over by the next miserable batch.

I stopped at a newsstand to peruse the various choices. Should I buy a *Downbeat*, maybe a *Newsweek*?

My reverie was interrupted by the phlegmy voice of the impatient proprietor, a toad-like apparition, the stump of a cheap cigar sticking out of the corner of a wide mouth set into his grizzled and unshaven jaw. "Hey, *schmuck*," he inquired sweetly, "whaddaya read?"

"Keep your shirt on, *putz*. Princess Di comin' for tea? You got pressing matters at the U.N.?" I picked up the *Downbeat* and threw down three bucks. "Keep the change. Maybe you can save up for a personality transplant." It wasn't just the cold that frosted me.

I walked east on 14th Street and stopped for the light. I turned to look back at the news churl, thinking we could exchange dirty looks until the light changed. As I watched, a crazy kid on a skateboard slammed into the newsstand, sending the carefully piled magazines onto the wet sidewalk. A sudden flush of joy went through me. There was some German word for joy at someone else's misfortune, *schadenfreude*? With an *umlaut* somewhere? I don't remember. God, what an ogre I was becoming. Maybe it was the encroaching winter, or the bad attitudes, or who knows what?

I crossed the street and walked with my shoulders hunched, trying to turtle my head into my coat. I shivered with relief as I approached the storefront facade of my office building, and entered.

The decrepit structure seemed more than usually grim, decorated as it was by lacy icicles. But my perception may have been colored by the mood I was working up. To me, the prevalent state of mind for humans should be a warm glow. Life is good. Bad feelings are abnormal, and should be examined for clues on how to blow them off.

The normal state of mind for pseudointellectuals like myself is depression, with every happy thought giving rise to a kind of existential terror. Not for me.

Anyway, the dank, dark, mildewed entrance hall with the unswept staircase created the perfect atmosphere for a reassessment of my worldview, i.e., if I didn't get my mental house in order, it could wind up looking like this hallway. Figuratively speaking, of course. I walked up the stairs to my floor and straight over to Yvonne's door, passing Feinbaum's empty office.

The place hasn't been the same since old man Feinbaum died. Feinbaum's Love Link had gotten famous in latter years, after it was featured in a *New York Times* piece. It turned out that old Feinbaum actually had a terrific record as a matchmaker. The mayor even threw a party for Feinbaum, and invited everyone who had been fixed up by the old man to attend. Hundreds of people showed up. This included the mayor's cousin Sheldon, who drooled and was flatulent. Feinbaum paired him with a slightly older widow who drooled a bit herself and had lost her sense of smell in an industrial accident.

No progeny had been brought into Feinbaum's business because, as it turned out, the old man had himself been a bachelor. So the love link was shattered. The office remained unrented, the legend on the pebbled glass door serving as a kind of epitaph.

FEINBAUM'S LOVE LINK, it read in gold lettering, PATHWAY TO YOUR HEART'S DESIRE, CREDIT CARDS ACCEPTED. What a romantic that old bird was.

Yvonne's door read, MADAME YVONNE, PALM READER, CHANNEL TO THE ULTIMATE REALITY, BASEBALL SCORES ON REQUEST (IN SEASON ONLY). She changed this, or pieces of it, as the spirit or spirits moved her. In my memory, she had never successfully predicted a baseball score, although she got half of one once. The Dodgers did indeed score seven runs, but Atlanta scored twelve, not three, as Yvonne had intuited. I lost ten bucks to Mishkin on that one.

Yvonne's longtime lover Arletta had the office next door. Her door read, SISTER ARLETTA, TAROT READER, DIVINER OF THE ETERNAL MYSTERIES, AND TWO-WAY STREET TO THE SPIRIT WORLD, as it had for years. This was indicative of one of the many differences between them. Yvonne was mercurial and effusive, Arletta conservative and loath to make quick changes.

"Conservative" must be taken in context, because in most

things Arletta was a radical. She would certainly have overthrown the U.S. government in a heartbeat.

I was temperamentally inclined more to Yvonne, because she was crazy, a former psychedelic ranger, and had never grown past her poor, Lower-East-Side-Yid-childhood attitudes about most things. "Most things," she once told me, "eat shit." She also had a vicious sense of humor, and could still describe in detail baseball games she had seen in 1934. Unless she was making it all up.

I knocked. "Yeah?" she croaked from the other side.

"Yvonne, it's me. Got a minute?"

I heard her shuffling inside. She opened the door. She was wearing thrift shop rags apparently discarded by drag queens with questionable taste. Her makeup stopped just this side of qualifying as Special Effects. She said, "For you I got thirty seconds. Talk."

"Aren't you gonna let me in, you old harridan? All you're doing is reading *Penthouse*, anyway."

Her eyebrows shot to her hairline. "How the hell did you know? Oh, yeah. You're Sherlock fucking Holmes. Did you ever read the letters in this magazine? Do people really *shtup* on speeding motorcycles?"

She ushered me to a chair, and sat behind her massive wooden desk, decorated with a crystal ball, a human skull (which she claims she found in a bus station locker, and in New York this might be so) sporting a dripping black candle, and a *Penthouse* magazine opened to reveal its usual low-fashion gynecology.

"How's business?" I opened neutrally.

"If I got time to talk to you, it stinks. Now, get to the point. I got a date with a two-dimensional coed." She gestured toward the magazine.

"Christ, Yvonne, aren't you getting enough at home? You gotta poison what's left of your mind with soft-core porn?"

"Hey, *schmendrick*, what are you, a social worker? Arletta and me are doin' fine. I just like to look at the young stuff. Don't tell me *you* never buy stroke books." She glowered.

"Okay. Touché. I'm just surprised that a woman of your age . . ."

"Never mind my fuckin' age. Are you here for something? This hygiene lecture is from hunger."

I sighed. "Well, truthfully, I came here for a friendly face and some witty banter. The weather is depressing, and people are working themselves into their annual foul holiday spirit." I put on my best hurt voice. "I was *hoping* that I could get a kind word from you."

She showed me a gnarled, be-ringed, and vertically extended middle finger. "Sit on this and rotate, whiner. No, seriously," she sighed, "I'm *kvetchy* because of the weather, too. I had a fight with Arletta this morning over *nothin'*. My fault. So, I'm moping. I like to check out the snatch mags when I feel this way."

Then, suddenly, "Gimme your hand."

I complied. She turned it over to see the back as well as the palm. She studied the palm for about a minute, occasionally touching something or tracing a line with one of her talons.

"Been bugged lately about something." It was a statement more than a question, but I nodded anyway.

"Okay. There's gonna be a surprise for you soon. Maybe today. And," she looked up at me and said archly, "you're gonna take a long journey over land."

I laughed. "Yeah, and I'll meet a tall stranger who'll remove my shorts."

"Hmph! Yeah, well, you got the tall stranger part right, but what he does with your shorts is your business as a consenting adult. Now, get outta here and leave me to consort with Tiffany Gluckstern here."

I rose. "You're putting me on. Is her name really Tiffany Gluckstern?"

"Yeah. All but the 'Gluckstern' part."

I waved good-bye. She picked up the magazine and waved a close-up of Tiffany's privates at me.

So, here I was taking a long journey over land. Actually, she was right about the tall stranger, too.

I sat back, ordered a Bloody Mary when the flight attendant asked, the beer selections being dismal, and contemplated my navel and my novel by turns. My navel was linty and devoid of enlightenment, and the novel was a techno-thriller that was long on hardware and short on insight. The Bloody Mary was fine.

I stared at the back of someone's head, trying to will him to turn around. I played eyeball games across the aisle with an attractive middle-aged woman dressed in a severe business suit. I riffled through the in-flight magazine. I fidgeted. The guy next to me in the window seat was deeply absorbed in a production report, and responded to my attempts at conversation with barely polite monosyllables that invited no further contact. Why get a window seat, if all you're going to do is read the production figures from the plant in Dismal Seepage, Ohio?

I love flying. I had another Bloody Mary.

The tall stranger was the reason I was on this plane, sucking down drinks. I met him right after I left Yvonne's office. I went and sat in my office suddenly feeling good for no discernible reason, unless my session with the Channel to the Ultimate Reality had actually helped. I started opening mail absently, as my mind drifted into a daydream of lubricity with a movie star who caused a sensation in one of her movies by writhing all over a piano while she sang. Just as I was about to demonstrate one of my more arcane sexual techniques, there came a knock at my door. Snapping out of it I lazily called, "C'mon in."

There entered a tall man (aha!) in late middle age, silver-haired, but erect and showing only the first signs of a spare tire. He was dressed in expensive casual clothes. His face was a bit leathery, with crinkles around his eyes. His eyes were a vivid grey, a bit too dark to be described as "icy," and clear. I motioned him to my new visitor's chair (recently purchased from the *goniff* downstairs, as my partner Mickey continued to spruce up the office).

He moved easily, with grace, and sat with both feet flat on the floor, and his hands on his knees like the Lincoln Memorial. I rose slightly and extended my hand.

"Hi. I'm Lenny Schneider. What can I do for you?"

His hand was large, fingers strong and tapered, veins and knuckles prominent as though he had labored for his living, but smooth and well cared for. He had manicured nails. He shook firmly.

And he looked awfully familiar.

"Mr. Schneider, my name is Elwin Rowan. I need the help of a private detective, and your name came up when I asked around."

His voice retained the rhythms of the South but had the edge of a man who had spent many years in New York. I squinted for a second, running his name and face through my mind. *Voilà!*

"Pardon me," I asked, "but are you Deacon Rowan? Did you pitch for the Dodgers?"

He nodded.

Without further preamble, I began to rummage around in my desk drawer. I retrieved a fresh baseball from a box of a dozen and proffered it to him. He took it and began to pat his pockets for a pen.

"Here, use mine." I handed him a ballpoint.

Suddenly, my rude behavior shamed me. "Oh, gosh, I'm sorry. It's just that I saw you pitch at Ebbets, and . . . Please forgive me."

He signed the ball, handed it and the pen back, and smiled.

"Actually, I'm happy to do it. No one's recognized me in a long time."

"Mr. Rowan . . ."

"Call me Deak," he interjected.

I blushed. "Deak, I thought you were great. Sure, there was Erskine and Newcombe, and all. But you . . . Man, I saw you pitch one game in '57, you didn't throw a fastball all game. Change-ups, at least two kindsa curveballs, sliders. Everything off-speed. What a gem. The Brooks only got two runs, I think Roberts was pitching, but that's all they needed. No runs on maybe six hits for the Phils. Beautiful."

He beamed. "Yeah. I remember that one myself. The reason you didn't see no fastballs is I couldn't throw 'em no more. Hell, my arm couldn't handle the breaking stuff after that season. It was wore out, and so was I. Shit, I got into organized ball in '39, with the old Sally League. The soup bone was played out."

"Now I remember. You didn't go to L.A. with the team."

"Right. I pitched mostly relief that last season in Brooklyn. Couldn't work up a decent start, but one or two. You saw the best one. When the team left, they wanted to trade me to the Senators for some kid shortstop. I retired. Couldn't see myself bustin' hump for Washington in 95-degree heat, and havin' Mantle rattle the fences with my pitches. I quit. I opened a heating and cooling repair business with my brother-in-law. He was a refrigeration mechanic, and I could fix about anything with a motor. Had to when I was a kid on the farm."

"You look great." He looked great.

"Well, I try to keep fit. I go to the gym, play some racquetball, tennis. I play in a over-sixty softball league. Fast pitch. None of that eephus, slow-pitch bullshit. I do okay. I'm an outfielder now. My peg is still good enough to hit the cutoff man, and hittin' against Maglie and Spahnie all those years . . . Hell, softball looks like the Goodyear blimp. Hit .340 last season."

The pride still showed. A major-leaguer all the way.

"What can I do for you, Mr., uh, Deak?"

"I want you to find my daughter."

"How long has she been missing?"

He shifted in his seat, and clasped his hands together. "Well, she ain't exactly missing. I know just where she is."

"Okay. Where is she?"

"Portland, Oregon."

"When was the last time you heard from her?"

"About three years ago."

"Well, then, how do you know she's still in Portland?"

"'Cause she's dead."

I recovered myself after a moment. I looked over at him, and he looked at my eyes. The pain was evident.

"Forgive me, Deak, but you'll have to explain."

He nodded. "Sure. My girl Sophie was named after my mother. She was the last of my four kids, and a terror. Tomboy, always in trouble. You know. Good in school, though. Marge, my wife, and me always thought she would go to college. She got mixed up with this guy who went to her high school over in Jersey. We been livin' in Jersey since about 1960.

"So, she got involved with this guy, Donnie Kimmel. She almost didn't graduate from high school, forget college. Basically, she gave up everything for him."

"What was it? Dope? Gang stuff?"

"Worse. He's a sumbitch ballplayer. Pitched and played outfield on the high-school team. Got looked over pretty good by the scouts. Right outta school he signed with a major league organization as a left fielder. Went from the rookie league right up to double-A in Florida. Come winter, he would head down to Central America somewhere. Sophie followed him everywhere."

"Couldn't you convince her to come visit you in the off-season, even for a while?"

He pursed his lips, and shuffled in his seat.

"Well, the boy and me had a fallin'-out, 'cause of her not goin' to college. Almost came to punches. He wouldn't let her see us. I couldn't figure out how a tough little monkey like her let him order her around.

"Anyway, about four years ago, he got moved up to Portland, in the PCL. Triple-A. He was on the verge of goin' to the bigs. Hit .324 in Double-A, stole a buncha bases. His first year in Portland, he was battin' over .300, was gettin' a lotta RBIs, stole more bases. They figured, maybe one more year in Triple-A, he was gonna get a shot in The Show."

He paused, and spaced out a little.

"What happened?" I asked.

He cleared his throat.

"One night, after the season was over, he smashed up their car. His shoulder was wrecked. Destroyed. He's held together by wire, I hear. She died. I got all this from the Portland cops. He never even called us.

"I wanna know where my little girl is buried. I'd like to bring her home to our family plot."

I rubbed my chin. I didn't quite know what to say, so I fell back on business.

"Deak, my fee is $350 per day, plus expenses. Any unusual expenses will be cleared with you first. I've never been to Portland, so I have no idea how long this will take. Maybe I'll have a better idea after I get there. Anyway, I'll call you to keep you informed, daily if you like."

He nodded. "Yup."

"Do you still have the names of any cops in Portland? They would be the logical starting place."

"Matter of fact, I got it right here."

He handed me a much-refolded paper, which had been torn from a steno pad. There were two names written on it.

"When can you start?"

Of course, I had no time at all. But for him I'd work something out.

"How about day after tomorrow, or so? I'll book a flight. Oh, and please call me Lenny."

He got up slowly, unfolding like a carpenter's rule, and offered his hand.

"Lenny, I want you to realize that this is so important to me that I'm willing to go broke over it. I ain't afraid to be broke even at my age. I just want my little girl back."

"Deak, I'll do this for nothing for you."

He smiled with real affection.

"Shit, boy. Never work for nothin'. I wouldn't throw

horseshit at an umpire for no pay. Well, maybe at an umpire, but just once."

I got his home number, some other pertinent details, and he gave me a thousand-dollar cash retainer. Mickey passed him, coming in as he left.

That started a whole other round of troubles.

The plane's engines had settled into a loud hum. I swilled my thinning drink, ice shards rattling in the plastic glass, looked out the window at the clouds and thought about Mickey's reaction to Deak Rowan.

She had flashed me a questioning look and gestured toward him with her head.

"Deacon Rowan," I replied.

Her eyes got big. "*The* Deacon Rowan? The old Dodger pitcher?"

"The same."

"Jeez, he looks real good. What'd he want?"

I gave her the *Reader's Digest* condensation.

Her forehead wrinkled with concern. "Did you take the case?" she asked.

"Damn right."

"Len-n-n-ny!" She drew my name out really long, like a whining kid.

"Yeah?"

"Do you know what your calendar looks like?"

"Sure. Little rectangular thing with boxes on it. Got numbers in the boxes."

She made a wicked face. "Seriously! I hope you told him you would get to it sometime in the spring."

I squirmed a bit. "Um, well, actually, I told him more like day after tomorrow."

"Goddamn it, Lenny! You've got solid work for the next six or seven weeks. You had better be able to do it after hours."

I squirmed some more. "Okay, it's like this. I have to go out to Portland, Oregon."

She smacked her forehead.

"Careful," I offered, "you'll give yourself a headache."

"You're the only headache I need. Do you think I bust my ass for nothing around here? You never *had* this much work before I joined you." She was really getting hot. The color was rising in her face. I watched as it met her red hairline.

I paused. I wanted to say this as rationally as possible, under the circumstances. It had been in my mind for a while, and I didn't want her to go off like a Roman candle. I cleared my throat.

"No, I *don't* think you bust your ass for nothing. I think you bust your ass for fifty percent of the profits. My calendar used to be a lot skimpier, but it used to be fun sometimes, too. All I get these days is the grunt jobs, lightweight body guarding, all the dull crap. I sometimes wonder whether you turn away the good stuff on purpose. Well, I'm sure you can find someone to do this while I'm gone. Truthfully, I'm glad to be going out there. I hear that it's real nice, and I can use the time away from this salt mine!"

Her face registered shock and outrage, her fists clenched and unclenched. She stuck her finger in my face.

"Damn you, you ungrateful shit! You don't remember how it was, do you? I hired people to do the dangerous stuff. I used to lose sleep because I never knew what was happening to you from day to day. I tried to make you into a businessman, and leave all the cowboy crap for the help. I tried to make you into a *mensch*, instead of a . . ."

She began to unravel here, from rage and I don't know what else. Our romantic relationship had suffered as our partnership had flourished. When we saw each other socially, all she talked about was the business. She often put in late hours, and more than a few weekends. Hell, last year we never even got to see a ball game together. I snuck in a few while she was putting in overtime.

Worse, our tender, active sex life had deteriorated to a perfunctory occasional coupling. She was beginning to remind me of Faye Dunaway in *Network*, quoting Arbitron ratings to William Holden while she was boffing him.

Naturally, I didn't tell her any of this. Instead, I put on my quiet and apologetic voice.

"Mickey, listen. I really have to get away, and this is the perfect opportunity for a working vacation. I don't mind telling you that you could use some time off yourself."

Now she got hot.

"Don't tell me what I need, you son of a bitch! I've got just what I need, a boyfriend who's asking for a separate vacation! Maybe your bitch ex-wife is going with you, huh? Well, the two of you can go straight to hell, for all I care!"

She turned and sped out of my office, slamming every door she went through. I *was* going to suggest that she come with me to Portland, but she would never believe that now.

It got worse the next day, but I didn't want to think about that now. I undid my seat belt, got up and walked back to the bathroom. There was a line four long at each of the two heads. I decided, "To hell with it," and made my way back to my seat, slowing deliberately when I spotted the businesswoman. She was curled up on her seat covered with one of those ridiculous little airline blankets. Her shoes were off, and her stockinged feet protruded ever so slightly beyond the hem of the blanket. She looked so adorable I wanted to tuck her in, but I didn't need the lawsuit.

I sat back down in my seat, careful not to disturb the drudge with the calculator. I recalled kneading my face with my hands for a while, as I sat in my office after the fight with Mickey, and then grabbing a cab for Dirty Ernie's. I needed the juice of one keg of beer.

When I got downtown the temperature had dropped, and the precip was now small but relentless snowflakes. It seemed like there might be a real snowstorm cranking up. I paid the cabbie, and ran into Ernie's to avoid contamination from the weather.

The place was nearly empty, with just a back booth holding a couple of late lunchers hunched over the dregs of some wine. They leaned toward each other conspiratorially, like a couple of Haymarket anarchists.

Ernie was in post-lunch mode, but he noticed me come in, and dug my mood. That's why I was here. Ernie and I had known each other since . . . I forget when. His role as my bartender, i.e., confessor/advisor/dispenser of fermented absolution, was enhanced by his genuine compassion and his deep knowledge of my life. He knew me well. He could tell when I was miserable.

"Hey, Lenny! What's up? You look miserable."

"Thanks, Ernie," I replied. "You look unwholesome as usual."

"The wages of sin, my boy, is the living death you see before you. I got some new beer on draft. It's pretty good."

"Hit me."

Ernie ambled over to the taps. He pulled one that said "Full Sail Amber Ale." It was a very satisfying brown color. I took a sip from the pint glass.

"Hey, this is good! Where's it from?"

"Portland, Oregon. The new mecca of beer worshipers. I also got a nice porter. But enough about this. What's eatin' you?"

I sighed. "Ernie, never go into business with someone you love."

He shrugged. "Helga and me have been in this bar for more than twenty years, and we're doin' fine."

I stroked my beard and contemplated this datum. "Yeah, well, you two are exceptional people. I guess that I don't have your gift for relationships."

"Bullshit," he rejoined, "we got to this state of bliss by workin' out the bugs little by little. We coulda killed each other a coupla times. What you need to decide is whether the business or the woman is what matters, and by how much. Then, each time somethin' comes up, you got a way to figure out how important it is." He shrugged. "Sooner or later, nothing seems so important that it should break up the partnership, or the marriage."

"Ernie, the Zen masters say that each human being can be your teacher. They must have been thinking of you when they said that."

He shrugged again. "All those years of watchin' *Kung Fu* on TV, *somethin'* had to sink in. You wanna talk about it?"

I drank the ale, ordered a rare burger and a salad, and had a Black Butte porter for dessert. Porter is wonderful—ale that tastes like chocolate. Ernie hovered around, both from concern and from lack of other business. I decided to open up to him.

"Look," I began, "you know business has never mattered much to me. I do what I do simply to pay the freight. Ambition and me parted company long ago. When I met Mickey, she was a widow. Lost her husband and son in one swell foop."

Ernie nodded. "Yeah, I remember."

"She had been an elementary school teacher, but she didn't want to do that anymore. Goffin, her old man, is an entrepreneur. He's started and lost a couple of businesses, but he learned something every time. Finally, he opened the millinery factory I met him in.

"Get this. When I first saw him, he was being chewed out by some *jiboney*. I thought the guy was his boss. Turns out, Goffin hired the guy to run the operation so that he could stick to production, which he likes best. So, even though the guy is listed as company president, he really works for Goffin."

Ernie smiled. "The old man's a character."

"Big time. But I love him. A better-hearted person doesn't exist, unless maybe it's Helga." Ernie bowed slightly, but we both knew that this observation was more than a mere courtesy.

"Well," I went on, "Mickey has a lot of her father's business ability. She came into my disorderly, undercapital-ized, and seedy detective agency and, before long, we've got bread-and-butter accounts, a list of reliable casual employees, an ad in the yellow pages. . . . Ernie, I sometimes feel like I've become redundant in my own business."

"Sort of like, your name's on the door, but she really owns the company?" He permitted himself a wry smile.

"Yeah," I sighed. "A lot like that. I'm simply the only full-time employee besides her. But it gets worse. We used to have a real nice relationship. That's about gone. She never liked Sue, but Sue and I haven't had anything going for a while, certainly not since I hooked up with Mickey. But Mickey's jealous of Sue, for some damn reason."

Ernie assumed his best ironic look, one eyebrow upraised.

"Oh, a woman who doesn't like your ex-wife? That's novel."

"You've noticed that, too, eh? There isn't a man in the world Sue couldn't turn into a zombie in a couple of hours, but she sees all other women as threats, rivals, who knows? Unless, of course, it's in her interest to make nice with some other female.

"But you know, Ernie, Sue is smart and intuitive, and she's been more of a help than I'd comfortably admit to most people. And she's funny and has a nasty mouth. So, for many reasons, I'm not about to shit-can almost thirty years of history with Sue because Mickey's insecure."

Ernie rubbed his chin. "The Chinese character for 'trouble' is two women under one roof."

"Very droll, Ern. But we all have separate residences."

"What you need, Schneider, is separate continents."

I went on about my discontent for a while, with sympathetic noises from Ernie as punctuation. I told him about the Rowan job, and he was about to comment when Mishnik walked in with a couple of his disciples. They were arguing loudly about whether fusion was jazz at all. Mishnik, ever the purist, held that, like a mule, fusion was a sterile hybrid with no hope of stylistic issue, unless you counted pop-jazz "Fuzak" or New Age, and he made gagging gestures as he mentioned each. Then he took off on Keith Jarrett for sinking noodling to a new depth in his Köln concert and being the spiritual father of New Age.

"You know what you get when you play New Age music backwards?" He paused. "New Age music!" Mishnik was on the verge of popping a blood vessel.

Ernie excused himself to shush the group and get their drink orders. I finished my porter and went home, the better to contemplate the throbbing welt on my psyche. By the time I got home, Ernie's soothing talk, and even more soothing new ales, had put me in a mellow mood.

It was an odd thing, Portland, Oregon, suddenly looming in my life. It occurred to me as I crunched the ice shards at the bottom of my drink, annoying the number cruncher in the next seat. This kind of thing happens from time to time, the Powers That Be waving a flag. I wondered if it had any real significance. I returned to the pages of the novel.

Just as the book was starting to get interesting, and the hero was having virtual sex with a set of Siamese triplets, the pilot clicked on the intercom and drawled, "If you can see down through the thin clouds, you'll notice that the roads are laid out perpendicular, north to south, and east to west. They are a mile apart, so each square bounded by the roads is a square mile. For some reason, that's the way they've done it here in the Midwest."

Probably for the sheer excitement of it, I thought. The pilot sounded just like every other pilot I'd ever heard. I think part of their training includes the Chuck Yeager school of famous announcers. I dozed.

When I awoke, they were serving what is regarded in some circles as food. Next to me, Dismal Seepage was deep into a double scotch, and was working on adding some furrows to his brow. I stretched as much as possible in the seat and tried a tentative smile at him. His return look reminded me of the face on the iodine bottle, so I backed off. I wondered if I had snored in my sleep, or committed some other unacceptable act.

The flight attendant sidled up to my seat and gave me a

choice. Dinner was either chicken cordon bleu, or filet of sole almandine, or lasagna. I chose the lasagna, because it's always the fish that kills you in airplane disaster flicks, because what's a "cordon bleu" anyway?, and because I used to be able to eat canned macaroni. How much worse could this be? Actually, it tasted fine, but I kept a sample so the toxicology lab would have something to test.

As they were clearing away the trays, they started the movie. It cost more for the headphones than I had paid to see it in New York. Plus, they had edited out all the naked women. I spent the next hour trying to figure out whether airline food was a metaphor for airline movies, or vice versa.

The movie wasn't enough to hold my attention, the book was beginning to pall, and the nifty-looking woman across the aisle was still sleeping. So I continued running over the week's events.

The morning after my fight with Mickey, I attempted to get myself organized for the trip. I ran out for a quick breakfast at the Old Kiev and a *shmooze* with a Russian émigré who claimed to be Trotsky's love child. A bit skeptical, I asked him about the Theory of Permanent Revolution. He bristled. "I am his bastard, not his apostle!" I begged a thousand pardons, and escaped into the comparatively friendly streets of the Lower East Side.

The frigid air had warmed up enough to fill with a kind of freezing fog, somehow more substantial than fog generally is, and harder to see through. It was a good thing that I didn't have far to go. I hate most of winter's gelid manifestations, and this was a new one, a "fresh hell" as the sainted Dotty Parker would say. I hoped that global warming had kicked in in Oregon.

When I got back to the apartment, a situation assessment seemed in order. Most of my packing was done. I purchased my ticket by phone, and had it delivered to the office, where I would pick it up later. I needed to call Uncle Sol to touch base with him.

Sol was Mickey's uncle, and the reason we met. I was

hired to try to prevent Sol from taking his revenge on a Nazi
camp guard he had seen in good ol' New York. I failed
miserably, in the sense of performing this duty to expectations, but succeeded in keeping both me and the old guy
alive. Mostly. Since then, the old man had become my
unofficial surrogate grandpa, and I used him for legwork
from time to time to keep his mind active.

I rang Sol's apartment and, to my amazement, got an
answering machine. Sol's European-accented voice told me:
"Listen, if you hear this, I ain't here. Unless you're a
burglar. Then, maybe I'm here, but maybe I'm in the can
with *The New York Times*. So, you don't know. If you try to
break in, you'll be asking for trouble. So, don't be a bum.
Get a job and I'll buy you a coffee and Danish. Just don't
ask for no 'latte.' Plain coffee, like a regular person.

"So, you talk already." *Beeeep*.

So, I talked. "Uncle Sol, this is Lenny. I need to ask
you . . ." Sol picked up.

"*Nu, boychik*, how's the *baytzim*?"

"Sol, what are you doing now, screening calls?"

"Nah, watching Sally Jesse and toasting a bialy. They got
some guy on here who says dogs come from another galaxy.
He's got pictures."

"You need more to do. I got a question to ask."

"*Zug mir.*" I heard a toaster spring up in the background.

"What's up with Mickey? Is she pissed at me for some
reason?"

His voice suddenly became arch and teasing. "Say,
tattele, Mickey called me last night. Twenty minutes she did
nothing but *kvetch* about you. Oy, what she wished on you
should happen to Farrakhan! So, you're going to visit the
lumberjacks in the woods?"

"It's so nice that she feels able to share her feelings. I'm
going to Portland to track down the grave of a dead girl, a
young woman, really. Her father wants to have her moved
to the family plot. It's a long story. And, I just need to get

away. I'm not having any fun anymore. I need a change of scene."

"Hey, if God wanted you to have fun, you'd be born with a whoopee cushion stuck to your tush. Look, I don't give you much in the way of free advice, but Mickey's got a few things on her mind. Be a good boy and talk to her." I could hear the scraping of cream cheese being applied to a toasted bialy.

"Sure, Uncle Sol. I promise."

"Okay, now leave me alone. Is coming on now *Donahue* with a nun trapped in a priest's body."

My Russian grandmother had an expression in Yiddish, something like, "*A klug zu Columbus'n.*" Roughly translated, this was a curse on Columbus for discovering this place, and she used it when confronted by some peculiarly American outrage. I can't imagine what she would have said if she had seen talk shows.

So I went to the office, carefully avoiding Mickey. Once at my desk, I made a lot of calls to cover myself for a couple of weeks, or to postpone things that could safely be put off.

After I was satisfied that my affairs were in order, like just before I died, I ventured into Mickey's office.

"Mickey," I said softly, "let's go get some lunch. I'll treat at the Pine Tree." She shrugged, then nodded.

As my grandfather used to say, I lived to regret it. But I really couldn't bring myself to think about it. I'd deal with it when I got back.

I lamented the crooked ways of life, the mini-tragedies of bad timing or missed chances, the failed communications, the fact that a toasted bagel always falls cream-cheese-down. Then, I dozed some more.

I was awakened by the pilot's folksy rumble over the intercom. "Ladies and gentlemen, if you look out of the right side of the plane, you can see Mt. Rainier in Washington State. If you look out the left side, you can see Guam."

Mentally, I counted one-two-three-four.

Right on cue. "Just kidding, folks, heh-heh. Actually, you can see Mt. Hood and Mt. St. Helens."

I kind of wanted to see that. St. Helens offered a truncated cone of a peak, like some diagram on a geometry exam. The mountain was more than a thousand feet shorter since it vaporized itself several years ago. Although the top was shrouded in snow, there was still a wisp of steam emerging from somewhere in the crater. Spooky.

We were well into our descent. I prepared myself spiritually for the landing. The pilot said, "Well, it's raining in Portland. Welcome to the Northwest. But it's fifty degrees, sorta balmy after New York."

Wow, I thought, fifty degrees. And you don't have to deal with drifts, or shovel rain. I can live with this. It's not exactly rum and coke on the beach at St. Maarten, but it beats the winds howling across town redolent with the exotic aromas of northern New Jersey.

three

PORTLAND INTERNATIONAL
turned out to be practically a mom-and-pop airport compared
to Kennedy or LaGuardia. Having no luggage but my carry-
ons, I broken-field walked around and through the foot traffic
after I deplaned.

"Deplaned" is one of those modern words used only by
the airline industry. Have you ever heard a normal human
being use the word? Shouldn't the opposite activity be
"enplaned" rather than "boarded"? We don't debus, or
decar, or even dehorse, only deplane. Was the term used
before that munchkin uttered it on *Fantasy Island*: "Deplane, boss, it's deplane!" Who says that all the great
questions have been answered? Not me.

As I made my way to the terminal, I thought about Walter
Egon, my old friend, and how I came to know he was here
in Portland. No weird week, or any other time in my life,
would be complete without Sue, my ex-wife and lifetime
noncompanion. Someone once described our relationship as
"a divorce that works." No matter where our lives led us,
and with whom we became involved, Sue and I were joined
by some cosmic umbilicus.

Heaven only knows why we still needed each other, and
why we were closer and more affectionate than when we

were married. Maybe it was because we were older and wiser.

Nah. No one who knew either of us would testify to that under oath. Suffice it to say that we had entered some zone that surpasseth human understanding. My understanding, anyway.

So, the morning before I left for Portland, Sue showed up. And I wasn't prepared for her, mentally or spiritually. Running on automatic pilot that morning, I punched the button on the coffeemaker and listened for it to make its weird suck-gurgle. Sidling over to the refrigerator, I wondered whether there was anything edible.

I opened the door and gazed stupidly into the icebox. Stuck way in the back was a plastic container. I groped for it and opened it. Eureka! Linguine with white clam sauce cold from the fridge, my favorite breakfast. I sniffed it cautiously, to determine whether it had evolved into some pernicious life-form and would rise up and devour Manhattan, or if it would meekly submit to being eaten. Smelled OK to me, and it didn't reach out like the Alien to suck my face off.

I rinsed off the cleanest-looking fork in the sink and wiped it on my *Bird Lives!* T-shirt. While I tore into the pasta-and-bivalve, the coffeemaker delivered itself of its last gasp, and I poured myself a cup of Kenya AA. Nectar to go with my ambrosia. I flipped on the radio to get the NPR news, and then didn't listen to it. It just made a harmless drone as my mind wandered in search of a thought.

Oh, Christ, I thought, when the doorbell chimed. Whoever it was would have to see me in my sleepwear. "Yeah?" I growled into the intercom.

"Lenny, open up. It's Sue."

I winced. Not now, Lord. But my prayers had come too late. I buzzed her in.

When she entered my tiny but claustrophobic apartment, she gave me her best Bette Davis, "what-a-dump" look. Sue was actually beginning to look near her age, although the years rested lightly on her. Her dark, long hair was showing streaks of grey, and all it did was set off her gamin face to even better advantage. There was fire in her large brown eyes, and it was a sure sign of trouble.

She searched around for a place to sit down. I gestured toward a chair that had only a week's accumulation of bachelor detritus on it. She tilted the chair forward so all the stuff slid off onto the floor, righted it, and then sat down.

"Hey," I attempted brightly, "long time no see."

"Lenny, I have something serious to discuss with you."

Somewhere, way in the back of my head, a little alarm bell went off.

"Yeah?"

"I've come here to save your life."

Ask not for whom the bell tolls, it tolls for thee. "Um, yeah?"

"Can't you say anything but 'yeah' this morning?"

I resisted the temptation to say "yeah."

"Sue, I can honestly say that I am always thrilled to see you." Mentally, my fingers were crossed. "Do you want a cup of coffee?"

"That's what I'm here to talk about."

Maybe it was just too early. "You're here to talk about coffee?"

She made an exasperated noise. "No, *putz*, I'm here to talk about your pathetic state of health."

Uh-oh. Another of her "enthusiasms" was about to rear its ugly head. The omens were all there.

"Let me guess," I offered. "You've been reading nutrition and health books."

To my surprise, she looked surprised. "How did you know that?"

"I'm a detective, *n'est-ce pas*?" I tried to look inscrutable.

"Well, that's what it says on your business card. Okay, here's the scoop on you. You're getting older."

I guess I winced. This gave her immense satisfaction. She went on.

"Your diet can best be described as what a nine-year-old would eat if its mother left it alone for a month. Your cholesterol level is probably in the lard range, and your blood is no doubt a soup of toxins."

"Hey," I demurred, "what nine-year-old you know would eat smoked oysters washed down with Guinness Stout?"

She made another exasperated noise. Her arsenal of exasperated noises should be tape-recorded for the Smithsonian.

"Lenny, I wouldn't be here if I didn't care about you. You're digging your own grave with a knife and fork. I want you to sit down with me and work out a regimen of diet and exercise. The very first thing is to put down that coffee. And, yuck, can I believe what I see you're eating for breakfast?"

I was shocked, shocked!

"Excuse me, is this the same person who used to eat two-day-old pizza that had been left in the backseat of a car? Is this the same person who spent an entire summer with the Greasy Dildo Motorcycle Club living on cheap beer and Fritos? Is this the same person that used to stand in front of an open freezer to scoop ice cream into her face directly from the carton with two fingers? You, of all people, have the chutzpa to advise me on how to eat properly?"

She raised her head and assumed a look of injured dignity.

"I refuse to allow these intimidating tactics to deter me from my purpose. Do you have a food dryer?"

I gawked at her. "A food dryer? Sure, it's right there in the kitchen, next to the subatomic particle accelerator."

"Lenny, dried fruits and vegetables are very important to this diet. We need to get you a food dryer."

"Can't we just use the clothes dryer downstairs? Oh, gosh, I'll bet that the fabric softener will take the wrinkles out of the prunes, so that's out."

Another exasperated noise. "Lenny, why can't you ever take me seriously?"

Answering truthfully would have put me into yet another minefield, so I dissembled a bit. "Sue, you know I love you, but I can't always follow you down every path you take. You're right about my diet needing some adjustment, and we can talk about it in a while. For the time being, I will be on the road, and not always able to eat properly. Okay?"

She agreed to be mollified, and succumbed to curiosity. "On the road? Where're you going?"

"Portland."

"Maine or Oregon?"

"Oregon. Why?"

"Well, Walter Egon is out there. At least I think so."

"Walter? How do you know?"

"I spoke to him in Washington a few years ago, and he said he was thinking of moving out there. Then he sent me a postcard with a change of address. I'll bet I can still find it."

This was very good news. Walter was closer than a brother to me in the sixties. In fact, Sue had been his girlfriend briefly, before she and I were paired by a vengeful heaven. Walter was funny, talented, and very smart, a whiz with words, and a dedicated hippie. He had moved to Washington, D.C., and gotten married. I never met his wife, but I heard that she was working for the FBI at one point, and that had caused problems in the marriage. I hadn't seen him in years.

"Can you call me with whatever you've got?" I asked.

Sue shrugged. "Sure. No problem. When are you leaving?"

"Early tomorrow. It would be nice to see Walter. Maybe I can cop a place to crash, and save my client some money in the bargain."

"What's the job?" she asked. I didn't hesitate to tell her. For all her *mishigass*, Sue has often helped me to figure out knotty problems. She recognized Rowan's name immediately.

"I suppose it doesn't hurt that you're doing this for one of your boyhood heroes."

I smiled. "Not a bit. Now, if you'll excuse me, my breakfast is getting warm."

Yet another exasperated noise. But she kissed my cheek on the way out. I resumed my search for bits of petrified clam.

After my breakfast and a quick shower, it was time to make mental notes again. Everything was mostly in order. My flight left from JFK early in the morning. I needed to arrange a ride; perhaps Mickey would do me the honor. I was going to call the cops in Portland for some information, and maybe try to make reservations at a hotel.

On sober reflection, however, I decided to try to avoid the cops altogether by checking alternate sources first: newspaper stories, which are often useful and sometimes suggest additional avenues of investigation; and maybe the medical examiner's office, since their reports are usually quite complete. All this would have to wait until I got to Portland.

Plus, I wanted to call Walter Egon and probe the possibility of finding a place to crash. Per diem expense allowances don't go as far as they used to, and I didn't want to soak Deak Rowan for more than was necessary. Besides, seeing Walter would be a delightful bonus to this otherwise fairly grim matter.

So I bashed around the apartment, trying to come up with some last-minute details I'd forgotten, and inspecting my luggage to make sure I had enough underwear for a few days. I turned off the NPR news, which I hadn't listened to anyway, and put on a CD of Louis Armstrong. I especially wanted to hear him do "Sweethearts on Parade," the 1930 version where he sings. I like it better than the earlier version where some woman, maybe Eva Taylor, does the vocals. It might have been my break with Mickey, but I needed to feel a little sorry for myself, and Pops's singing prevents me from excessive wallowing in misery because I love it so much.

Sue called and gave me Walter's last-known phone number. I almost told her about Mickey, but decided I couldn't handle discussing it with her right now. I told her I'd call her when I got back, as I didn't anticipate a long stay in Portland.

I calculated the time in Portland, bringing to bear all my meager arithmetic skills, and decided that it wasn't too early, especially if he was getting ready to go to work.

The phone rang about six times, and a harried voice answered, "Your nickel!"

"This'll cost me more than a goddamn nickel," I cleverly retorted.

There was a second of silence at the other end, and then he asked, "Who the hell is this?"

"Okay, I'm really not in the mood to play stupid phone games. This is Lenny Schneider."

"The fuck it is! I thought you were dead."

"You wish, you little shit. How the hell are you?"

Walter laughed his famous humorless cackle, which people could never decide was a real laugh or not. "Christ, Lenny, is it really you? I haven't seen you, even talked to you for . . . twenty years? Could that be right?"

"Close enough for jazz. So, what's up out there in the great Northwest?"

"Not much is up at my age, man. Damn, I still can't believe it. Where are you calling from?"

"The Apple, specifically the scenic Lower East Side. But I am coming out to Portland tomorrow."

"Gawd, you don't still live in that horrible rat-hole, do you?"

"Affirmative. Except I've outlived four landlords, and at least one remodeling that Jimmy Carter worked on. He's a better painter than president."

"That place was like the legendary cockroaches' burial ground. Wound a roach anywhere in North America and they came to your place to die."

"Yeah, well, it's not so bad now. They do regular

exterminations. It really used to be bad once. I used to have to load my Water Pik with Johnston's No-Roach, and lay in wait. Every time a roach reared his filthy head, I would zap him with the No-Roach."

"I could almost believe that you really used a dental appliance to kill bugs. Didn't that stuff taste awful when you used it on your teeth?"

"Yeah, but it made my breath killing sweet. Enough of this bullshit on my time. Is there any way I could crash at your place, for maybe as long as a week?"

"Hell, yeah. Do you need to be picked up at the airport?"

I gave him my flight number and arrival time, and he assured me that it would be no problem, then we got to reminiscing again.

"Well," he asked, "is *she* still around?"

"By 'she' you can only mean Sue. Yup. I got your number from her. She hasn't changed much. Well, maybe she's a bit mellower."

"Oh, no more attempts to make powerful hallucinogens in the kitchen sink? No more disemboweling live animals trying to learn to be a Santeria priestess from a correspondence course? No more . . ."

"Whoa! We could be trading war stories about her for hours. I'll see you tomorrow, and we can fill each other in. Meanwhile, I've still got a bunch of shit to do before then. Let me sign off."

"Whatever. See you tomorrow."

We hung up. Walter sounded just like himself. I wondered if he'd changed any.

The rest of the day was spent making last-minute runs to the store, making calls to Bruno and Uncle Sol, calling Mickey to abase myself and beg for a ride to Kennedy Airport, and finally smoking some hash and going out for Ethiopian food.

I got home about ten, watched the local news, and fell asleep to some freak on cable access who was actually able to convince strange women to strip for his video camera.

God, I am *so* bourgeois.

But all that was prologue to what was happening now: looking for my old friend. As I reached the lobby of the terminal, I was accosted by a short plump person. He sneered and spoke to me in a Peter Lorre voice. "I'll sell you this ring for five thousand dollars."

"Ha!" I responded. "What kind of a chump do you take me for?"

"First-class. Perhaps you remember Melanie Haber?"

"Melanie Haber?"

"Perhaps you know her as Audrey Farber?"

"Audrey Farber?"

"How about Susan Underhill?"

"Susan Underhill?"

"Well, then. What about Betty-Jo Bialoski?"

"Oh, you mean Nancy!"

I dropped my bags and embraced my old friend Walter. We pounded each other on the back and hugged tight. After a minute, we stepped back to survey the damage time had wrought.

"Walter," I said, "you've put on a few."

He sighed. "Ah, too true, too true. Not enough amphetamine in my diet these days. But, hey, you look pretty good."

"Well, I *am* lucky. I eat like a man with two assholes most of the time. It's only lately that it doesn't all seem to go away by itself. I try to do a few workouts a week, but I'm not exactly rigorous about keeping the schedule."

"At least you still remember your Firesign Theater."

I chuckled. "Yeah, if it's worthless, I remember it. I can't retain anything useful. I used to use the Firesign Theater as a kind of IQ test. I recall that I became interested in you because you knew the answer to the question: 'My friend, what has happened to your nose?' "

Walter laughed. "Okay, enough of this crap. Let's get going." He hefted one of my bags, and we were off. He moved pretty quickly, doing the same kind of New-York-broken-field zigging and zagging I had done. Some things never leave you.

We walked out of the airport terminal into a fine, drizzling rain. There were three lanes for access to the airport, and just beyond them a row of short-term meters. I said, "Gee, there are certain advantages to living in a smaller city. You can't park this close to the terminals in New York unless you're a certified terrorist."

"Yeah, well, enjoy it while you can. This airport is the first-or-second-fastest-growing in the country. It'll probably look like Washington-Dulles the next time you come."

We stopped at a well-battered minivan. He opened up the back hatch and deposited my bags amid a clutter of boxes, books, and baseball gear. I wondered if the bats and gloves were going to spend the entire winter in the van.

As we hit the road, Walter said, "It's too bad that it's overcast today. Usually there's a good view of Mount Hood from here, and Saint Helen's just as we get on the freeway."

"I wonder why highways are called 'freeways' here, and expressways and parkways back east?"

"Don't forget thruways. I don't know. On the parkways in New York you're stopped as much as you move. Maybe a parkway is a highway you park on."

Our conversation went on in this witty way as we headed into town on Route 84. We passed an exit marked 43RD AVENUE, and Walter indicated that this was his normal exit, but that he needed to go to the radio station, and he thought that I might like to see it. I agreed. I'm a sucker for radio, having grown up listening to the last vestiges of network radio before it was done in by TV, and became the brainless, gutless aural wallpaper most Americans listen to.

After we got off the freeway, we drove around through city streets. My first impression of Portland was that it was like a city in Jersey. But the hills looming on the west side over a downtown skyline were like nothing I recalled back east. Pittsburgh, maybe.

We headed down Burnside Street. Walter spoke with an

apologetic tone in his voice. "Uh, I'm sorry you have to see all these street people. There are a couple of missions in the area and . . ."

I held up a hand to stop him. "I guess you haven't been back to The Apple for a while. The place is getting like Calcutta, or someplace, where entire families live out their lives in cardboard boxes on the streets. This place seems relatively free of homeless people."

"There are more than you might think, but I guess it's worse in New York. Of course, a few more years of Republicans running things, and we might make Calcutta look like Palm Springs."

I grunted agreement.

We pulled up to a parking place, only to find a guy down on his hands and knees in the street. He was inspecting the asphalt minutely. We waited, as he was blocking access to the spot.

"He must've dropped a contact lens, or something," Walter mused. I squinted over the hood of the van.

"I don't know about that. He's wearing glasses. What's he got in his hand? It looks like, I don't know, road debris."

We watched for a second. He was picking up stuff off the street: matches, twigs, paper, cigarette butts. And he seemed to be collecting it. Walter lightly honked his horn. The guy glowered at us, and picked trash more quickly. After another few seconds, Walter cranked down his window and bellowed, "Get out of the street, you goddamn nut!"

Another vicious look from the guy. Then he bent over and began sucking water from little puddles on the street.

At the same time, Walter and I uttered, "What the fuck?" Then Walter said, "Welcome to Portland."

"I take it that this is standard behavior here?"

Walter cogitated before answering. "No, but the nutcases here have a peculiar inspired quality that I've never seen anywhere else." Here Walter tapped his horn lightly, and the Street Sucker finally relinquished his watering hole, albeit resentfully. We pulled in. "New York certainly has more

than its share of loonies, and the protest crowd in front of
the White House in D.C. includes some of the most seriously
pixilated individuals I've ever seen, but Portland . . . well,
let's just say that the eccentricity here is equal to a much larger
city in percentages, and is often far greater in creativity."

I was intrigued. "You'll have to tell me sometime, over
some of your excellent beer."

"Done deal!"

We walked around the corner. The radio station was on
the east side, not far, Walter said, from his house. A squat
building with antennas and a satellite dish on the roof, the
station was in a light industrial area featuring a rooms-by-
the-hour motel and a collection of sorry-looking hookers
who occasionally strolled by. Unlike their counterparts in
New York, there was no flashy fake fur and spangled
minidresses. Strictly jeans and down jackets. Very homey:
Screw the girl next door. The only high heels I saw were on
a pair of cowboy boots. The station's call letters were
KOOK-FM, in chipped and faded paint on the front of the
building next to the door.

The station lobby was crowded with people moving in a
random fashion. The receptionist looked like the guitarist in
a London punk band, circa 1978. Candy-cane red hair was
arranged in a kind of rooster cut, with shaved sides. He had
six earrings in his right ear, all silver hoops, and what
looked like a severed finger dangling from his left ear. He
had a stud *and* a hoop in his nose, and a stud piercing his
lower lip. His beat-up black motorcycle jacket covered a
torn Ramones T-shirt. He was busily engaged in a vain
attempt to keep up with ringing phones, and growing
increasingly snappish with each new caller. His lip stud
clattered against the mouthpiece in a staccato accompani-
ment to his snarls. All the lights on the phone were lit up.
We walked past him apparently without his taking any
notice of us.

Then he raised a hand. "Hey!" he challenged. "Where are
you goin'?"

Walter made a sour face. "Back to see the station manager. That okay with you? Hmmm?"

"You gotta sign in." He gestured to a clipboard. Then said into the phone, "I gotta call you back. Some old dudes are tryin' to sneak in." He hung up the phone, which immediately began to ring as soon as the line was free.

"Sign in," he demanded.

Walter leaned over the desk. "Listen, I've been at this station since before you got your brain pierced. Since when do we sign in?"

"Hey, pop, you got a problem with this, you can hit the street. They tell me to get signatures, I get signatures."

"Well," Walter replied unctuously, "it's nice that you do your job. America would be better off if more young people were as conscientious as you."

He signed "John Dillinger" with a flourish. I followed with "George Sand." The kid looked at the clipboard and nodded.

"Okay, that wasn't so tough, was it, pop?"

"Mr. Dillinger, to you."

"Yeah, whatever."

So much for security.

The interior of the lobby was dominated by a bulletin board of enormous size displaying everything from station manager and committee reports, to personal messages, to flyers for various events like concerts and benefits and protests, to angry letters directed at one program or another, or just ranting about how the station had failed this or that cause or community. The rug looked as if mud wrestlers had practiced on it, and the paint job was old and dingy.

All in all, a typical left-wing, listener-sponsored, community radio station. Not much different from a similar one in New York.

I followed Walter around a series of turns which led to a suite of small and squalid offices. Along with bunches of stapled, taped, and glued items, one door had a sign reading

STATION MANAGER, under which someone had penciled an obscene suggestion. Walter knocked.

"Come in," said a muffled voice.

We entered a magnificently cluttered office, in which no horizontal surface including the floor was free of rubble, mostly paper and books, with some records, cassettes, and CDs distributed haphazardly. Sue thinks my apartment looks like a rummage sale in hell; she should see this place.

Walter gestured toward the thin, nervous man sitting at the desk. He looked like Don Knotts, only not quite so rugged or relaxed.

"Lenny, this is Slim Reed, our station manager."

Reed arose and extended his hand. His greasy and unraveling sweater couldn't cover the flayed, red skin on his forearm from recently scratched nervous eczema. I hesitated before shaking his pale hand, worried that bits of flesh would drop from his fingernails. Then I noticed that his fingernails had been bitten to the quick, so I took his cold hand. It was as limp as a nervous bridegroom.

"Good to meet you," he said in a quavery voice. "Walter told me that you and he are old friends from the sixties."

I looked at Walter, who had his trademark smirk working.

"Yeah, good to meet you, too. Walter and I go back to before we were hippies." I wasn't sure what else to say to this guy, and an awkward silence ensued. Walter stepped in and took over.

"So, Slim, anything new and horrible lately? What's with the sign-in sheet?"

Reed suddenly developed a tic in his left eye that twisted his whole face out of shape. "Somebody got attacked here last night."

Walter's eyebrows shot up. "What do you mean, 'attacked'? I came by here about nine to pick up my mail. Nothing was wrong then."

"We had a programming committee meeting last night. Broke up around ten-thirty. You know how it is, people straggling out the door, talking on the street, hanging out. I left about ten minutes later. Well, finally it was down to about three people, Carl Gibbon and two pals of his."

Walter looked over at me and made a face. He turned and spoke to Reed. "So, did Gibbon attack someone?"

Reed shook his head. "Just the opposite. Someone popped out of the alley by the motel and took a swipe at Carl as he walked by. Cut him on the arm."

I was trying not to listen, but this was too good to ignore. Reed noticed my interest and said to Walter, "Maybe we should talk about this another time."

"One more thing," Walter asked, "did anyone see who did it?"

Reed shook his head, and scratched his forearm. "Nope. It was dark, Carl was in shock, I guess, and the guy, or whoever, was down the alley and gone by the time the other two got there."

Walter leaned in to speak quietly to Reed. "You know, I saw Augie Stabile's van parked around the corner when I got here."

Reed actually broke out in a sweat. "Aw, jeez. Don't tell me that. He's capable of anything."

"Yeah, well it is too bad about Gibbon. He hurt much?"

Reed shook his head. "Nope. Got a few stitches, but he's lucky, all in all."

"Yeah, too bad." Walter seemed oddly insincere. "Anything else?"

Reed gave a kind of spastic shrug. "Only if you want to read B.B.'s newest love letter. Actually, you figure quite prominently in it." He half-turned and began excavating the jetsam on his desk. "Aha!" he said, and pulled out a sheet of paper with thumb and forefinger, which dislodged several other items that promptly fell behind the desk. Reed gave them no notice.

"Here," he said to Walter, "you're welcome to xerox it for your files. It's the usual."

Walter took it and held it so that he and I could read it

together. It was two pages of single-spaced typing, beginning with, "Dear Jack-Off Cretins . . ."

"Something tells me," I said to Walter, "that this will more than supply your maximum daily requirement of venom."

"Oh," he said airily, "I didn't know assholes oozed venom."

He read the letter, giving us the odd passage aloud.

"Blah, blah . . . can't hear anything but angry dykes anymore . . . discrimination against straight white males . . . violations of Oregon Law Number so-and-so, against your charter, violations of your own bylaws . . . censorship of views not approved by your Board of Fascist Directors . . .

"Ah, here's the good part: 'But these other morons are nothing compared to Walter Cocksucker Egon, whose father-in-law is a corrupt FBI storm trooper, and is probably a plant sent by the ghost of J. Edgar Hoover to destroy dissent in the Northwest and kill the institution of free radio.'"

Reed laughed a nasal little chuckle. "I told you," he said. "It gets even better on the second page. He thinks you're the Antichrist, or something."

"He certainly has a way with words," I interjected. "Can you sue the guy?"

"I suppose so," Walter said after a couple of seconds, "but I'm not sure I could collect anything. Besides, it's attention that he craves. A lawsuit would give him a permanent erection. Nah, I'm just gonna forget it. I might send a reply, just to piss him off. Besides, there are worse than him."

Reed reached out for the letter. "I'm gonna post it on the bulletin board. I'll xerox it and put the copy in your mailbox."

Walter nodded. "Yeah, okay. Put it in an envelope with my name on it, just to avoid confusion. Things have a way of going astray here."

We took our leave of the station manager and wound our way back to the lobby, and its milling crowd. Just as I turned to say something to Walter, a microphone nearly got shoved up my nose. The mike was held by a long, porky, tattooed arm, which was attached to a body of excessive height and corpulence. As I followed the course of the body to the head, I was faced with a person of, um, *unusual* appearance. Her hair was in dreadlocks, each braid dyed a different unnatural color. The eyes, as malevolent as a starved rottweiler's, were sunk into fleshy cheeks, and the open mouth revealed uneven teeth, where there weren't gaps or decayed stumps. I was so astonished, it took me a second to realize that this person was talking to me.

I stammered, "Wha—what? Did you say something?"

"Yeah," she responded in an asthmatic wheeze, "I asked you if you think that PMS is a valid murder defense."

My higher centers finally caught up with my animal brain. "Not alone. I certainly think that PMS should be considered as an extenuating factor, if a woman is provoked enough to commit murder. But just to use it as . . ."

She made a disgusted sound and pulled away before I could finish my thought. "Hey," I asked, as she moved her vast bulk in another direction, "what's this for?"

Annoyed, she yelled over her shoulder, "I'm doin' a program on myths about menstruation."

"Oh, sort of a period piece."

She stopped, looked me over, and flipped me the bird. Then she was sticking the mike in some other poor schmuck's face.

I turned back to Walter, who looked like he was going to bust a gut laughing. "Let's get outta here, before I *plotz*."

We walked out. There was a fine mist falling. Several grunge types were hanging out in front of the building smoking cigarettes. One raised his hand in greeting to Walter, who returned a wave. Then he burst out laughing.

Between whoops, he made several attempts to start a sentence, but to no avail. Finally, he calmed down enough to talk.

"Congratulations, you've been ambushed by Bella Durke."

"Vastly amusing, I'm sure. What's *her* story?"

Walter shook his head and emitted another chuckle. "Bella is an old-timer at the station. She's even held one of the few paying jobs at this place. Basically, she's a profes-

sional lesbian. Very active politically, a real presence in the
gay and lesbian community. But also a man-disdainer, if not
a man-hater. Some say she treats everyone with equal
contempt, but I don't think so. My take is that she has a
hierarchy of values, and that straight white males rank just
above septic tanks, but below rabid hyenas.

"The interesting thing about her is that she's a quirky,
surprisingly good interviewer. She keeps everyone a bit off
balance with her snide aggressiveness. Sometimes it works
perfectly with certain subjects.

"But she's also a hypocrite. She's come on to just about
every woman in the place, at one time or another. If she
were a man, her considerable ass would have been banned
from the station long ago." He shrugged. "Just one of our
little double standards here at KOOK." He pronounced it
like it was spelled, rather than as letters. It seemed fitting.

"That letter the station manager showed us?" I inquired.

"Yeah, the one from B.B. Wolfe. What about it?"

"The guy explicitly said that the place was run by a cabal
of lesbians. Any truth to that?"

He made a face and waved a hand dismissively. "B.B.
sees conspiracies everywhere. This month it's lesbians.
Next month it'll be the logging industry that runs the station.
Or the Rosicrucians. Or the Elders of Zion. He's just fulla
shit. He's a big fish in a little pond, the number-one
conspiracy nut in town, with a gaggle of followers ranging
from serious paranoids to people who put aluminum foil
under their hats to keep the Martian lizards from reading
their thoughts. He's mostly harmless, but he's got a big
mouth, and a jones for the station."

I nodded. "Did I hear you say that there were worse than
him?"

"Worse than him? Shit, yeah! There are some fourteen-
karat twistos out there. People who are beyond the counterculture malcontents our audience mostly comprises. This
Gibbons guy who got cut last night? Biggest hypocrite I
ever met. Claims to be a fervent proletarian, a friend of the

underdog. The minute he got elected to the board of directors, he started voting himself privileges. You know, it's like Orwell said, 'We're all equal, but some of us are more equal than others.'" He made a retching noise. "When I said it was too bad he got cut, I meant it was too bad it wasn't his throat."

I winced. "Wait a minute, isn't that a bit harsh? Aren't there a lot of people who are sincerely interested in making progressive changes in—"

He waved a hand dismissively. "How can you still be so naive? The only thing the sixties taught me is that change is not possible, except in the short run. Where're all the goddamn improvements that we made? Nixon killed 'em, or Reagan. They made racism acceptable again. They stole from the working class and the poor to give tax cuts to their fuckin' fat-cat friends, they—"

"Whoa! Enough. Let's go get a beer and something to eat."

Walter puffed out his cheeks and expelled breath slowly. The pink of his cheeks started to fade.

"Good idea," he agreed. "Do you need to go to the house first?"

"Nah. Let's just get some food and a beer."

"What do you want?"

"Surprise me. It's your neighborhood."

As we headed for the car, I could see a lot of myself in Walter. Maybe a lot of what I used to be, and especially what I could have become.

I wanted the world to be better, with an end to racism and poverty, and useless wars. I still do. Somewhere along the line I decided that things went in cycles, and that the only bit of received wisdom that I found to be true was: And this too shall pass.

More than one of my friends from the sixties considered this a cop-out. I kind of hoped it was "perspective."

four

WE CRUISED UP HAW-
thorne Boulevard. Walter, silent for most of the time since
we left the station, asked, "Do you just want a beer, or do
you need some food, too?"

"Food, please. The stuff they serve on the plane is
probably designed to stay down during landings, rather than
for taste or nutrition."

"Well, the reason I ask is that I could take you to a good
Thai place with no draft beer, or a place with several draft
beers but mediocre food."

I considered briefly. "Let's go for the Thai food."

As we drove along Hawthorne, I saw more and more
young people in various forms of antisocial dress and
attitude: grungers, punks, hippies, bikers. The stores began
to change, too, from more light-industrial and standard
stores to used record shops, used clothing shops, book-
stores, and the ubiquitous coffee shops. Finally, I saw a sign
for Thanh Thao, catty-corner from what could only be a
head shop called the Third Eye. A head shop!

Walter pulled over to the curb, and we got out. "It's a
good time to get here," he allowed, "because there'll be a
line out the door in a couple hours."

The place consisted of a bunch of mismatched booths and

tables in Formica. Ambience was at a minimum. Walter suggested the salted squid and eggplant in garlic sauce. I ordered a Singha, since the selection was in bottles, and all stuff I'd had before.

We made small talk until the food arrived. I could tell Walter had something itching inside him, but it wouldn't come out. I knew what it was, so I short-circuited the process.

"What's making you squirm like this, Walter? If you don't get it said, we'll both be nuts."

"Tell me about Sue."

I pulled at my beard. What is there about that woman that holds men even after long years and other relationships? I made a mental note to talk it over with Walter, sometime.

"Well, she still looks great. Her clothing budget is more than my rent. Plus, she's still doing freelance design, so she gets samples, or at-cost garments, from a bunch of manufacturers."

"Damn! She finally became a designer. She always talked about it when we were together, but she was doing shitty office work for no pay when I left."

"You've been away longer than I remember. Sue's been supporting herself with designing for maybe twenty years."

"Where was I? Oh, she wears her hair pretty much the same as she used to, only it's going grey. Looks good on her."

Walter waved his hands. "Get to the good stuff!"

I shrugged. "I don't have much dirt for you. Sue's calmed down quite a bit. She's currently on a health kick, exercise, natural foods, I don't know. As far as I know, she's not as, um, active as she used to be. With men, I mean."

"What's it now, women?" Walter's eyes were popping.

"Whoa, pal. Isn't it beyond your interest, never mind your control, at this point?"

Walter was strangely agitated. I wondered if Sue was the cause. His expression suddenly changed, and he took a new tack.

"Anybody else in the picture for you? You *are* still out there in the fray, aren't you?"

I rolled my eyes, and he laughed. "You sure you want to hear this?" I asked.

He batted his lashes and gave me his best movie vamp impression. "I'm all ears."

I figured "what the hell?" and gave him the details, including the scene with Mickey the day after Deak hired me. It took place at the Pine Tree, one of the last of the dairy restaurants in New York, and the best in midtown. Dairy restaurants serve vegetarian fare and dishes made with dairy products. No meat. This is for Jews who keep kosher, and won't go to a nonkosher place, or are interested in something like blintzes, which would be dicey in a kosher restaurant that served meat.

Jews are called the "chosen people" because they have been chosen to observe dietary and behavioral laws that would drive most folks nuts. "Whaddaya mean, you can't eat meat with dairy products? You don't eat ham and cheese sandwiches?" Yeah, something like that. Heaven forfend that one day I am forced to explain *t'fillin* or *tzitzess*.

I go to dairy restaurants because of food like fried potato pirogen, blintzes with sour cream, or, as substitutes for meat, Rumanian eggplant salad, or mushroom cutlets with kasha and *varnishkess*. To die for. Almost quite literally, since the cholesterol count on some of these is figured exponentially.

Mickey ordered blueberry blintzes, and I had the pirogen, with sour cream and onions-fried-in-butter as garnish. It was, of course, scrumptious.

After lunch, and over coffee, I ventured a discussion. "Mickey, I'm sorry about yesterday. Let's talk."

She nodded. "Yeah, it's time. This is gonna be hard to say. I've been seeing someone."

I guess I must have gone pale. She quickly clutched my arm, by way of comfort.

"I'm sorry to spring it on you like this, but, um, we

haven't talked much. Lenny, I had no idea what was going on with us. I panicked, a bit. My cousin's cousin, Arnie, he's just divorced. He's got a good job, a piece goods salesman. He makes a bundle. He called and asked me to dinner. Who knew? I thought it was innocent enough. But one thing led to another. . . ."

Arnie? I had met him at a bar mitzvah, with his ditzy wife, who left him for a conga player in a salsa band. A schmuck-with-earlaps. Snappy dresser, though. Custom suits to hide the paunch.

I looked stern. "Are you asking for my blessing?"

She looked as if she were about to cry. "Yes. I guess so." Then she began to cry. "He asked me to marry him. I said I had to talk it over with you, but I said 'yes' first."

"And that little performance in the office yesterday?"

She blushed. "Mostly guilt. God knows, Lenny, it isn't easy to work with you all the time. You're completely disorganized. . . . But, still, it's been good for me. I hope we can stay friends, and business partners."

I was nonplussed. I felt deeply for Mickey, and we had meant a lot to each other, but instead of the deep pain and anguish I would have expected there was just this hollowness. It was probably a good thing. She had always been much too conventional for my, well, *unusual* life. She was starting to relate to me more like my mother than my lover. One mother is all we get. And all we need.

Absently, I whispered, "Only time will tell just who has fell, and who's been left behind, when you go your way and I go mine."

"Was that another Bob Dylan quotation?" she asked. I nodded. "Well, I'm sure Arnie won't be mystifying me regularly with obscure references to music and whatever." She frowned. "I might just miss it. Still, he is a smart guy."

"Yeah? Well, if he's so smart, maybe he knows what Billy Joe McAllister threw off the Tallahatchie Bridge."

She laughed. "If you're not careful, I'll throw you off the Brooklyn Bridge!"

"Let's get back to the office. I've gotta call Portland, and you probably have a lot to do, also."

Her eyes narrowed. "Well, yes. Especially if you're running off to Oregon."

As we were leaving, I stopped her, clutched her shoulders, and looked into her eyes. "Mickey, look. I feel very bad about this. I just want you to know that I still care very much for you, and that there is no one else in my life, especially not Sue."

She nodded, and her eyes were glistening. We caught a cab.

When I finished the story, which Walter listened to with rapt attention, he asked, "So, what does Sue think about this?"

The conversation was getting old, so I changed the subject, indulging my curiosity.

"Answer me something. What's going on at the radio station? Is violence common there?"

I could see Walter's mental gears grinding. He sighed.

"No, not the physical kind. However, this incident is not the first in the so-called community."

"What do you mean, 'community'? Portland?"

He shook his head. "No, no, I mean the people who work, volunteer, or hang out at the station. Plus the active listeners, I guess. The KOOK Community."

"What else has happened?"

"Are you sure you want to know?"

I spread my palms. "I'm curious, and if it keeps you from tripping out on our mutual ex, it's cool with me."

He nodded. "Point taken. There have been at least two other incidents that I know of, although neither involved serious attempts at hurting people. And Stabile was somehow in on both of them.

"I got this secondhand, of course."

Before he could elaborate, the food arrived, carried by a tiny woman who was almost invisible under and behind the plates. It was not first-rate by New York standards, but it was certainly delicious, and I'm too much of a parochial food snob. The salted squid turned out to be fried in a tempura-like batter and not at all salty, and the eggplant was cooked in a thick, sweet-hot sauce. The cold Thai beer went down perfectly.

"Now," said Walter, "let's go get us a beer."

We drove back down Hawthorne until we got to a place called the Barley Mill. Walter said, "This is as good a place as any to start. I'm pretty sure it was the first brew-pub in Portland, or nearly. And the people that run it have several now, including movie theaters that serve beer and pizza, and only charge a buck for admission."

The place was festooned with Grateful Dead posters, posters for other bands, and the usual assortment of dreck found on barroom walls these days. We bellied up to the bar.

"What should I have?" I asked. The beers had names that didn't tell me much about them.

"What do you feel like?"

I shrugged. "I need to relax and get some sleep before tomorrow. Maybe a stout?"

Walter waved down the bartender. "Two pints of Terminator, please."

"Terminator? Sounds lethal."

He laughed. "Not really. But it's quite respectable stout."

The stout was more than respectable. Dark brown and rich, but not like Guinness. Less bitter. We traded war stories from the sixties. Even the bartender had to laugh at some of them.

"Remember," I asked, "when John moved into an apartment in my building, and decided that he wasn't going to pay Con Ed for any more electricity than he had to? He bought a bunch of candles, and never turned on a light. After about two months, he realized that he was paying more than double for candles than he would be paying for lighting the place up like Yankee Stadium."

"Yeah." Walter shook his head as if in disbelief. "That building was really something. Half the people in it were recently divorced guys who decided to be hip and live in the East Village. The rest were hard-core hippies and dopers. What a gas.

"Remember the time we were all in your place totally wrecked on acid? This guy from upstairs knocks on your door in a panic because some maniac was out on his fire escape with a knife in his teeth. He's hoping we're gonna help him, but all we do is treat him like he's on a bad trip. 'Just touch us, man. It'll be all right.' What a joke!"

"I wonder what ever happened? He wasn't in the building much longer."

"Probably went back to the wife and kiddies in Staten Island."

And so on. After another round, we headed for Walter's house. I forgot about the radio station stuff.

five

WE ARRIVED AT WALTER'S
house, a pleasantly seedy Victorian pile, on a street of
similar-style houses in all sizes. Most were in a decent state of
upkeep, with paint jobs of various colors, and yards exhibiting
casual care. The house across the street was three shades of
purple, with trim in two shades of blue, and white accents.
Walter noticed me staring.

"Welcome to Portland, home of the so-called 'painted
lady.' You'll find more than one, um, *colorful* paint job. This
neighborhood was one of the hippie enclaves in the sixties,
but was usurped by dope dealers and bikers. Some of the
people on the west side are still reluctant to come over here.
They think that it's *Mad Max*, or something. It's slowly
returning to a real residential area, but the residents are not
what you would call yuppie types. The counterculture dies
hard here."

Walter's house was big and turreted, with three floors,
and the prevailing color was a sky blue, with trim and
gingerbread accents done in a variety of contrasting colors.
The effect was jarring, but not unpleasant after a while. Like
a mild acid flashback.

We entered the front hallway, which was lined with
built-in bookshelves on both sides. The shelves were broken

by a doorway on the left, and the hall terminated in a staircase leading upstairs. We turned left into the doorway opening to the living room. It was a large, high-ceilinged and well-windowed room. A picture rail ran around the walls a couple of feet short of the ceiling, and framed photos and jazz posters hung from the rail. The furniture was a motley assortment of chairs, tables, and lamps, with one threadbare mohair couch. The couch faced the television set and stereo, which was set up in an ersatz period home entertainment center.

Off to the right, large pocket doors were open to reveal a formal dining room, and a kitchen visible beyond that. Nice place. I told Walter so.

"Thanks," he replied. "I was able to get it with the money I made selling a house in the D.C. burbs. I lived on the rest until I could pick up some work here. The job market was tough, but I've been able to get into the freelance writing and editing thing. I make enough to survive, and I rent out the top floor and the basement to help cover the nut. In fact, you'll be staying in the basement, since my next boarder isn't gonna be here for a month or so. Follow me."

I grabbed my bags and followed him through the kitchen and down a flight of stairs to the basement. He flipped on an overhead light. There was a comfy little apartment set up there, with a big bed, a TV, a phone, and a separate bathroom. It was great, especially at the price. I was thrilled.

As I looked around, I noticed something skulking along the corners of the room. When it came into the light, it turned out to be a large orange cat. The animal pinned me with slitted eyes.

"Does the room come with the cat?" I asked.

Walter knelt down and made a noise with his mouth. Warily, the cat sidled over to him, never breaking his surveillance of me. Walter scratched and petted him, and the cat began to purr, no louder than an idling Ferrari. One eye was always fixed on me.

Walter stood up. "This is Love, Lenny. Love, meet my friend Lenny."

The cat looked up at me, as if expecting an acknowledgment.

"Love?" I asked. "Is this some kind of residual hippie thing?"

"Well, not really. You know that Beatles song, I'm Looking Through You?"

I ran it in my mind. "Ah, yes. The line about 'Love has a nasty habit of disappearing overnight'?"

Walter looked impressed. "Very good. Yup, that's it. He's neutered, so he doesn't really roam, but he does neglect to come home now and then. We think that he has another place somewhere, and he stays there when the spirit moves him.

"And, despite his literal lack of balls, he beats the crap out of every other cat in the neighborhood. He's also a hunter, and brings in the odd rodent or bird every so often. You may wake up one morning to see us scurrying around trying to catch a rat."

"Walter, despite my years living on the Lower East Side, I am not looking forward to that. Rats are not my favorite drop-in guests."

He shrugged. "Well, just like the TV, it kind of goes with the accommodations. You may luck out. He hasn't brought one in for a while.

"Why don't you settle in, and then come upstairs. My housemates should be home soon."

I agreed, and set about it. Love kept me company, and I found myself talking to him. It'd been a long time since I had a cat, and he was pretty cool. I stopped to scratch him a few times as I unpacked. He was enormous. His ears showed the signs of battle; I wondered what the other guys looked like.

It was getting to be around five o'clock, eight my time. I tuned my portable radio to NPR and listened to the sad litany of the day's news, and a particularly infuriating commentary by some right-winger complaining that the liberals were calling conservatives nasty names. I wondered where this guy was when reactionaries like him were blacklisting, assassinating reputations, and destroying lives with red-baiting and groundless accusations. I decided that he was just pissed off that the conservative franchise on mindless viciousness had been violated.

Love was snoozing contentedly. I sat next to him on the bed and idly rubbed his belly. He stretched out to his rather amazing full length to take advantage of my attention. Walter's voice filtered down from above.

"Hey, Lenny! C'mon up. I want you to meet someone."

I excused myself, but the cat grabbed my hand as I tried to leave. He wasn't satisfied yet, I guess, and I had to extricate myself gingerly to avoid major damage from his claws. I went upstairs, bleeding only slightly.

When I got up to the kitchen, Walter was standing next to a tiny, wiry woman of about thirty-five. Her short, dark hair was beginning to grey and was squished down from a bicycle helmet. She was wearing spandex bike gear and a vest advertising a messenger service. She sized me up with large blue eyes as Walter made the intro.

"Frieda, this is my old friend Lenny Schneider. Len, meet Frieda Kerr, my partner." I shook her hand. I was uncomfortable with the word "partner." It was too vague. I never knew anymore from the word whether people were in business together or were sleeping together. My uncle Murray always used to tell me that his partners were screwing him. Maybe I misunderstood him all those years.

"Hi, Frieda, it's nice to meet you. It's hard for me to believe that anyone could put up with this guy for any length of time."

To my surprise, she got huffy. "My relationship with Walter is a good one, and I fail to—"

Here Walter stepped in. "Easy, hon, he's just kidding. Just that back-east humor." She seemed relieved to hear that.

"Okay, then, I'm glad to meet you, too."

I gave her my best sincere smile. "No offense?" I asked.

She shook her head. "Nope. If you'll excuse me, I'm going to shower. See you all later."

After she had left the room, Walter said, out of the side of his mouth, "Sorry. A lot of people out here are very literal. They don't pick up the joke like you're used to. And many of the people I deal with are PC. You have to be politically correct with certain things: race and gender names, no ethnic stereotyping, like that. It took me a while to realize that the New York sense of humor is beyond understanding here."

"Thanks for the tip." Just what I needed. What happened to the laid-back West Coast? Did it ever exist?

"Want a beer?" he asked. I gratefully accepted. At least the beer was uncomplicated.

We talked about this and that. I found out that Walter and Frieda had been together about four years; that he had met her at the radio station; that she had been a technical writer, and very overweight, when they met; and that she quit her job to do what she wanted to do, i.e., ride bicycles. She was very defensive about Walter because he had stuck by her come-what-may, and she had taken the political and personal attacks on him with even less grace than he had.

I heard the front door open and close. Walter said, "That'll be Lois."

Lois walked in, long black hair flying in all directions, carrying a bunch of books and files, all of which seemed to be leaping from her hands. Instinctively, I got up to help.

"Here," I said, "let me help you." I started grabbing falling items until the avalanche had stopped.

An olive-complected face with piercing black eyes and a strong aquiline nose came up to meet me. She looked at me uncomprehendingly and said, "Uh, sure. Thanks." Then she looked over at Walter.

Walter said, "Lois, this is my old running pal, Lenny. Lenny, Lois Newsom."

When she had gotten herself somewhat more organized,

she said, "Oh, yeah, the one from New York. Excuse me while I put this stuff down." She dumped her armload on a chair, and I put my few things beside them. She removed a wrinkled and weathered trench coat, and smoothed down her vest. She had on a man-tailored Oxford shirt and a pair of khakis, covered by that suede vest. She had well-worn hiking boots on her feet. She was easily six feet tall, maybe more. Her hair had the kind of shine and texture found with Asians and American Indians. I guessed that she was the latter.

"Hey," she said, extending her hand, "how you doin'?" Walter's been filling my ears with tall tales about you two."

I looked abashed as I shook her hand. "Alas, they are probably all true." She had a good grip. I thought I detected something in her voice. "Are you from New York?"

She made a sweeping bow, extending her arms. "At your *soivice*. Born and raised in Brooklyn, NYU journalism degree."

"Forgive me, but are you Native American?"

"No need to ask forgiveness. My dad's a Mohawk Indian who worked the high iron. His last job was on one of Donald Trump's monstrosities. He's retired now. My mom was a Canadian Blackfoot. I'm one-hundred-percent Injun."

Walter interjected. "Lois works for our local rag, *The Portlander*. Crime beat reporter, former sportswriter. She covered the local triple-A team. I figured you two would have a lot to talk about."

Just then Frieda came down drying her hair roughly with a towel. She had changed into jeans and a UNLV sweatshirt.

I looked at Lois. "As a matter of fact, you may be uniquely able to help me, but we can talk about that later. Is anybody hungry?"

They spoke affirmatively with one voice. We decided to get some pizza. They wanted to have it delivered, but I whined until Walter agreed to go pick it up. I hate pizza that's been steamed into mush in one of those insulated bags the deliverers use. The cardboard box is bad enough. So we called in an order, which I insisted on buying for the house. Lois went upstairs to change, Frieda sat down with the local newspaper, and Walter and I took a leisurely drive to the pizzeria.

A light rain was falling as we headed there. I noticed that few people on the street carried an umbrella. Walter believed that true Oregonians only used umbrellas in the worst downpours, and then grudgingly. I contrasted this with Londoners, who seemed to carry their "brollies" everywhere.

And, with this erudite and sociological conversation, we passed the few minutes to the pizza place. I was not surprised to see a Starbucks on the corner of the block. After all, we were near enough to Seattle, the navel of the espresso revolution. I remember when the only places you could get espresso were Italian restaurants, where it was served thick and bitter in tiny cups, with a twist of lemon peel on the side, or in the ubiquitous coffee houses of the Village. Same with cappuccino. Now, of course, there are more coffee shops in the average town than casinos in Vegas. I wondered if the Starbucks in Vegas had slot machines. I wondered if the casinos had espresso machines.

Walter broke into my reverie. "Okay, pal, here we are."

We parked on the street and ambled into the pizzeria. A kid with four nose rings and at least a dozen hoops in each ear waited on us. He looked like he had been hit in the face with a spring from a screen door. We negotiated the purchase and walked out. Walter looked at me quizzically.

"I noticed that you haven't said anything about the multiple piercings or tattoos yet."

"Huh?" I asked. "You think I come from Kansas, or someplace? I haven't seen anything here that choirboys don't wear in New York. Walter, I've seen two women walking down Eighth Street with their nipples pierced and chained to each other, and holes in their T-shirts displaying it all. I shuddered when I thought of one running to make a traffic light, and the other deciding not to chance it. The

Apple is still The Apple. It's probably getting weirder just
while I'm away."

Walter thought on that for a minute. "Yeah, I guess the
years I spent in D.C. gave me a warped view of the world.
I was there not too long ago, and very little of this kind of
thing has caught on. A *very* conservative place. Even the
coffee at the local Starbucks tastes weak."

"Remember what Leadbelly called D.C., a bourgeois
town?"

"Amen," said Walter.

The trip back was more silent, but it only lasted a few
minutes. I ruminated on the divergent paths Walter and I had
taken since our time together in the sixties. He had been
formed largely by his experiences living in D.C. In a way,
I was a case of arrested development, never having lived
anywhere but New York. I was long past the idea that
civilization stopped at the city limits, and I had traveled
some, but my universe was still New York, and, heaven help
me, the Lower East Side.

We pulled up to the house and carried the pizza to the
door. Frieda let us in and took the steaming boxes from
Walter's hands. After we doffed our coats, we went into the
kitchen to discover a set table and beer glasses set out. Lois
came in, dressed in baggy sweats and barefoot. She walked
over to the fridge and pulled out four beers.

Dinner was filled with pleasant chatter. The pizza was
acceptable, which far exceeded my expectations. The sauce
was a bit strange, with a sweet quality. But the mushrooms
were fresh, the pepperoni fair, and the crust thin and crisp
without being crackery. I gave it a seven. The beer, a local
brew called Blue Heron, was excellent.

After we finished eating, we poured a second round of
beers. We exchanged life stories. Lois began.

"I dunno, there's not much to tell. I was the only Indian
kid in a Jewish/Italian neighborhood. They stopped treating
me as a curiosity sometime in elementary school, although
I always got the jokes about eating buffalo parmigiana, or

lox pemmican. I played all the right games, but I was a bit of a tomboy. I always read a lot, and I did okay in school without working too hard. I was this tall by junior high, and so I played basketball, which I didn't like much. I quit in high school because I was a head, you know, a freak, a doper?

"My dad beat me up and grounded me regularly because of my weird friends and bad grades. One day—I guess I was a sophomore—I was in the school library pretending to study. I picked up a book that turned out to be H. L. Mencken. I couldn't believe what the guy was doing with the language, and how nasty he was about the 'squares,' the 'booboisie' he called them.

"Well, one thing led to another. I read more of Mencken, and generally got into writing down my own thoughts. I spent less time with the stoners listening to Def Leppard, and more time reading and writing. My mom died when I was a senior, and she died happy because she believed I saw the light, or something.

"The rest is J-school, and picking up jobs where I could find them. I got the sportswriting gig here because I could talk basketball in this hoop-crazy city, and because I'm tall enough not to get intimidated by the jocks. I moved to the crime beat because I got bored.

"Okay, now somebody else talk for a while."

Frieda begged off, and Walter took over. He lubricated his throat with cold beer, and dove into his favorite subject.

"I was born a poor black child . . ."

Satisfied with our groans, he proceeded.

"Okay, born in New York when it was still the best place on earth. I was a product of the public schools, which I kind of breezed through, and then I promptly flunked out of college. No study habits, but several other bad ones, which I pursued vigorously. I wound up in the garment center with a succession of stupid little jobs, which I hated and had no future I could relate to.

"Then I got involved in the civil rights struggle, which led me to radical politics in general, and to the so-called counterculture. It was during this time I met Lenny, which should indicate to you the appallingly low class of people I hung out with."

I bowed to acknowledge the recognition. Lois clapped silently.

"May I go on?" he asked rhetorically. "Good. At this point, say 1968, I was in a kind of personal worst."

"Hot dog!" I interjected. He made a pinched face.

"*If* I may. Anyway, I had just broken up with Sue, and an evil, tawdry breakup it was, not alleviated by the fact that she took up with this lowlife immediately thereafter." He hooked a thumb at me. "So I disappeared into drugs for a while and eked out a living selling acid and speed. Don't *ever* sell speed. Your customers never sleep, and they think nothing of ringing your doorbell at four a.m. I didn't think much of them doing it myself.

"Then I met Gail. Actually, I knew her sister, who was one of my speed-freak buddies. She introduced us after Gail returned from school in Europe. It was pretty quick. We got married in a few months and moved to Washington, D.C., where she was from. I figured, what the hell? I wasn't doing Jack shit and I needed to change my luck. Why not try a new place?"

He sighed. We all shifted in our seats and drank some beer.

"Her father," he continued, "was an FBI man. As any old rad will tell you, the Bureau is the spawn of Satan. Completely without morals or scruples. They tell me it's changed since that porked-out closet queen Hoover died, especially lately, but I don't believe it. I'll always believe that it's one step away from planting evidence on the Rosenbergs, or suborning perjury, or executing a death sentence without benefit of judge and jury.

"Needless to say, I was uncomfortable with the situation. It got worse when Gail went to work for them. I couldn't help making nasty insinuations about her job. 'Frame any innocent people today?' She and I would fight constantly. To make a long story short, we divorced in an oddly civilized way, remarkably free of anger or recriminations. It sucked. I wanted one big blowout, with all the shit festering inside of me coming out. Instead," he shrugged, "it was so fucking polite, I wanted to puke."

He put on a mincing little voice.

"'Oh, would you like the bedroom furniture?' 'Sure, do you want the couch?' 'Have you signed the papers?' 'Of course. Some more wine?'"

Frieda put a hand on his arm. He rubbed his forehead.

"Okay. So after a while I moved out here to get away from the East Coast, while still avoiding places like L.A. or Seattle. It suited me here, and I needed to cool out. Then, of course," he snickered ruefully, "I fell in with the radio station. KOOK is a haven for social misfits and losers. It reminded me why I got out of radical politics in the first place.

"You know," he leaned forward and waved a finger at me, "the reason the Left will never amount to shit is that lefties hate each other more than they hate the enemy. It's been going on forever. The Bolshies hate the social democrats, the Stalinists hate the Trotskyists . . . shit! They'll sell each other out in a minute. Remember the Smith Act trials? 'Under the spreading chestnut tree/I sold you and you sold me.' Orwell was right. Why—"

Frieda covered her ears and yelled, "Stop it, for Christ's sakes! Why the fuck don't you quit that place?"

Walter took a deep breath and puffed up his cheeks. He exhaled slowly through pursed lips. He looked at Frieda.

"What? And give up show business?"

The laughter broke the tension in the room, but Frieda hadn't joined in. She stood up and said, "Please excuse me, I'm going to bed. Nice to meet you, Lenny."

I stood up. "Same here, Frieda. See you in the morning."

We sat silent for a few minutes after she left.

Walter looked at me. "Wanna smoke some dope and watch the tube?"

I put my palms together and bowed in his direction. I was secretly happy I didn't have to tell my own story. "Lois?"

She thought for a second. "Um, okay, but just for a while. I'm pretty beat myself."

We moved to the living room, carrying our drinks with us. Lois's bare feet made a light slapping noise on the floor. When we sat down, Walter reached into a drawer in one of the tables and withdrew a wooden box. Inside were a pipe and a medicine bottle full of pot. He filled the pipe, lit it with a lighter, and passed it. While we were smoking, he picked up a remote and turned on the television.

Lois and I got into a conversation about her life in Brooklyn as Walter surfed through the channels. We were comparing notes on the French toast at Cookie's, when Walter shouted, "Hey, look at this!"

Lois swung her head toward the tube, and rolled her eyes. Now I was curious. I saw a badly lit guy seated at a table, with a pile of papers at his side. The poor lighting caused ominous shadows on his face, but the guy's demeanor was so startling it transcended the bad production. Madness shone from him like a beacon. He reminded me of Renfield in the old Bela Lugosi *Dracula*. You know, the deranged one who ate spiders.

"Walter," Lois moaned, "do you *have* to?"

"Yeah, yeah. I want Lenny to see this guy." He turned up the sound.

". . . want to silence me because I tell the truth about them. They can't stand to hear the truth. They're stealing your money and lying to you. And, when I tried to tell you about it, they threw me out. But, heh heh heh, they can't stop me!"

"What the hell's this guy ranting about?" I asked.

"Ssshhh," said Walter, "just listen for a while."

He went on, in a thick Boston accent. As he spoke, he

leered, snickered at inappropriate times, and his eyebrows appeared to be trying to bounce free of his forehead. His face and body twitched spasmodically. He was the perfect picture of a madman.

"Is this guy institutionalized?" I asked.

Walter shot me a look. "Ssshhh!"

"He oughta be," Lois whispered.

The guy paused, and drank something from a cup with "KOOK-91.2 FM" on it. "Isn't that your station?" I asked Walter.

"Yup. His name is Caliban Strunz. He used to do public affairs programming there. He was prone to slanting his pieces by editing material out of interviews that he found, um, unsupportive of the point he was trying to make. He once used only one sentence from a half-hour interview, after he had browbeaten his subject to get something out of him. The whole rest of the interview worked against his preconceived idea, so it got cut.

"Strunz has the personal and journalistic integrity of a pimp. He claims to have a journalism degree, but I think he slept through the ethics class."

"Have you got a personal beef with this guy?" I asked. Lois nudged me subtly. It was too late.

"Yeah," Walter replied, "you might say that. The cocksucker spread the word around that I was an FBI spy, and that I was sent here to bring down the station and stop it from operating. And that I was reporting names back to Headquarters in D.C."

"But that's obvious bullshit."

"Well, maybe you know that, but some of the wetbrains at the station were prepared to believe it. I had told a couple of them, really because I thought they would find it funny, that I had married into an FBI family, and that my ex-wife worked for them." He sighed. "I don't know. They're so provincial out here that they still have that yokel distrust of new people. Whatever, he made my life miserable for a while."

"Why isn't he at the station anymore?"

"He likes to claim that it's censorship. The truth is that he was so vile as a person that people were afraid of him." He smiled ruefully. "Caliban has what could be called an 'anger management problem.' In other words, he's a gold-plated asshole with a vicious temper and a persecution complex. Nothing is *ever* his fault. 'They' are always out to get him. Whoever the fuck *they* are."

Lois leaned toward the TV set. "Uh-oh. Walter, make this louder."

Walter thumbed the remote, and Strunz's voice rose.

". . . tellin' you that his father-in-law is Gabriel Tourn-cot, notorious *provocateur* for the FBI in the sixties and early seventies. This is the guy who used to work his way into peace and civil rights organizations, and cause them to commit criminal acts, so the FBI could bust 'em. A real bad guy, and Egon is his son-in-law.

"Now, where the hell did this Walter Egon guy come from in the first place? We don't know! But he gets into KOOK, and pretty soon he's got his own show, and he's a big shot. And where's he get his money from? He don't seem to have a job. Still, he lives in this big house and all. If you ask me, his papa-in-law's footin' the bills while he rats on us back to the FBI!"

Walter screamed like a scalded ape. "Goddamn that fucker!"

Lois and I tried to calm him down, to little avail. Finally, Lois grabbed the remote and turned off the tube, while Strunz was still in full rant.

"Gimme that fuckin' remote!"

"No, goddammit!" Lois shouted back. "You'll give yourself a heart attack. For crissakes, Walter. This guy's got about fifteen regular viewers, and you're one of them! Wise up. Just go to bed and forget it."

Walter waved his hands in frustration as Lois held the remote way over his head. "Don't you see, Lo," he wailed, practically in tears, "whoever sees this is gonna think he's right. They don't know me, but he's got a fucking TV show!"

I put my hands on Walter's shoulders. I said, in as soothing a voice as possible, "Hey, man, *nobody* can believe that guy. He's crazy as a shithouse rat. I saw that from the get-go."

It took a few more minutes to get Walter calm enough to go to bed. In all my years of knowing him, I'd never seen him that mad.

Lois sighed loudly when he was finally out of earshot. I just stood there kind of stupidly for a second.

"Lois, I'll admit that I haven't seen Walter in a long time, but I hardly recognized him just now. What's up?"

She shrugged her helplessness. "I've been living here for a couple of years, and he wasn't like this then. Based on what I can figure, including some conversations with Frieda, he's beyond disillusioned, into some kind of anguish. She told me that he's been trying to work on his personal issues and become a nicer person. You know, treat people better, not be so cynical, blah, blah, blah.

"Well, he was doin' fine until he got caught up in radio station politics. He used to be a member of their board of directors, but he quit when he decided that they were a bunch of grandstanding neurotics who've turned their psychological peculiarities into politics. He said that they were congenital losers who blamed their personal lack of success on the government, the right wing, God knows what. He got tired of their whining and their lack of any idea of what a radio station should be. So he quit the board, and they savaged him publicly at the next meeting when he wasn't there to defend himself."

"Gee, I, well it hardly seems likely that the whole group would be like that. Sounds a little paranoid."

"Yeah, I guess. But my impression was that the ones he considered his friends failed to defend him in his absence. And it doesn't help that a fuckin' loony like Strunz slanders

him on cable access. Also, he's had public fights with both
B.B. Wolfe and Augie Stabile."

"I was with him at the station today when he read a letter
from Wolfe. Most uncomplimentary. Who's this Stabile
guy?"

She made a cross with her two index fingers. "Whoa! It's
too late to start explaining *that* dude. Another time. I'm the
breaker tomorrow, and I'm gonna spend my day with my
ear glued to a police scanner. I'm goin' to bed."

"One question." I felt like Columbo.

"If it's a quick one."

"Is this Stabile guy capable of violence?"

"From what I know, quite possibly. He's fascinated with
it. Look, I gotta go to bed."

"Fair enough. Good meeting you, and thanks for everything."

"No problem. G'night."

She moved across the floor like a ballet dancer, graceful
as a breeze. I smoked some more of Walter's weed, and hit
the sack.

six

I WOKE UP EARLY, STILL on East Coast time. I decided to get up and pee, and return to bed to sort out my business. When I returned from draining the snake, I snuggled under the covers and turned on the news on my little radio, not quite loud enough to disturb my train of thought. Next thing I knew, Love appeared from nowhere and leaped up on the bed. After inspecting the terrain for a bit, he settled down between my legs and went to sleep. Great cat; terrible name.

I took stock of my task and possible resources. I wondered whether there was a newspaper morgue available to civilians. Lois might know. I needed to find Donnie Kimmel, too, although this might have been more for my curiosity than anything else.

Naturally, I couldn't help thinking about Walter. He was much the same outwardly as he had been in our time as close friends, but maybe for very different reasons. He was still cynical and a bit snide. Now it seemed that this emerged from another place inside him.

In the sixties, it was easy to be disillusioned. The country our parents had given us wrapped in a glittery package had turned out to be a festering mess. The happy family images on TV were only images. The reality for many of us was anger, infidelity, drink, Valium prescriptions, or worse.

The real TV reality was fat Southern cops turning fire hoses on neatly dressed young people who were asking only for what the culture had promised them. It was a honey-voiced hypocrite of a president who promised us peace while gearing up for war, and then hitting us with a trumped-up bullshit story about an attack in a faraway gulf. It was the realization that going to college and getting the good job was a hollow exercise in futility.

The final revelation was that you couldn't even bring your ideas home to your family without anger and discord. So we chose drugs, sex, and facetiousness, and vainly demanding the American Dream we had been promised, or else we would continue to behave weirdly.

And instead of Robert Young putting his arm around our shoulders and saying, "Okay, let's go into the study and talk," we got foulmouthed anti-Semite Mayor Daley beating the shit out of us on national television. Father, and Mother, not only *didn't* know best, they were all too often narrow-minded thugs.

All I could think of when they asked us, "What are you rebelling against?" is what Brando rejoined in *The Wild One*: "Whaddaya got?"

But that was a long time ago. Now most of us had jobs, mortgages, kids in school. A lot of us voted Republican (a sure sign of drug-induced brain damage) and threatened to kill our kids if they smoked grass. So what else is new?

With Walter, the disillusionment was no longer that of youth discovering that the prize package contained a gilded turd; Walter seemed to be suffering more than anything from a deep disappointment with The Way Things Had Turned Out. And not just on some abstract philosophical level. It was personal.

Love stirred himself, stretched lasciviously, and departed to destinations unknown. I could never bring myself to call him by that name. Didn't matter much. He wasn't my cat.

"Okay, Schneider," I said out loud, "time to get your aging ass out of the rack."

I got up and performed my ablutions. The shower was a bit small. Every time I tried to move my arms, I banged into something with my elbows. When I bent over to wash my legs, my tush scraped the shower walls. Still, there was water pressure and the price was definitely right.

The NPR news was featuring another terrorism story. The local news segment featured a story about a Portland cop who had shot an unarmed citizen in the back. Allegedly. The alleged victim had four alleged slugs in him. The weather would be clouds and possible drizzle early, with periods of clearing later, temps in the forties. No snow; no ice storms. Sounded good to me.

I dressed in jeans, boots, a work shirt, and a leather jacket. Turning off the radio, I headed upstairs to see what I could do about breakfast.

As I reached the top of the stairs, I smelled coffee, good and strong. Frieda was running around in the kitchen in her bicycle clothes, rattling cereal boxes and coffee cups.

"Good morning!" I offered brightly.

"The same," she came back warily. She didn't trust me one bit.

I was determined to relax her, and convince her I meant no harm to her man, or her life.

"Can I help you do something?"

"Um, no," she said, shifting various burdens in her hands. "Sit down and I'll give you some coffee. Cream? Sugar?"

"Black, thanks."

She poured me a cup of steaming, aromatic coffee. The cup read, "KOOK-FM, 91.2, NEWS, VIEWS, BLUES." I drank it gratefully.

"Mmmmm. . . . Good coffee. Mocha-Java?"

"Uh, yeah. Actually, half Mocha-Java and half Celebes. You know about coffee?"

"Well," I tried to sound modest, "only a little. But I really like all those South Seas coffees. I figure that they don't call coffee 'Java' for nothing."

She considered that. "Never thought of it, but yeah. Glad you like it."

"So, where's Walter?"

"He, uh, had sort of a rough night. He didn't sleep much. But," and here she turned and looked me in the eye, "he's very glad to see you. You're from the old days in New York, when he was still happy there." She made it sound like it had occurred on another planet. She paused, and her eyes went slightly out of focus. "A lot has happened since then."

"And not all of it good, I'm surmising."

She started to cry. I made a gesture toward her, but she waved me off. "No, no, I'm all right. I'm just an emotional wreck this week. I guess it's my period."

I blushed. I'm still uncomfortable with this confidence, especially from women I hardly know.

"I'm just real scared. We've been through a lot together, and he was so happy to be on the radio." She sniffed and dabbed at her eyes with a wadded paper towel. "It gives him something I can't understand. Not ego jollies, although that's a part of it. He loves giving people music. He loves it when they call and ask what he played. He doesn't want Gershwin or Rodgers and Hart or Duke Ellington forgotten in favor of Snoop Dogfood, or whoever. But the politics . . ."

She started crying again and turned away for a second. When she had more control, she continued.

"They eat each other alive there. Everybody suspects your motives, nobody gives you the benefit of the doubt. Jesus, what's wrong with these people? They think they know better than anyone. They accuse conservatives and radical Christians of wanting to run your life, but they would do the same thing, only from nobler ideals, see?"

"Yeah, I see." I had seen this before, and would see it again.

Now she was getting angry. "And the bottom line is that

someone else is telling you what to do, so where's the freedom anyway?"

"Frieda, look." I stood up and went over to her. "I've been out of organized politics for years. Mostly because, lame as it is, I've had a life. I try to keep up with issues, and I still consider myself a person of the Left, but it's mostly an illusion I let myself have. It's a way I have of keeping in touch with the feeling of being alive I had when I was active.

"Of course, I was simply much younger then, more sexual, and more innocent on the most basic level. I know this intellectually, but I need to maintain the illusion of vigor by keeping the illusion of caring more deeply than I really do.

"Is any of this making any sense to you?"

She nodded and smiled through her tears.

"Look," she said, "I didn't mean to dump all this on you. You haven't even had breakfast yet."

"It's okay, I just wanted you to know that I understand, and that I'm no threat to Walter. I'm here on business, and when I finish, I'm gone like a cool breeze. Now, what's for breakfast?"

After some back-and-forth, I settled on shredded wheat with skim milk. I guess Sue's warnings had taken hold. Frieda busied herself making a lunch to take with her, and I read the morning *Portlander*. I was finishing up when Lois came downstairs in her work drag. Red silk blouse over a navy skirt cut short enough to display her long, shapely legs, but not too short to be a lady. Red heels. She looked smashing.

She caught me looking. "Uh, nice," I tried.

"Men are such pigs." She repeated the formula with an exaggerated mechanical tone, so I would know she was a good sport about it.

"Lois, is there a newspaper morgue I can use?"

"Well, it's not really open to the public. The old prune face that runs it will give me a hard time if I bring you there, and expect payback for the favor. However," she arched an eyebrow archly, "I can be bribed."

I laughed. "Well, I would be happy to ply you with food, alcohol, or your most secret desires. But I really don't want to cause you any trouble. Is there any other place I could find what I'm looking for?"

"How far back do you want to search?"

"About three years."

"Public library has microfilm of the paper. And you don't have to deal with hatchet face."

"Bingo. Can I have your number at work, you know, just in case?"

She reached into her large handbag and fished around, coming up with a silver card case. She extracted one and gave it to me.

"Call if you need me." She put on her rumpled trench coat, said her good-byes, and left.

"She's great," I said to no one in particular. Maybe to myself.

"I love her. She always comes through for you," Frieda responded.

"Frieda, I need to get downtown to the library. Can you tell me how to get there?"

Her face actually lit up. "I'm glad you asked. We have an extra bike around here that nobody's using. Take that."

I guess I made a sour face, because she laughed.

"Hey, I don't know about this, it might rain . . ." My arguments declined into muttering.

"Trust me, it won't rain. I'll be happy to pump the tires for you, clean off the chain, whatever. Have another cup of coffee. It'll take me about ten minutes."

I smiled wanly, done in by another woman with a mission. Frieda ran off to do her thing, and I sighed and poured another cup of joe. Lois's byline appeared in the Metro section, and I read her story about how some guy shot a kid to death who had rifled his pickup truck at three in the morning. The kid and a couple of his pals had worked on, but not managed to cop, the guy's stereo. When the guy came out of his door wielding the ol' 12-gauge, the kid took off, got stopped by a fence, and doubled back. The truck owner said that the kid threatened him, and he blew open a hole in the kid's gut. The kid's friends say he threw his arms out and begged the guy not to shoot. No sale.

The kid bought the farm. A cop who didn't want to be identified speculated that the guy would get off, because protecting your life and property is looked on sympathetically out here in the Wild West.

I'll take New York in June, how about you?

After a few more minutes, including a run at the comics and a lament for the lost Calvin and Hobbes, Frieda returned. She was beaming, her face lit with the glow of the righteous having snared another black sheep.

"Okay," she said, "the bike's all clean and lubed, and the tires are full. You're gonna love this."

I responded with a grin of false enthusiasm, which she read correctly. She waved her hand at me. "You'll see. It's just like when you were a kid. I live to ride bikes."

We marched out to the hallway, where a red bike with fat tires and a real seat awaited me. I breathed relief.

"Man, you have no idea how good it is to see a seat that doesn't look like a sigmoidoscopy tool. I hated those skinny little bikes with the low handlebars. Not only did they put you in the proper position for a rectal exam, those skinny little seats gave you one."

Frieda looked amused. "Whatever gets you in the spirit, I guess."

Tentatively, I swung my leg over the bar. I diddled the brakes to remind myself which was the front and which was the rear. I didn't want to panic-stop and go ass-over-breakfast because I hit the front brake. I looked with incomprehension at the gear shift.

"There are twenty-one gears," Frieda explained. "You won't use more than four, and the shifter is set at the lowest

of the four. All the others are for serious mountain biking."
She demonstrated.

"Hey, your average molehill looks like Everest to me, if
I have to bike over it."

"Let me show you a map you can take with you."

We pored over a map, while Frieda explained the downtown setup, the several bridges across the Willamette River,
and how to get back to the house from any one of three of
them. Then she showed me where to find Powell's Bookstore, but insisted that her favorite was Great Northwest
Books, just down the street.

"Now," she said, "this is important. Pay attention, Portland drivers are nothing like east-coast drivers. We have our
share of maniacs and red-light runners, but the average
Portland driver is courteous to a fault. Walter insists that
getting behind a wheel puts people in a kind of temporary
brain death. And we have lots of intersections with no stop
signs in either direction. You'll find drivers deferring to
each other so that no one moves for a while until they work
it out. Drivers from back east are worked into a state of
hysteria while this is going on.

"Walter once was waiting for a light behind three or four
cars. The light turned green, and the guy in the first car
didn't move. No one honked. The light cycled one more
time through green and red. By this time, Walter was nearly
insane with frustration. He got out of his car and discovered
that the guy in the first car had fallen asleep. He woke him,
and they all made the next light. Walter still wonders how
long they would have sat there before somebody did
something."

I thought of the usual New York scene, where the first car
has one nanosecond to move when the light turns before the
horns start. This scene would have resulted in a homicide,
and no judge in the city would have convicted the perps.
Frieda went on.

"So don't expect instantaneous reactions from drivers,

don't expect stop signs at every intersection, and don't yell or gesture obscenely. It's bad manners."

I scratched my beard. "Let me get this straight. Hanging people up at a green light because you're meditating on the last Grateful Dead concert is *not* considered bad manners, pointing this out is?"

"Well, that's one way to put it. When in Rome, you know."

Having armed me with cultural data, Frieda now provided me with a bike lock, and a rain slicker, just in case.

I opened the door, and was immediately assaulted with a foul smell, something like swamp gas. I screwed up my face as the acrid stench hit the back of my throat.

"What the fuck is that smell?"

Frieda actually looked embarrassed.

"Um, well, that's the paper mill in Camas, Washington, just east of here in the Columbia Gorge. The winds come from the east fairly often and carry the smell with them. It's worse in the mornings, when the air is damp."

"Jeez, so much for clean air out here. A paper mill, you say?"

"Yeah, and the worst of it is that dioxin is a by-product of the process."

"Ah, so while the air may be foul, the water is poisonous."

She smiled such a pathetic little smile that I had to laugh.

I carried the bike down the stairs, and with a prayer to the gods that Mickey had remembered to pay our major medical, I took off. Much to my surprise and relief, the old cliché is right: You never forget how to ride a bicycle. Damn, it was fun. So much fun that I forgot to watch for traffic and wound up causing some guy in an ancient DeSoto to slam on his brakes and utter oaths. Obviously not a native.

As instructed, I headed north to Burnside Street and west to the bridge of the same name. Along the way I spotted several old cars, many of more than thirty years' vintage. I had noticed the same thing all over the West and Southwest, attributable to mild, or nonexistent, winters and no salt on the roads to eat away your pride and joy. The most fun was seeing a couple of those little Nash Metropolitans, the cartoon car itself. All it needed was eyeballs for headlights and teeth in its grille.

When I got to the Burnside Bridge, it was opened to river traffic. At first, I was pissed. How do they expect to be a real city if commerce is suspended every time some pissant boater with an overgrown mast comes down the river? It occurred to me almost immediately that this was just fine. Too many other cities had become slaves to speed and business whores. This little inconvenience was just right to remind us that not everything has to be done in a hurry. There are still cities in the USA that have train tracks intersecting large streets, and everything has to wait for 200-car freights to go by. Maybe we need more of this kind of thing.

Listen to me. In Oregon less than a day and I'm mellowing out already.

I made a quick left off Burnside, and made my way through the downtown to Tenth Avenue and Yamhill Street. There, in all its grey glory, was the main library. I locked the bike at a handy rack and headed inside. I was greeted by what I thought were security metal detectors, but were antitheft devices. You passed through them on the way out.

The woman at the information desk told me where to find the periodicals room on the third floor. I walked up, suddenly getting a hint of how much I had abused my aging-to-decrepit leg muscles. By the time I got to the right room, I despaired for cycling back. No matter.

An earnest young woman with tattoos and a Pebbles Flintstone hairdo got the proper microfilm volume and set me up on a viewer. I fast-forwarded through fires, floods, fights, and farces. Finally, I turfed up the story in the Metro section. It was sketchy, probably a quickie before deadline. It mentioned that Donnie Kimmel and his wife Sophie were involved in a terrible accident on I-84, that the truck was totaled, and that they both had sustained severe injuries, which probably "spelled the end of his baseball career." They were listed in serious condition at Providence Medical Center. Nothing more.

A few days later, Sophie Kimmel's dire condition was noted, and death expected to be imminent, from "injuries sustained during the wreck." Drugs and alcohol were suspected, but no charges had been filed against Kimmel, who was now listed in "guarded" condition, but whose left shoulder was scheduled for reconstructive surgery "as soon as doctors feel he is up to it." The story then went on to say that "D.K., as he is known to fans and sports reporters, popular outfielder for the Portland Webfeet," would never play again. His manager, speaking from his winter home in Phoenix, said, "Donnie was a bright spot in last year's disappointing season. He batted .323, and drove in nearly eighty runs. He stole twenty-six bases, and the brass were looking to move him up to the majors next year, sometime during the summer. They were sure going to give him a look-see in spring training."

Two other items I found interesting. First, there was a persistent rumor, resolutely undenied by the team owner, that the team would be moved to Salt Lake City, Utah. As opposed to Salt Lake City, Pennsylvania, I presumed. Second, that this same team owner had arranged for Kimmel to get a job with the stadium administration when and if he was able.

As a Brooklyn Dodger fan, I felt sympathetic agony for Portland, but it was the second thing I found puzzling. Why would this team owner, who didn't care about breaking a whole city's heart, give a shit about a ballplayer who had ruined himself and killed his wife? Why go out of his way for Donnie Kimmel?

I figured Lois would know, or at least be able to point me in the right direction. I rewound the microfilm, returned it to

Pebbles, who wished me a nice day, and decided to bike
right over to the stadium, which was pretty close by.

It only took a few minutes, but it was getting colder, and
Frieda's promise about not raining seemed as good a bet as
George Bush demanding a progressive income tax. The sun
seemed to have done a farewell for the day. It still wasn't as
cold as New York had been when I left it.

The stadium was smack on the fringes of downtown, a
real urban ball yard. I locked up the bike at the entrance and
walked in through an open gate. There were signs directing
me to the stadium office.

The office was of painted cinder block and cheap grey
metal desks. A guy in expensive sweats was sitting at one of
the desks. His hair was blow-dried into a TV evangelist's
pompadour. He looked up at me and smiled.

"Hi, can I help you?"

"Uh, yes, I hope so. I'm looking for Donnie Kimmel?"

His brow furrowed briefly, but his smile relit. "D.K.?
Yeah, he must be around somewhere. He's usually around
by this time. Look for him down on the field, or in the
stands. He's got a couple of maintenance things going."

It occurred to me how much "D.K." sounded like "Deak."
But then, I always was a fan of cheap ironies.

"Thanks. Just go on out there?"

"You bet, and have a good one!" That 100-watt smile again.

I nodded. I didn't ask what I should have a good one of.

I wandered around the concourse for a bit, and I walked
through a gate. Even in winter, I knew that I would
experience the thrill of emerging from the tunnel onto a vast
meadow of . . . artificial turf. Take me now, Lord.

Just managing to submerge my disgust, I wandered
through the stands and down to the field level. After about
ten minutes, I gave up. If Kimmel were there, his location
was beyond my poor powers to discover.

I went back to the office. Smiley was still there.

"Pardon me," I began.

He jumped.

"Sorry if I startled you. If Kimmel is here, I can't locate him."

The furrow returned to his brow, this time accompanied by a frown made grimmer by contrast with his smile.

"Um, may I ask who you are?"

"Sure. My name is Lenny Schneider. I'm a private investigator hired by Kimmel's father-in-law. I need to speak with him about a family matter."

The frown deepened. "You're not going to make trouble for him?"

Why was everybody so concerned about this guy's welfare?

"Not at all. Can you tell me where to find him?"

Smiley sighed. "Sit down, Mr., uh, Schneider, is it?"

"Schneider it is." I held out my hand, and he gripped it. "My name is Richard Smiley."

Another cheap irony. I thought, Maybe there is a master plan.

He sat down and tented his fingertips. "Donnie has, ah, a bit of a problem. And it's getting worse. He drinks. It never affected his work until recently, and he never used to drink on the job.

"Now . . . well, some days he shows up late, and some days not at all. We don't want to be, ah, unfair to him, but it is becoming a problem. We'll do the best we can for him."

I thought, Unfair? To him? How unfair was he to Sophie? But I said, "It's admirable of you to feel that way."

He shrugged. "I assume you know something about his, ah, circumstances. Don't you think he's had it rough enough?"

"At least he's alive. Thanks for your help. If Kimmel comes in, please give me a call at this number." I wrote Walter's number on a scratch pad lying on his desk. "I would really appreciate it."

"Sure. No problem. I'll tell Margie, too. She works afternoons."

I walked out. Smiley didn't smile.

seven

W<small>HEN</small> I GOT BACK TO
the street, it still hadn't begun to rain. I decided to press my
luck and visit Powell's Bookstore. The place was just a few
blocks down Burnside from the stadium.

Powell's is a tourist attraction in Portland, and with good
reason. I had heard about it from other book freaks, but I
had never been there before, and I was anxious to see it. It
takes up a whole block, and is multileveled. And there are
books *everywhere*. New, used. Even a rare book room. The
place is divided into sections, each given a different color,
the Rose Room, the Gold Room, etc. Each section contains
specific types of books. The only store that even comes
close is Foyle's in London, which is two five-story buildings
full of books, but the damn place is arranged by *publisher*,
so that you could go nuts if you're looking for a specific
subject area.

It was kind of overwhelming. I wandered for about
twenty minutes, stopping here and there, browsing, vowing
to come back when I wasn't on a damn bike. As I stood
absorbed in a Mencken collection, I got a tap on my
shoulder, and almost jumped through my thinning hair.

"Sorry, didn't mean to scare you." It was Lois.

"Hey, no problem. I haven't had a coronary yet this week."

"What are you doing in Powell's, besides the obvious?"

"Not much." I showed her the Mencken book before I replaced it, and got a nod of approval. "I was in the neighborhood, and decided to check out the legendary place itself."

"Yeah, quite a joint. You know, there are more readers per capita in Portland than in New York." She struck a prideful pose.

"Really? Well, this is a bit like a bookworm's Valhalla."

She leaned in conspiratorially. "Actually, my favorite bookstore is Great Northwest Books, just down the street. Tell John or Phil that Lois sent you."

I did a looking-around take. "Affirmative. But what are you doing here?"

"I came to look for a book of Emily Dickinson's poetry, and to have a bite. You can get soup and sandwiches in the Coffee Room, and there are tables for reading and shmoozing. Wanna go?"

I shrugged. "Sure. I always prefer meals in the company of beautiful women. It aids my digestion."

"Pig." But she smiled.

We wandered through sections of mysteries, science fiction, and children's books, and came to a large room full of tables that were full of people. As we looked around, a small table opened up, and Lois made for it like a cruise missile.

She gestured for me to sit down. "Hold the fort. I'll treat. Soup du jour and a chicken sandwich?"

"Yeah, fine. And some coffee? Black?"

"You got it."

Lois moved in and around the close-placed tables, toward a line at a counter. More than one head turned to follow her.

I looked around. The place had racks and racks of magazines, and books on gardening. The walls were decorated with aprons, of the Donna Reed/June Cleaver 1950's-mom variety. Lace, flower prints, rickrack, froufrou galore.

The crowd seemed, based on my limited experience, to be a cross section of Portland. There really did seem to be an unusually large amount of ultrahip eccentricity in this small city, balanced with a yuppie or two, and those who were clearly in here to escape the street for a while. I had observed before, on trips to Seattle and San Francisco, that the upper-left-hand corner of the U.S. was where all the old hippies had come to live out their existences. Portland fit right in.

I was rescued from a fate worse than sociology when Lois returned with a tray. I stood and helped her with the various items. We snacked on the soup, served bewilderingly in paper cups, and plastic-wrapped sandwiches. Certainly more a convenience than a gustatory delight. While we ate, we chatted pointlessly.

I looked up from my, ahem, repast to people-watch, as a steady stream came in to have coffee, browse, see and be seen. One new visitor grabbed my attention immediately. Tall, slender, with a haystack of straw-colored hair, he was striking anyway. But the thing that got me, and held me like a chicken hypnotized by a snake, was his eyes. Remember that *Life* magazine cover of Charlie Manson, eyes burning out of his sockets and into your uneasy consciousness? Well, this guy's eyes were like that.

Restlessly, his eyes took in the room, slashing through his surroundings with a razor-blade edge. The temperature seemed to drop ten degrees in his presence, and a chill shook me. Lois noticed my slack-jawed stare and turned to follow my gaze. She made a sort of small gasp.

"I might have known," she whispered, "that it was him."

Snapping out of it, I asked, "You know this guy?"

She nodded. "Augean Stabile. He has this effect on everyone, no matter how many times you actually see him. I've spoken with him many times, and I'm sure I still look at him like he was dressed in black robes and carrying a scythe. Another one on Walter's shit list. And the feeling is mutual."

"Oh?" I became more attentive.

"Yeah, Augie Stabile was once partners with Caliban Strunz."

"The maniac on cable TV?"

"The very one. We talked about this a little last night. Strunz was a volunteer news reporter on KOOK, and a real pain in the ass. He hogged the production facilities and bullied people who tried to ask him to give up some time so they could work. He got into several shouting matches and terrified most of the women who had to work around him."

"Shit, he terrified me just watching him on the tube."

"So you can imagine the pleasure it must have been to be there with him. Anyway, he hooked up with Stabile, somehow. I think that it's because Stabile wanted to get onto KOOK, and figured the best way was to piggyback on Strunz."

I nodded. "But, to mix a metaphor, he backed the wrong horse."

"Big time," she agreed. "Strunz got Stabile on for some series of specials about the Portland police being the shock troops of the oncoming fascist takeover, a not-uncommon idea here in the Land of the Conspiracy Nut."

"And?"

She shrugged. "Well, I didn't hear it, but the word is that they really were too much. They made a series of wild, half-baked charges, and then demanded that people call the station to get them a regular time slot. It didn't help that the slot they wanted was Walter's. He took it personally. To add injury to insult, they called on listeners *not* to pay their pledges to the station unless they got a show."

"I guess this is a no-no on a listener-sponsored station?"

"Right again. Slim Reed, the station manager, could have acted here to, I don't know exactly, calm things down or clear the air, or lay down the law. Whatever. Instead, he did nothing. Walter took it upon himself to read the riot act to these guys, and it almost wound up in a fistfight between Walter and Strunz.

"The next night, on Strunz's cable TV show, these two bad-mouthed KOOK, including slanderous personal attacks. They even dug up some black guy who used to do a music program there to swear that he was kicked off the station because the program director and station manager were racists. Walter tells me that he was really 86ed because he was stealing records and CDs, and got caught at it.

"Stabile and Strunz also resurrected the 'KOOK is run by a cabal of dykes, and a straight white guy can't get a show' charge."

"Any truth to that?" I was keeping my attention on Stabile, who seemed to clear a path before him just by walking, even in this crowded room.

"You know, I've lived in a couple of cities now, not excluding New York. They have all had left-wing community radio stations, and they have all been accused of that. It's mostly bullshit. There are plenty of lesbians at KOOK, but they sure don't run the place, and plenty of white guys are getting shows."

"So what next?" I was truly rapt, deep into a fascinating story from a fascinating woman.

"Well, the program director fires Strunz off the station. Stabile never really had any formal status there, except as Strunz's guest. Immediately, they start a campaign on cable and in the local alternative press claiming that they were being censored for their views. It was a real mess. People withdrew their support from the station, and a claque of Stabile's supporters started disrupting the station's board and committee meetings. It took months until things calmed down, and the station's never really recovered."

"So what's this about Strunz and Stabile falling out?" The hot soup was starting to erode the glue on the paper cup. I was in a race to swallow it before it escaped.

"It's hard to say what really went on. They were sharing a house, Strunz and his wife, Stabile and his now-former girlfriend. I guess they were just too nuts and egocentric to survive under one roof. Stabile owns two big dogs, mastiffs or something, whose house-training left something to be desired. Stabile felt that, if Strunz lived there, he should clean up dog poop without complaining. Stabile is also a gun and knife collector, and would brandish various weapons from time to time.

"Strunz, on the other hand, throws temper tantrums at will. You never can tell what will piss him off. He's supposed to have punched out his wife a few times. It was inevitable that they would get in each other's faces."

Before I could ask the next question, a dark shadow fell over us. I looked up and saw Augean Stabile looming at our table. I felt like Frodo Baggins in the lair of Smaug.

Stabile's voice was a wind from a tomb, tinged just slightly with a European accent. He eyed me balefully, and his hand went to his waist. I broke my stare and followed his hand with my gaze. He had a large and unusual knife hanging sheathed from his belt, the hilt carved with what appeared to be demons or gargoyles. He fingered it as he glared at me. I thought about the incident at the radio station.

"Hello, Lois." He kept looking at me, even as he addressed her. "I have not seen you in a while. Are you still sharing a house with that vicious little toad?" Stabile chuckled nasally, reminding me strangely of Joe McCarthy.

"Hello, Augie. Yes, I'm still living with Walter. Are you still sharing a house with Caliban?" Her face was the image of innocence.

Stabile hissed like a reptile. "Aaagh! Don't mention that name to me! Hadn't you heard? Surely you heard?"

Lois spread her arms and mimed ignorance.

"Enough about that." Stabile switched gears. "Who is your friend?" he asked with whatever he could muster for pleasantness.

"Oh, this is Lenny Schneider. He's a friend from New York."

I stood up and extended my hand, albeit reluctantly. I would rather shake hands with Freddy Krueger. His grip was clammy.

"Hi, good to meet you." Another socially required fib.

"What are you in town for? Are you thinking of moving here?"

"Ah, well, I'm here for a client, a kind of personal services thing. And, no, I'm not thinking of moving here, despite the presence of women like Lois."

Lois nodded graciously. Stabile grimaced.

"Good. There are too many New Yorkers here already. No offense," he lied ineptly.

"None taken. It's a pretty little place, but the food and culture could stand improvement, and I'm told the city is lousy with paranoid conspiracy nuts."

Another grim reaper smile, and a quick look toward Lois.

"If you'll excuse me . . ." and he turned and was gone in a blink. His absence was a rosy dawn after a werewolf night.

"Gee," I wondered aloud, "I wonder how much he'd charge to haunt a house."

"He'd probably charge by the room."

I had to laugh. "Not bad. So, speak of the devil, eh what?"

"No doubt the devil would be better company. There's more to tell about him, but suddenly I've had enough Augean Stabile for one day. You never really told me why you were in town. Can you talk about it?"

"Ah, Lois, I would tell you anything. If I had two cigarettes, and I smoked, I would light them and give you one."

I made my best Charles Boyer bedroom eyes. She leaned across the table, batted her eyes, and said, "You are so fool of sheet."

"Chevrolet coupe, my dear. Okay, I'll tell you, but only because I think that you can help me some more. Thanks for the library tip, by the way.

"I'm here to find Donnie Kimmel for Deak Rowan, so I can locate Sophie Rowan."

She whistled. "Boy, I remember that can of worms. What does Rowan want D.K. for? To apologize?"

I guess I looked shocked. Lois gave me an inquisitive stare.

"What in the world would Deacon Rowan have to apologize to Kimmel for?" I asked incredulously.

Some kind of understanding broke on her face. "Lenny, what do you know about Kimmel's accident?"

"I was told that Kimmel was stoned and/or drunk and he wrecked their pickup somewhere out on the freeway killing her and ruining himself in the process."

"I thought so. Okay, here's what really happened. D.K. was a terrific ballplayer. This kid had Major League written all over him. He was also good-natured and a hunk. I was tempted to throw myself at him more than once. He was a pussycat.

"He was also very loyal to Sophie, as foulmouthed and unpleasant a bitch as I've ever run into."

"What!?"

"Let me finish. She was so awful, it was a mystery to all of us why D.K. stayed with her. When she was sober, she was just grumpy and irritable, but she was hardly ever sober. When she was loaded, she was like a Hell's Angel on speed: crude, obnoxious, loudmouthed, insanely jealous.

"The night of the accident, in the off-season, they learned that he might be called up to The Show. He was invited to attend spring training with the team, and, when they settled some roster changes, he would get a shot. Meanwhile, he was probably going to spend some part of the Triple-A season with Portland, only Portland was losing its team to Salt Lake City. Bottom Line: they might have to move temporarily to Salt Lake to await being called up.

"Sophie went bugshit when she heard. She ranted about how boring Utah was, and a bunch of stuff about Mormons, and who the hell did they think they were making him cool his heels in the minors, blah, blah, blah. She got shit-faced drunk, and she was already loaded on some kind of downer. She demanded that they go out to the Gorge to Multnomah Falls. She liked it there. I do, too. No matter.

"Anyway, it was cold and foggy. She wouldn't let him drive. They fought about it, but she drove stoned most of the time. While they were driving out there on 84, she lit a cigarette. D.K. asked her to open a window, 'cause he hated the smell of smoke. But the stench of the paper mill pissed her off, and she took her eyes off the road to complain to him. They hit a patch of black ice . . ."

I interrupted her. "What the hell is black ice?"

She took a breath. "Black ice forms pretty easily on the roads here in the winter. It's a patch of unshiny ice that just looks like the road is wet, but it's as slippery as hell. When she hit that black ice going too fast, and fucked-up to boot, she started to skid, panicked, and careened from one side of the freeway to another, nearly killing people in several other cars. Finally, she went off the road and flipped the truck. Naturally, she wasn't wearing a seat belt.

"She was mangled, and nearly died on the way to the hospital. D.K.'s shoulder, and his baseball career, were crushed. He made the cops tell her father that it was his fault. The only reason they went along with it was because everybody here loved him, and he was desperate that her folks be spared the truth."

I was flabbergasted. I didn't say anything for a while.

"Close your mouth, Lenny. Your dental work isn't that attractive."

"Huh? Oh, sorry. It's just that, my God, I had no idea. Deak thinks Sophie was . . . and that Kimmel . . ." My voice trailed off.

"So it seems."

"Deak asked me to come out here and find out where Sophie was buried, so he could have her moved to the family plot. You know anything about this?"

"Nope." She furrowed her brow, and a funny look blew across her face. "I guess you'll have to speak with D.K."

"They told me he was a drunk today when I asked about him at the stadium. An unreliable one, at that."

"He is *now*. He never even took an aspirin before the accident. The club owner was a freak for drug testing. He even made the groundskeepers pee in little cups. Kimmel couldn't have used anything even if he wanted to."

I whistled. "Well, goddamn. I'm glad we had this little talk. Now I really have to talk with him, and not just about the grave site. Thanks a lot. It certainly explains why everyone is so protective of him."

"Hey," she brightened, "I knew there was something to tell you. There's a KOOK party tonight, not far from the house. You should try to come. You'll meet the good, the bad, and the ugly."

"I've already met Bella Durke, so two out of three are covered."

"Yikes! Cold, but accurate. Remind me to tell you about the time she cornered me in the bathroom here at Powell's. But you might have to get me drunk to tell it."

"Sounds good to me, in any case. Can I get you another coffee?"

"Nah, I really got to get back to work and hit that old police scanner. See you tonight."

She got up, put on her coat, and hurried out. I watched the watchers watching her. She was fine as wine.

eight

I SAT THERE FOR A FEW more minutes deciding whether I would buy the Mencken book, and trying to shake off the encounter with Stabile, of the sociopath eyes. As my mind was trying to wrap itself around the eternal mysteries, the sun broke through the clouds and blasted in the windows of the Coffee Room.

What a mood elevator! Flushed with good feeling, I purchased the book, the clerk wishing me a nice day, and I allowing as how the sunshine helped. The clerk, a magenta-haired fellow with a Virginia Woolf T-shirt, frowned.

"I left Phoenix because I was tired of the sun. Sunlight just depresses me." I advised renting a couple of Ingmar Bergman films and drinking a bottle of cheap Aquavit. He thanked me. I wished him a gloomy day.

The bike ride back to Walter's was uneventful, unless my shock and horror that it was all uphill once I crossed the river qualifies as an event. It was nice to get back on a bike, but tomorrow it would be *real* nice to rent a car.

It was about 3:15 local time when I arrived at the house. No one was home, and I decided to call Deak, the time difference being what it was. I mulled over telling him what I had discovered, and concluded that I would try to talk with Kimmel before I gave a complete report.

"Deak? This is Lenny Schneider from Portland."

"Hey, Lenny, whaddaya got for us?"

"Well, I found out where Kimmel works. I tried to see him, but he hadn't come in. I should get to him within a day or so."

"That bastard's still hangin' around, eh? Do you really need him?"

"I suppose I could call the county clerk and try to get Sophie's location. I'll try that as soon as we get off the phone."

"Oh, yeah, it's still the middle of the afternoon there. If you get something today, call me right back."

"Check, Deak. If not, you'll hear from me around this time tomorrow."

"Thanks, Lenny. And, oh, treat yourself to a beer and a good meal. On me."

"You're a nice man, Deak. Talk to you soon."

I hung up, feeling only a little guilty. I called Sue.

"So, how's Walter?" she asked archly.

"Funny, as in peculiar. He's working at a radio station here that gives him more grief than goodies, but he loves his show so much he won't quit it."

She made a *humph!* noise. "Typical. Is the grief real, or is he just unable to completely enjoy himself, as usual?"

"If you're basing that question on your relationship with him, you might ask yourself who *has* completely enjoyed being with you."

"Len-n-n-ny. Must you, even on long distance?"

"Okay, cheap shot for cheap shot notwithstanding. Walter's station is one of these highly political places where anger and ideology often substitute for thought. He's definitely being harassed by some unsavory types. I can't figure out yet how much he brought on himself, but it's not all his fault."

"What's his girlfriend's name?"

"Frieda. She's very sensitive and intense, and very

protective of Walter. It's nice to see such loyalty and passion in a woman."

Coldly, "What are you trying to say?"

I sighed. "Hey, don't get your knickers in a bunch. No implications meant. He's had a few knocks, and it's good to see him getting support from his lover, that's all. She's a bike messenger, wiry as a monkey. She's a bit afraid of what I represent, but she's okay."

"You mean the 'bad old days'?"

"Yeah, I guess. Walter's still got some issues to work through. Everybody's not like you, you know."

"Meaning?"

I was on thin ice here. My mind raced.

"You know, uh, able to reinvent yourself and let things go." That sounded cool.

"Yeah, yeah. Right. What about the case?"

Whew! I gave her the highlights. She *oohed* and *aahed* in the appropriate places.

"You know," she said, "I'm getting a feeling about this whole trip. I think you're in for some shocks before this is over, and it's not related to your actual job there."

I always take Sue's intuitions seriously. She could start her own psychic hotline, if she could learn not to alienate people she feels superior to, a group which includes most of the human race, especially those of the female persuasion.

As we were talking, Love galumphed down the stairs and leaped onto the bed.

"Walter's cat just came in. Great cat. A real bruiser, kinda like a small wildcat, but with a goofy name."

"Goofy name?"

"How about 'Love'?"

"Over the telephone?"

"No, silly. That's the cat's name."

"Ooh, icky."

"Yeah, and it doesn't fit him. It's like Mike Tyson was named Percival, or something."

"I once knew a biker named Percival."

"Sue, I don't *even* want to hear about it. I'll talk to you soon."

We rang off.

I stretched out on the bed to think. Love wanted to play, so I leisurely ran my hand over his fur. Apparently, this was not what he had in mind, because he grabbed my hand in his claws and bit me hard. The little fucker had a bite like a pit bull. I yelled and yanked my hand. Big mistake. His claws raked me a few gashes. The bloodletting must have been satisfying, because he let go and assumed a smug look.

"Listen, you furry assassin, if we're gonna get along, you'd better play nice."

He flopped down on the bed and meowed, whether in agreement or disdain I can't say. I decided to take a walk, in the hope of preventing my muscles from charley-horsing. When I stood up, the cat leaped off the bed and began rubbing up against my legs. I knew that meant he was hungry.

I walked upstairs with the cat dogging my heels. When I got to the kitchen, I noticed a full plate of food over in the corner, next to a bowl of dry food. I walked to the food plate, with Love trotting next to me, and indicated that he had stuff to eat. He sniffed it and with monumental revulsion, backed away from it like it was on fire.

"He won't eat it."

I jumped. It was Walter.

"Christ, you scared me. Why won't he eat it?"

Walter shrugged. "He's a funny little bug. If he doesn't scarf it immediately, he won't ever touch it again. Even if it's something he usually likes, his rejection is permanent. You might as well chuck the stuff. He's the pickiest and most oddball cat I ever had."

"Guess who I met at lunch today?"

"You don't know anyone here, so it's tough for me to imagine."

He seemed a bit grumpy. Maybe he hadn't got a lot of sleep.

"Well, I was in Powell's and ran into Lois, so we decided to have lunch there."

He made a face like he had eaten there. I went on.

"So, while we're eating, in walks Augie Stabile."

He made gagging noises and mimed sticking his fingers down his throat. "Did he give you the creeps?"

I nodded. " 'The creeps' doesn't begin to describe it. He would unnerve a grave robber. He's got a Manson quality to him. What's his story?"

Walter sighed.

"Hey," I came back quickly, "I don't want you to have another cow like you did last night. Forget I asked."

"Nah, what the hell. Sit down, I'll make some coffee." Love yowled and rubbed against Walter's legs. "How silly of me. I meant that I'd feed the cat, and *then* make some coffee."

I paid attention to the mechanics of the process in case I was called upon to perform the duty. I hadn't had a cat in a long time, and I was really liking this scruffy feline hoodlum. When Love noted his satisfaction with the new choice of cat food by purring and bolting the stuff like a wolf, Walter made some coffee, grinding the whole beans and using a drip cone. Perfect.

Walter sat across from me and began to rub his beard with one hand, the coffee cup suspended in the air by the other.

"Where to begin? There really is no beginning here. B.B. Wolfe is the nexus of the conspiracy-nut universe around here. He's been investigating things for years, the Kennedy and King assassinations, the CIA running drugs, the shadow government, the international military/industrial cabal, what-have-you. He reads dozens of publications that cover the spectrum from crazy Right to loony Left. He reads books, he monitors shortwave, I don't even know what.

"As a result, this guy is astonishingly well informed about political activity around the world. There's only one thing, no, two, that bother me. First, whatever your problems with, say, *Time* magazine, they use reporters who at least have some bona fides. If they screw up, they print retractions, or at least explain why they stand by their story. And they are always being second-guessed by *Newsweek,* or *U.S. News*, or whomever.

"The stuff that B.B. reads has no such checks and balances. Oh, sure, the occasional argument ensues among these rags, but it's more of a pissing contest, or an attempt to prove that the other guy is a tool of the enemy. Second, if you read some far-out bullshit in one source, and another source has the same story, even if it's only reporting the fact that the story appeared, this does not constitute two sources as confirmation."

He began to gesture and slopped coffee out of his cup. I almost challenged him on the trustworthiness of corporate whores like *Time* and *Newsweek*, but figured it wouldn't do much good.

"Walter, why do you give a shit? Let these people have their fun. What's it got to do with you?"

He made a frustrated noise. His face got red. I held up my palms.

"Whoa, pal. Calm down. I don't want you to have a conniption."

"Okay, this is the problem. Wolfe commands the loyalty of a small but vocal group of people. They hang on his every word. When he goes off on the radio station, he can poison a lot of minds. Plus, when Stabile and Strunz went around bad-mouthing KOOK, he supported them. This gave them credibility they didn't deserve. And he was most likely doing it because he has issues with the station, rather than on the merits of their case. Their case had *no* merit. I was on the board of directors when all this shit went down, and I refused to let them make it a censorship case. It was . . ."

"I know. Lois filled me in."

"Yeah, so they proceeded to assassinate my character in public. I fought back, until Frieda threatened to leave me. She said I was becoming obsessed with them, and that it didn't matter. But it mattered to me. I've tried to be fair and open to everyone, and they were making me out some fascist, or FBI plant, whatever. I *still* meet people who react badly to me from all this, and it was two years ago."

I decided to change the subject. "Lois tells me there's a party tonight."

It took him a second to change direction. A wry smile crossed his face.

"Yeah, it'll be mostly KOOK people. You should go. It might be educational."

"Okay, what time?"

"It'll get rolling about nine-thirty or so. The place is only a couple of blocks from here. We should all go together. The girls'll be home by six; we can cop some eats and still have plenty of time to get there."

"Solid," I agreed. "What should I wear?"

He laughed. "You're already overdressed. Chill out. This is Portland. You could pick your wardrobe out of a dumpster and nobody would notice."

"Yowza. I'm gonna head back downstairs and relax. I'm still struggling with West Coast time." This was a lie, but I needed some time to think.

Walter saluted, and I stood up. "Is there a cold beer in the fridge?"

He looked hurt. "Is a fat hog heavy?"

"Gotcha."

He got up and headed toward the stairs. "I'll be up in my room catching up on some work if you need me."

"Yeah, well, I'm just gonna get a beer and go down to my little dungeon. See you later."

I tossed down the last of the coffee and rinsed the cup in the sink. There was a pile of saucers in the sink, each with a residue of cat food on them. What a spoiled animal! If my cats didn't like what they got, they went hungry until their next feeding.

The refrigerator had a variety of beers. I chose Obsidian Stout. Finding a beer mug in the drainer by the sink, I poured the stout and went downstairs.

The job for Deak Rowan would probably resolve itself quickly. I had to think of some way I could break the news to him that Sophie was the bad guy in this morality play. In the meanwhile, I called the county clerk's office and was informed that there was no record of any interment.

So now I *really* had to talk to Kimmel. He could have had her cremated and stashed in a shoe box under his bed. I felt that idle speculation was useless, if not morbid, so I went on to contemplate Walter's situation. This seemed equally useless and morbid, but a lot more fun.

I turned on the radio and looked for KOOK. They were playing African pop music, for which I have only a small tolerance, so I hunted around the low end of the dial where the public stations usually dwell.

I found a station broadcasting Catholic Church doctrine, with some Christian pop music. Ixnay.

I found a classical station that was playing one of those overblown Sibelius symphonies. Not in the mood.

I found a jazz station that alternated decent stuff with guitar-and-synth "soft jazz." I settled, and was soon rewarded with Jon Hendricks and Thelonious Monk doing "In Walked Bud." Cool.

Sitting on the bed and sipping my beer, I let my thoughts wander. How was Mickey, and her new beau? A call to Uncle Sol for that, although I had better check in with Mickey at the office so she thinks that I really give a shit.

Then Walter and his peculiar situation insinuated themselves in my thoughts. My better judgment told me to stay as far as I could from what was a tar-baby mess. The more you got into it, the more it would suck you in. The horror, the horror.

Hey, if all went right, I would be done with Kimmel and out of here in a day or two. I could take Walter and Frieda out for a nice dinner, thank them profusely for their hospitality, listen with great sympathy and compassion to their plight, ask Lois if I could call her every now and then, and be outta here like a big-ass bird.

Sounded good. I finished my excellent stout and took a nap.

After what must have been a couple of hours, I felt someone's presence hanging over me as I slept. I woke to find Lois, arms akimbo, at the foot of the bed.

I stretched and groaned, and rubbed my eyes. I said sleepily, "Oh, have I died and gone to heaven? Who is this angel I see before me?"

"God," she laughed, "you can bullshit even roused from a sound sleep. It's about dinnertime, seven or so. We're all famished waiting for Sleeping Beauty to haul his ass out of bed. By the way, you snore like a two-hundred-pound bumble-bee."

"Ah, it speaks, this angel. Do I have time to take a quick shower?"

"If you take more than ten minutes, we'll come in and haul your naked ass to the restaurant."

"Okay, let me get in the water. Unless you want to scrub my back."

"Lenny, you don't know me very well. So far, you've been on good behavior. I'm not amused by sexual banter, even if it's not serious."

I held up my hands. "Ouch. Sorry. *No mas*. I'll see you upstairs in a trice, whatever that is."

She nodded and walked away. I stripped, showered, and dressed in eleven minutes.

"You're late!" they said in unison as I burst into the kitchen.

We all piled into Walter's van and went across the river to a deli called Korn's. There were pictures of Olde New York on the walls. I ordered a cold beet borscht and a tongue sandwich on club with sauerkraut. The waitress told me they didn't have beet borscht, only cabbage, didn't serve tongue, and what was club bread?

Walter blushed deeply, and then even more deeply when I ordered a corned beef on white toast with lettuce and mayo and a glass of milk. The waitress was about to place the order when I called her back, and changed it to chopped liver on rye, a potato knish, and a beer, some local brew if they had it. She made a face. I gave her an innocent look.

After she left, Walter apologized. "Lenny, as you are certainly now aware, this is not Katz's deli. Sorry."

"Hey, don't worry about it. I'm still learning that my concept of what's funny isn't necessarily so here, not to mention my concept of what to eat. Is this the best Portland can do?"

"Not really. This is just the easiest place to get to. There aren't many more places, but they're both better. One is in the Jewish community center, so it's closed now. The other has two inconvenient locations, unless you live in the burbs."

The food was fair when it came, except that the knish weighed in about the same as a bowling ball. I made a great show of liking it, which neither Walter nor Lois bought, but which pleased Frieda. Even *ex*-New Yorkers are skeptical of everything.

I paid for dinner, amongst perfunctory protests and requests to pay the tip. I let them come up with the tip. We left and headed back to the east side for the party. It was being thrown at a group house, all of whose inhabitants worked at KOOK in some capacity.

When we pulled up, I could just make out a huge gabled old Victorian, that looked like the Addams family lived there. It was really nice, in a spooky, altogether ooky sort of way.

A group of cigarette smokers, banished to the outer darkness, congregated in front of the house. As we passed them, a Klaxon voice rang out. "Oh, shit. I guess they'll let anyone in here. Lois, why don't you ditch that bunch and come over here."

I turned toward the sound, which turned out to originate in the rotund body of Bella Durke. Walter yelled, "Lois is afraid you'll sit on her face and suffocate her."

This drew a few snickers from the other nicotine heads, but Lois hissed agitatedly at Walter, "Mind your own damn business. I can take care of myself. She wasn't talkin' to you!"

Undaunted, Walter said, "Hey, Bella, why don't you quit smoking. Oh, I know, it helps you keep your weight down."

Now Frieda chimed in. "Aren't things bad enough with her without you provoking her?"

"He don't provoke me," Bella snorted. "He ain't even on my radar screen."

"I hope your feet are on your radar. It's the only way you'll ever get to see them."

Now Frieda grabbed Walter by the arm and rushed him toward the doors. "God*damn* it! Don't you know when to stop?"

I looked at Lois, but she was looking at the ground and muttering disgustedly.

It was just ten when we got there, if you could believe the magnificent old grandfather clock in the front hallway of the house. Coats were piled in careless abandon on a couch along the wall. Loud music and chatter seemed to be coming from everywhere. We dumped our coats in one pile, and entered the house.

Another big, high-ceilinged living room with dark wainscoting, picture rails, and pocket doors greeted us. I wondered what a house like this, fixed up a bit, would fetch in the New York suburbs. More than I had. Of course, a decent apartment was beyond my means.

The furniture was the same kind of fifth-hand castoffs most people I knew had been using since the fifties. The walls were festooned with framed snapshots, jazz and rock posters, and handbills announcing political events. There was even, heaven help us, a poster proclaiming that war was not healthy for children and other living things.

The people were a mix of assorted boho types spanning all eras: brooding middle-aged beats, sixties-style longhairs, punks, grungers, and nondifferentiated counterculturalists. Over in one corner, a few people were passing a pipe around. I was intrigued that tobacco smoking inside was verboten, but not weed. Maybe because it was illegal, but that may not have even been a consideration.

Slim Reed was sitting on a couch chatting up a pink-cheeked woman-child no more than twenty years old. He saw us and acknowledged us with a wave. Walter waved back. I was fascinated. I hadn't been to a real party in years. Most of my contemporaries had kids and mortgages, and tended to limit their conversations to few subjects more than that. Discussion of the issues of the day was perfunctory, but bring up plumbing repairs or soccer practice, and everyone's eyes lit up.

This party, though, was more like it. Walter and Frieda were called over to join a group in hot pursuit of an idea. Lois hung back, and I decided to stay with her.

I stepped back, the better to appreciate her. There was a lot to appreciate. She was dressed down, in a casual/preppie kind of way. Much-washed and baggy khaki slacks, snug in a couple of attractive places, with a faded navy-blue knit alligator shirt that clung lovingly to her upper torso. Seemingly, no bra intruded to hinder its caress.

She wore a red bandana around her neck, a rope belt, and deck shoes with no socks. The whole thing was topped by a blue hopsack blazer. This kid had style.

She caught me looking, again. I affected wide-eyed innocence. "I was just admiring your . . . ensemble," I stammered. She nodded.

"No, really. Well-made casual clothes, all put together with a classy touch. Very impressive."

She smiled. Bull's-eye!

"Thanks. I don't find many people out here who would notice. I guess I move in the wrong circles."

"Lois, I've met very few people whom I would less suspect of going in circles."

She arched an eyebrow. "If you're coming on to me, let's have a beer. I want to see what happens when I weaken my resistance with alcohol."

"Sounds good to me."

Lois raised a finger in a just-a-minute sort of way, and headed off somewhere. Oh, great, I thought, she's probably escaping out the back and going home. I continued to affect a casual stance.

To my delight, she soon returned with two bottles. I didn't even notice what kind it was. My eyes were on her.

"Okay, do your thing."

I assumed a pained expression. "Look, Lois, I don't know enough about you to be sure if you're putting me on. I'm doin' the best I can here."

"Aw, poor baby. Is the big, bad tough guy intimidated by li'l ol' me?"

I got a bit hot. "Hey, Lois, you know what? Screw this shit. Women are always bitching about men playing games. Guess what? It's no better coming in the other direction. So . . ."

"Okay, okay, I'm sorry. Time out." She laid a palm on top of her beer bottle to make a T. "I'm so used to jocks and cops playin' grab-ass with me I'm not fit for polite company anymore.

"I'm sorry if I offended you, or hurt your feelings. You seem to be a nice guy, and I'm way too jaded."

On impulse, I leaned over and kissed her.

Big mistake. Whatever thaw had been in progress stopped. Before anything else could happen, Walter and Frieda came over.

With his usual sensitivity, Walter chose to make a big deal out of it. "Do my eyes deceive me, or did I see a public display of affection here?" He and Frieda were leering obscenely.

Neither Lois nor I said a thing. Something passed between us that approached understanding. Walter quickly discerned that his remark was as welcome as RuPaul at a Southern Baptist bible camp.

"Oops," said Frieda, not quite under her breath.

"No problem here," Lois recovered. "Lenny was just saying 'see you later' and got carried away. Right, Lenny?"

"Yeah, and the quicker I get carried away, the better." I excused myself from my group and set out on some serious mingling.

I scoped the place out. There were intense little conclaves everywhere, so I eavesdropped long enough to see if I was interested. Topic shopping, as it were.

I avoided the ones that were personal gossip, or KOOK politics. I zeroed in on one about Cuba. The dominant speaker was an intense, shaven-headed man of about thirty-five, in a U.S. Army fatigue jacket and surplus *Bundeswehr* wool pants. He was holding forth on the blockade.

"The U.S. is trying to starve the revolution, but Fidel is tough. His people can't get medical supplies, or oil, and so they've reinvented the revolution. They use organic techniques for farming, and animal power rather than tractors. It's inspiring."

One of his listeners, an equally intense, multi-pierced and tattooed young woman, asked, "How will they survive? The Soviet Union can't help them anymore."

"The world has to defy American economic imperialism. Eventually, we'll see the futility of our behavior and lift the embargo. The Cubans will have to tough it out until then."

I asked hesitantly, "Um, are they still relying on sugar and tobacco as export crops? It doesn't seem like these have much of a future in the modern world. Wouldn't it be better for them to develop a subsistence agriculture, and train their people for modern light industry? It's never gonna change for them until Castro croaks. He's still hung up in Stalinist economic and social ideas. Not to mention the rumors of mistreatment of anti-Fidel dissidents."

Everyone turned and looked. I felt like I had farted at a christening. The man looked at me with bemused contempt.

"Listen, I don't know who you are, but Cuba and North Korea are the last hope of the revolution. Even China is going capitalist. You got a problem with Fidel?"

"I've got a problem with dictators. The Right is willing to

support savages like Franco and Noriega, and even Saddam Hussein until they fuck up. The Left is blind to the faults of Castro and Kim Il Sung, or whoever's in charge over there. You either have a free society or you don't. The revolution is bullshit if it results in a North Korea or a Cambodia. Fidel is a tyrant who is kinder to his people than Batista, but that's no big trick. And he was a lousy pitcher, too."

The *Fidelisto* looked around at his listeners. "Let's go outside for some fresh air." He looked right at me. "It's starting to stink in here."

Boy, I thought, a hit right away. What a guy I am.

I looked around some more. A woman approached me. Plump, not fat, blond, blue-eyed, and with a humorous curl to her mouth.

"Say," she opened, "you sure cleared them out in a hurry."

I had to laugh. 'Yeah, I'm like a speech-seeking missile. I detect a conversation, home in on it, and destroy it."

"Well, some people are unable to deal with opinions that aren't theirs. My name is Molly. I thought I knew everyone at the station, but you're new."

"Ah, well, I'm not a KOOK person. I'm here from New York on business. Walter Egon is an old friend of mine, and I'm staying with him. My name is Lenny."

"As in Lenny Bruce?"

"I wish, but yes."

"May I ask what brings you to Portland?"

"I guess so. I'm a private investigator, and I'm here to track someone down. That's basically it."

"Skip-chaser? Bounty hunter?"

"No, no. Nothing as adventurous as that. It's a family matter."

Her eyes went slightly out of focus. "Sometimes the family stuff is the worst." Back to me. "How long are you going to be here?"

"Truthfully, I don't know, but it can't be more than a couple of days. Why, may I ask, do you ask?"

She shrugged. "No sense being coy. I like what I see. I thought we might get together. Unless, of course, you're after Lois like everyone else."

"Yikes. No, I'm not. She's really something, but no. She doesn't seem to have much of a life beyond her work."

Molly looked at me skeptically. Were my fingers crossed behind my back?

I slapped my forehead. "My God, here I am gossiping about someone I hardly know with someone I don't know at all." I put on my best Scarlett O'Hara voice. "What *must* you think of me?"

She laughed. "Don't go getting the vapors on me. I won't judge you on this. Station politics being what they are, nothing short of vicious rumors requires apologies, if that."

I considered my next question carefully, then asked it anyway. "Um, I wonder if I could ask you a few things about KOOK. As you might suspect, I'm getting a somewhat skewed viewpoint from Walter."

"I'll make a trade. Have dinner with me before you leave town, and I'll let you pump me for information."

I made a face of concern. "Curses. You drive a hard bargain, woman. Yes, sure. Do you want me to cook, maybe at your place?"

"I've got two teenage boys. The more I get out, the better I like it, and I haven't gotten out much lately."

"Say no more, say no more," I replied in my best Eric Idle voice. "Why don't you give me your phone number, and I'll call you."

As we were searching for pen and paper, a contretemps arose across the room. I turned to see—who else?—Walter and Bella at it like a couple of alley cats. Molly and I walked over together.

They were standing practically toe-to-toe, and both red in the face. Durke towered over Walter. Slim Reed was attempting to intervene, ineffectually. Bella was in full foghorn voice.

"You fuckin' homophobe! You just hate queers, admit it!"

"Don't you accuse me of that, you goddamn hypocrite."

"Whaddaya gonna do, tell me about how you got so many gay friends? You're fulla shit!"

Reed interjected here. "Hey, this is a party, can't you guys—"

As one, Walter and Bella turned toward Reed and said, "Shut the fuck up!"

Molly leaned over to me and whispered, "Well, at least they can agree on something."

Walter went on, first to Reed. "You're pathetic, Slim. If you had any balls, the whole thing with Stabile and Strunz would never have happened. So stay the fuck out of this." He swung back to Bella.

"And you, you festering mountain of suet, if you had any balls, you wouldn't keep trying to cut them off every man you meet."

"Kiss my ass, you queer-hating prick!"

"You'll have to mark a spot, honey, you're *all* ass."

"I'll dance on your grave, you son of a bitch!"

"Yeah, well, if I could believe that I'd be buried at sea. But you're such a goddamn hypocrite, if you were a man your fat ass would have been banned from the station years ago. No man could get away with the sexual harassment you been putting on women. How many women here have you cornered and put your hands on?"

"That's a fuckin' lie! Nobody's ever accused me of anything!"

"Yeah, that's what Bob Packwood said."

Reed finally inserted himself between them.

"Enough, goddammit! Bella, don't you have a show to do?"

Bella looked panicked. "What time is it?"

Reed held up his watch. "Ten to eleven. You'll have just enough time to get to the station if you quit yelling and go."

"Fuck you, Egon, and you, too, you wimp." And she swept out, followed by a small entourage.

Reed grabbed Walter by the shoulders. "What the hell is the matter with you? Why don't you just ignore her?"

Walter shook himself loose. "Ignore a cancer? I don't think so. Why the fuck don't you bust her for harassment, you gutless wonder. You make me sick!"

He left the room, with Frieda following. After a few seconds of shocked silence, the party began slowly to reassert itself.

"Wow," I said inanely, "does this happen often?"

"Well, we have a lot of true believers at the station. Some of them don't have much in the way of tolerance, or even a sense of humor. You just saw a clash between two people with a severe personality conflict, but they always try to put it into some other context."

"Is Walter's charge true?"

"About the harassment? Sadly, yes. I'm one of her victims. But I haven't mentioned it much."

"So there really is a double standard?"

"It's not that so much as I've decided to let it roll off my back. There's hardly a woman in America who hasn't experienced something like it at work, or socially, or whatever. I just don't want to make an issue of it."

"So, it *is* like the Packwood thing."

She made a face. "Can we change the subject?"

I nodded. "Okay. I'll save the other questions for another time. I'm beginning to form a mental picture here, anyway."

Molly held up a finger. "Don't jump to conclusions. There's a lot more here than meets the eye."

"Well, if I've learned anything, it's that there almost always is. So, what do you do at the station?"

We chatted amiably for a while. She introduced me to several people, and we talked about the state of jazz, alternative rock, even folk music. It was all very pleasant, and I was gratified at the knowledge and passion people brought to the subjects that came up. Informal chat with smart and interesting people is one of the great joys of existence.

I saw Walter and Frieda move in and out of the room we were in several times. Mingling, I guess.

About midnight, I excused myself, making sure to get Molly's phone number. I really liked her.

I walked the few blocks back to the house, the chill of the night getting into my bones. I'd be glad to get into a warm bed.

When I got there, I went into the kitchen for a glass of water. I heard a thump and the patter of little feet, and Love padded into the room. He immediately began to rub my legs, so I decided to feed him. I retraced the steps I had seen earlier and wound up with a little mound of cat food on a plate, which I set before him in his corner. He sniffed at it, and tried to cover it like he was burying a turd.

A profound rejection.

"Screw you, ayatollah. Eat it or wait."

He rubbed against my legs furiously. I began to walk away, and he went in circles. It would avail him not, the spoiled brat. I went downstairs to get into bed.

When I emerged from the bathroom, I heard movement upstairs in the kitchen. I grabbed my robe and went up. The cat food was eaten, the plate licked clean. Aha, I thought, all you need to do is stop catering to him, and he falls into line.

I went back down and read myself to sleep.

I got that feeling again that someone was staring at me while I slept. I tossed uneasily a few times before my eyes opened. Walter, unmistakable even in the near-complete darkness, sat at the foot of my bed. Alas, not Lois this time.

"Hey, man," I asked woozily, "what's up?"

"Sorry, I didn't mean to wake you. No, I mean I guess I did want to wake you."

I sat up. "What's goin' on? What time is it?" I groped for my clock.

"It's about four o'clock, or thereabouts. I got to talk to you."

"Yeah. Shoot."

"Bella Durke is dead."

I shook loose a couple of cobwebs. "Huh? Bella, the one you were arguing with?"

"Yeah, yeah," he said impatiently, "what other Bella is there?"

"Bella Abzug? Belladonna? Okay, okay. Tell me what happened."

"Are you awake?"

"Yeah, sufficiently. Go ahead."

"The station was broadcasting dead air. Gloria, the program director, who was at the party, called down there and no one answered. Bella was supposed to be there. So, she walked over to the station, and Bella was lying on the floor in a pool of blood."

"How did she get it?"

"What?"

"What killed her?"

"I don't know. I just told you all I heard. Lenny, I'm afraid the cops are gonna come for me."

"Why?"

"Whaddaya mean, 'why'? Everybody knows I hated her."

"What time did you leave the party?"

"About three-thirty."

"And had you already heard that she was dead?"

"Yeah. Gloria called back to the party when she got there and found Bella. She was in a state. We had to tell her to call the cops."

"Finding a bloody corpse will do that to you."

"Lenny, what's gonna happen?"

"Relax. Yeah, I know it's easy for me to say, but really. They'll investigate, and probably get around to you sooner than later, because of the argument you had with her. But if you were at the party, you're covered. Don't get excited until you have to."

"Yeah, okay."

"Walter, you didn't kill her, did you?"

"Lenny, she weighed 350 pounds and smoked like a

chimney. She was gonna croak eventually. Why not let nature take its course?"

"Right, but someone must have been in more of a hurry than that. Okay, go to bed. We'll talk about it in the morning."

"Okay. G'night."

I was asleep before he left the room.

nine

I WOKE UP A FEW HOURS later with one of those uneasy feelings, like I'd had a nightmare and the poison was still floating around in my mind. So I turned over to go back to sleep. The next thing I felt was a rough cat tongue licking my cheek. I opened my eyes, and my blurry field of vision was filled with a furry orange face.

I groaned. "Gimme a break, cat." I rolled over, and he leaped to the other side to wash that side of my face. "Okay, okay. I'm up."

I got slowly out of bed. Love sat on the corner of the bed and waited patiently, closely following my every move. I lurched to the bathroom, bled the weasel, and washed my face. The cat came in to spectate as I brushed my teeth.

I threw on some sweats and went upstairs to find a tableau of despair. Walter was sitting at the table, head down in his folded arms. Frieda was whispering in his ear and patting his back. Lois stood there in a flannel nightgown, drinking coffee and scowling. It occurred to me that I should go back to bed immediately, but Walter lifted his head and wailed my name.

"Lenny, I'm fucked. Help me!"

"Coffee," I announced with authority. Lois pointed me

out a cup, and I poured from a carafe. I took two short and one long drinks of the stuff before I broke the near-silence.

"How have you been fucked since I saw you this morning at whatever ridiculous hour it was?" The hypnotic, spattered mist was slowly lifting as the caffeine did its work.

Walter's voice was muffled, as he hadn't raised his head off the table. "One of my knives is missing. They'll trace it to me."

"*One* of your knives?"

"Yeah, a French bayonet."

"Walter, will you pick your head up and look at me? Did you say, 'a French bayonet'? One of those triangular things from World War One?"

He lifted his tear-stained face. "No, a real antique, something from the seventeenth century."

"Let me guess," as I fortified myself with more java, "you're a major collector? And the most distinctive piece of your collection is missing? This thing must have cost a bundle. Where did you get the money for it?"

He looked perplexed.

"Okay," I offered, "one thing at a time. You have a collection?"

"Uh-huh. Not a major one, but I've got a few major items."

"Can I see this collection?" He nodded. "Is this the primo item, this bayonet?"

He nodded again. I refilled my coffee cup. Lois watched us like she was watching a tennis match. Frieda continued to rub Walter's back and make cooing noises.

"How many people have seen your collection and could identify the bayonet?"

"A few. Ten or twelve. It's up in our room, and generally I don't show it around. Lots of people know I'm a collector, though. I tend to carry interesting knives."

"I'm a bit of a collector, myself, although the knives are usually pocketknives I may need in my work. Was this knife expensive?"

"Bayonet. Yeah. I had to sell my car to buy it."

Frieda chimed in. "You mean you had to sell *my* car to get it."

He waved his hand. "Yeah, yeah. You were getting rid of it anyway, when you chose to bike it. You got an expensive bike out of it."

"Okay, kiddies, don't fight. So you bought the thing after you moved to Portland. Does it matter from where you bought it?"

Walter looked at Frieda, and then at me. "Well, it might. I bought it from Augean Stabile. Now, *he* is a major collector."

"Am I missing something here? I thought you two hated each other."

"We got along fine until the KOOK thing with Strunz. I always thought that he was a little nuts, but I could talk to the guy. When I found out he collected knives, we traded a few things back and forth. I bought the bayonet when he was strapped for cash. He was refocusing his collection, anyway."

"Refocusing?"

"Yeah. He was getting away from classic stuff, like the bayonet, and concentrating on hard-core twentieth-century items, military fighting knives, ninja swords, what he calls 'edged weapons.' It's mostly junk, but he's still got a few good pieces."

Something occurred to me. "Um, Walter, why are you so concerned about this bayonet? How do you know that Durke was stabbed?" I felt very Sherlockian.

"Lois told me."

Rats.

"Yeah," Lois added, "I got it from my police contact. I'm not even sure that it's been announced by the cops yet. Another reporter has got the case. I told him what I learned."

I looked over at her. "What else do we know?"

"Not much." She shrugged. "Death was not instantaneous, because she bled a lot. She was stabbed several times."

"Front or back?" I inquired.

"Front. We have to wait for the autopsy results before we know what kind of weapon was used, other than just a sharp instrument. Nothing likely was found at the scene."

I rubbed my chin in a semblance of thought. "Durke was a big woman. Whoever did her in probably had to stab her more than once just to get lucky and hit something vital. Also, she was meaner than a barbed-wire jockstrap. I imagine that she might have inflicted some damage on her attacker if she was approached from the front."

Lois nodded. "No doubt. Whoever it is might look like the loser in a catfight."

"Walter, there is really nothing connecting you to the case, except that there was *tsuris* between you and Durke. No weapon was found at the scene. Is there anything distinctive about this shiv?"

"Very distinctive," Walter replied, with emphasis. "It's not only unusual-looking, it has a little stud on the blade that causes two spring-loaded prongs to jut out from the sides. That's what I liked about it, that it was a kind of ancestor to the switchblade. I have a lot of them in my collection."

"I thought switchblades were illegal."

"Not here in Oregon. You can own them, and even carry them, if they're not concealed. We have several knife makers in Oregon who make them. Only please refer to them as 'automatic' knives."

"Amazing. I might have to get one."

"Well, you'll run into trouble if you get caught going across state lines. They're highly illegal in New York, as you well know."

"Yeah, it's always amazed me that you can buy and own an Uzi, or an AK-47. But not a switchblade. Weird. Back to the case at hand. Okay, look: my advice hasn't changed since early this morning. Stay calm until they call you. Don't volunteer any information when they *do* call. You can always ask if you're under arrest. If you are, clam up and lawyer up. However, I really don't think that you have anything to worry about at this point. Now, I'm going to shower and pursue Donnie Kimmel."

I left the kitchen scene pretty much as I had found it.

After a quick shower, I mulled over the bike thing. I wasn't sore from the previous day's exertions, and I had almost enjoyed it. I wasn't too sure about the weather, but I figured, what the hell?

When I got outside, the paper mill stench hit me. I wondered how much healthier the air was here than back in The Apple.

I was suddenly aware that I hadn't had breakfast, what with all the excitement, so I grabbed the bike, took off toward town, and looked for a likely spot to eat. I saw a little place called the Cafe Lena on a corner of Hawthorne Boulevard. The thing that made me stop was a glimpse of a William Burroughs poster on the wall. Any cafe clientele that could handle food and Burroughs at the same time was all right with me.

Thus refreshed and surfeited, I got back on the bike and headed downtown to City Stadium. It was just past noon when I rolled up to the entrance, locked up, and headed for the office. Smiley was there, along with a motherly woman whom I took to be Margie, if memory served.

"Hi," I opened brightly, "remember me, Mr. Smiley? I'm here to see Donnie Kimmel."

Smiley forced a smile. "Hi, there, Mr. . . . uh . . ." He looked at me expectantly.

"Schneider. Lenny Schneider."

"Schneider, right. This is Margie."

I nodded in her direction. She looked at me kind of vaguely over half-glasses.

"We were just discussing D.K. when you came in. He, uh, well, he's not here. He *was* here, but now he's, uh, not here . . ."

His voice trailed off. I stroked my beard.

"Did you tell him I was looking for him?"

"Well, yes. It seemed to upset him. He was none too steady when he arrived, but I think that he has a bottle stashed up in the stadium seats somewhere. At any rate, he nearly fell and broke his neck from the upper deck. We sent him home, but . . ."

Margie spoke up. "This whole thing is really upsetting to all of us. D.K. was never like this, and we can't seem to help him." She sighed deeply. "I guess he has to hit bottom before he'll change."

"Let's hope it's not from the upper deck. Look, is there a home address? I promise you that I'm not after him for anything. I just need to talk to him." I put on my most sincere and concerned face. It makes Mother Teresa look blasé.

Margie riffled through a Rolodex and scribbled something on a piece of scratch paper. "Here, but I'm willing to bet you'll find him at the Long Run."

I walked over to take the paper from her hand. "The Long Run?"

"Yes. It's a tavern over on Burnside. He's a regular there. He used to have a beer there after home games, when we still had a team."

"Hey, I'm a Brooklyn Dodgers fan. I sympathize. Thanks."

I walked out onto the street. If the rain were coming, it didn't seem like it would be soon. The grey skies had actually lightened since the morning.

Burnside Street was a block down. When I got there, I looked left and right, and spotted the Long Run. I walked the block or so to the place, and went in. None of the clientele, most of whom seemed to be drinking up pension checks, resembled a twenty-something ex-ballplayer.

I walked over to the bar. The bartender, a big-haired, middle-aged woman with too much eye shadow on, was watching a soap, a cigarette curling smoke clutched in her stained fingers. Two people writhed around on a bed with a startling lack of clothing for daytime television. "Ma Perkins" it wasn't.

"Excuse me, but has Donnie Kimmel been here?"

"Who wants to know?" Her face closed up like a fist.

"I'm his social worker. He was late for an appointment today, and I'm checking up to see if he's okay."

She relaxed. "Good. He said some cop or something is after him. I'm glad he's getting some help. You'll find him down the street at the Night 'n Day convenience store. You only missed him by a minute. He'll be buying that cheap beer." She leaned over closer to me. Her breath was redolent of Marlboros and crème de menthe. "I lent him the money. Don't tell the boss, okay?"

"Your secret is safe with me. Thanks." I split.

I saw the Night 'n Day just up Burnside and headed for it. As I reached the door, a guy about 6′2″ wearing a City Stadium coverall came out. I sized him up.

He was unshaven, bleary-eyed, a stump of a cheap cigar hung from his mouth. He carried a brown paper bag clutched in the crook of his left arm. His right arm hung limply by his side, and his right shoulder seemed oddly sloped down from his neck. His left shoulder, by contrast, was big and square. My deductive powers told me that this was Kimmel.

"Donnie Kimmel?"

"Who the fuck wants to know?" He spun around to face me.

"My name is Lenny Schneider. I just want to ask you one question. Can we do this nicely?"

"Blow me, asshole."

"Ah, another New Yorker. I can always spot 'em."

He made a noise and turned to leave. I reached out and grabbed his left arm. The paper bag slipped from his grasp and hit the sidewalk. Two bottles of Olde English 800 malt liquor smashed, and the thin, urine-colored liquid began running toward the gutter.

Kimmel was horrified. "Motherfucker! Why did you do that? You replace them bottles, NOW!"

"Hey, I can't believe that you drink that panther piss in a town that has such great beer."

"Fuck you in the neck! I'll kill you!" He lunged at me. I stepped out of his way, and he careened into the Night 'n Day doorway. He started to cry, and the cigar butt fell to the ground. It was gruesome and pathetic.

"Donnie, look. I know the truth about Sophie and the accident. I'm not here to bust you. I just want to know where she's buried. Her family wants to know. You used to be a decent guy, I've heard that. Tell me where she is and I'm outta here."

He wiped his eyes and his snotty nose on the sleeve of his jumpsuit. "You workin' for Rowan?"

"Yup."

"Well, then, fuck you in the neck anyway."

I sighed. "C'mon, Donnie. He's her dad. Whatever went on between you two, he just wants to know where she is."

"I don't even know where the fuck she is."

"Didn't you pick up her body at the funeral parlor? Did you have her cremated, or something? It's not important, only just where is she?"

"You a private eye?"

"It says that on my card."

"Maybe you can find her."

"How is it that you don't know where her grave is?"

"She ain't dead."

Now it was my turn to reel as if loaded. I actually got light-headed and saw stars.

"Are you bullshitting me?"

He shrugged, an action made a bit grotesque because of his ruined shoulder. He looked at me with watery blue eyes. Not a bad-looking kid, just a mess from self-neglect and cheap beer.

"Believe me, she ain't dead. The last I saw of her, she was sittin' on the back of a Harley headed east toward Idaho, or maybe Montana. I don' know . . ." He hung his head and started to cry again.

"Donnie, is there someplace we can go talk? Get some coffee? I'll buy, and go for lunch, also, if you're up for it."

He shrugged again, and pointed to a McDonald's nearby. Despite my moral reservations about Mickey D, I agreed.

There was a smattering of people inside, from schoolkids to some who looked homeless. I asked Kimmel what he wanted, and talked him into a real lunch, including a double cheeseburger analog and a chocolate alleged milkshake. He scarfed like he hadn't eaten in days. It was agonizing watching him work around his mostly useless arm. I didn't pump him. In fact, we hardly talked until he ate. I sipped coffee, which I briefly considered pouring into my lap for lawsuit purposes, but it had already been done. The coffee was adequate.

When he finished, politely burping into a napkin, I saw my chance.

"Donnie, what went on here? Deak Rowan was told that you were stoned, or drunk, and wrecked the truck, that Sophie was killed. . . . I know that you were not responsible for the accident, but this Sophie thing. What the fuck is going on here?"

He made a sour face. "I still don't know whether I should trust you, just 'cause you bought me some food."

"Look, Donnie, what can I do to you? I'll sign a paper saying I won't divulge your whereabouts to Rowan. We can have it notarized, if you like. Deak wants to find Sophie. At first, it was just to know where the grave was. Now, well, who knows? I haven't told him much yet. I wanted to talk to you first. I'm glad I waited."

"He's a real asshole," Kimmel muttered, unable to meet my eyes.

"He's her *father* for crissakes. He had no idea what she was like. How long had she been, uh, like she is?"

"You mean a stoner?"

I nodded.

"Since junior high. She cleaned up a little when we started goin' together. It didn't last long. Her shithead pals from seventh grade grew up to be bikers and small-time crooks. They broke into cigarette machines, soda machines, that kind of shit. They wound up robbin' an all-night gas station out on the Turnpike. She actually went to see them a few times in the slammer."

He shifted and sucked the dregs of his chocolate shake through a straw. "She always had a crush on this guy, Goombah. Goombah sold dope, planned their jobs, whatever. He made friends with the local bunch of bikers, who were moving meth. He got into the shit, which didn't help his attitude much. She started using. He'd left a big stash when he got busted. She sold about half of it, and tried to put the rest up her nose. We almost broke up over that."

I watched him squirm. He was uncomfortable talking about this. I asked him, "What were you getting out of this relationship?"

He shrugged his lopsided shrug. "When you love somebody . . . . It wasn't all bad. We had good times. She's a major baseball nut. She's the one who coached me out of my batting slumps, and she also told me what I was doin' wrong in the field. I couldn't field a grounder clean until she worked with me. Shit, she could probably play minor-league ball, if she wasn't such a fuckup. You oughta see her hit."

"Did she make you play winter ball down south?"

He nodded. "Her old man pitched a shit fit, but she convinced me that I needed it. She spent most of the time down there looking for a coke connection. No personal-use bullshit, either. You could get enough for your own head easy. She was lookin' to move some weight. She was gonna ship it out in hollowed-out bats. She made a joke about the bats bein' 'coked' instead of 'corked.' Ha ha."

"Did it come off?"

"Fuck, yeah. She sent Goombah's people a few kilos

before we had to leave to come back. And this was pretty pure shit."

"What happened here?"

"When we got out here, she cooled a little, 'cause she was blown away by being with a Triple-A club. We saw major-leaguers coming through for rehab, or on their way down sometimes. She could always talk to them, because she knew about them. They got to like her, a nice-lookin' chick who can talk to you about the game? They loved her." He made a face.

"One guy loved her a bit too much. He was sent down because his habit was killing his skills. He got her into downers and booze, but it didn't take much effort, to be honest. So he's playing in the Mexican League now, pretty much hangin' on by a thread, and she's gone."

"How did that happen?"

"Fuckin' Goombah. He got out and tracked her down. It was pretty easy, 'cause everyone around town knew we were out here. He went to see her in the hospital. She snuck out, and they went off into the boonies on his ElectraGlide. I haven't seen or heard from her since."

"What's with this thing about her death?"

He rubbed his face. "Aah, God, I don't know. It just seemed easier than tellin' her old man. I begged people to go along with the story if they got asked by anyone from out of town. I even got a couple of cops to play along. I'd done a bunch of baseball clinics for the police boys-and-girls clubs. They loved me. They're the ones who called her old man."

"Did anyone try to find her?"

"Yes and no. Most people thought I was better off. But one of the cops used his own time to do some lookin'. The last place there was any trace was at some truck stop out on 84. That ElectraGlide got noticed, and it was a guy and girl on the bike. I guess the descriptions fit."

"Nothing after that?"

He shook his head.

I thanked him, and got his address and phone number

again, just to be sure. I told him I would report back to Deak. He nodded. I told him I would call him.

When we got out on Burnside, it was raining. Nothing hard, just a steady drizzle. The bike was still over at the stadium. I had to go home in the rain, with no raincoat or anything.

I finally felt like I had been welcomed to the Northwest.

ten

I GOT BACK TO WALTER'S baptized in Portland rain. I was soaked through. Some of it was from the inside out, as I had worked up a sweat bundling myself against the downpour. My tweed jacket would never be the same.

I hauled the bike up to the front porch and leaned it against the house. Taking off my jacket, I shook it and resisted an urge to wring it out. Then I shook my head like a spaniel to get off the excess. I was saturated.

I walked into the house and headed straight for the basement and a towel. I was rubbing my hair when I heard Frieda's voice from somewhere upstairs.

"Lenny, is that you? Lenny?"

I walked over to the stairs and bellowed, "Yo, Frieda. Down here!"

A few seconds later, she clomped down the stairs. "Oh, Lenny, my God!"

Uh-oh, I thought. "What's up?"

"It's Walter. The cops came to question him. They took him to the station." She was breathing in gasps.

"Whoa, take it easy. You'll hyperventilate."

She nodded, and began to take long, slow, deliberate

breaths. After a moment, she tried to speak. It was still a bit strained.

"They took him about an hour ago. What are we gonna do?"

"Well, first, don't panic. We sort of expected this. He *did* have a loud public argument with Durke the night she was, uh, the night she became stabbed." I was trying to be as neutral as possible. "And Walter is known to collect knives, and one or another knife is likely to be the mur—the weapon used. Oh, did they arrest him?"

She made a perplexed face. "I don't think so. How can I tell?"

"Did they tell him he was under arrest, or read him his rights?"

She shook her head.

"Aha. Well, the chances are that they just took him for questioning. They like to scare people that way. Did he seem willing to cooperate?"

"Oh, yes."

"Good. He has nothing to hide, and it looks good for him to help."

"What about his missing bayonet?"

"That *is* troublesome. It hasn't turned up, I gather?"

"No, no. It hasn't."

"Frieda, can I see this knife collection?"

She blushed slightly. "If you don't mind that the room is a mess."

I assured her that my bachelor digs at home were on the Martha Stewart "Ten Most Wanted" list. She gestured for me to follow her.

We went up the stairs to a large landing, with three doors along a hallway. Some of Walter's framed photos adorned the flocked walls. Frieda played tour guide.

"That first door, over there, is a bathroom. This middle one is our room, and that one," she indicated another closed door toward the next staircase, "is our study, office, what-have-you. There's a sofa bed in there. If the basement apartment was full, you'd be staying there. Is the basement okay?"

I assured her that it was fine.

"Those stairs go up to where Lois lives. She has about the same arrangement, but the rooms are a bit smaller."

"Where's the collection?"

"In our room."

She opened the door, and I followed her inside. If this was "messy," then my apartment was "toxic." The room was large and L-shaped, to fit around the bathroom, I surmised. The ceilings were high, and one wall was breached by magnificent glass French doors which opened onto a small balcony. The long leg of the L held the bed, dressers, and a large closet. The short leg, where we stood, held a chair with a reading lamp and a small TV, a desk, and, covering most of a wall, a collection of knives of all sorts, with a conspicuous plurality of switchblades. Conspicuous also was the bare space, from which the bayonet was presumably abstracted.

I whistled. "Do you know what all these things are?"

"Only a few. Walter's automatic knife collection is a good one. You know, Keith Richards supposedly has the biggest one. Automatic knife collection, that is."

"The bayonet fit here?" I indicated the bare space.

"Right."

"Is there a picture of it?"

"Sure. In fact," and here she picked a book up off of the desk, "this book has a picture of it."

She handed me a book entitled *Ancient Weapons of War*. There was a place marked, and I opened it. The bayonet was featured, complete with carved scrollwork on the blade, or blades, as the two side blades were deployed. It had almost a trident look about it. I read a little.

"According to this, the bayonet was made to be stuck into the end of the barrel of a gun. I guess the kind that attached directly to the rifle came later. Is this the very one in the book?"

"No. The one in the book is a much finer piece, but Walter's was very close in appearance. Even the springs still worked."

"So if you push this button here at the base of the blade, these doohickeys spring out?"

"Yup. Very scary. I didn't like it much."

"And how many people knew about this bayonet?"

She spread her palms. "At least a dozen, maybe more. Certainly Augie Stabile knew about it."

"How secure is this house?"

"What do you mean?"

"Could anyone get in here easily, maybe cop the bayonet?"

"I guess. We're not too swift about that sort of thing. We leave windows open. I've forgotten to lock the back door more than once. We don't make a big thing about it, because someone is often home."

"Did Stabile have a personal beef with Bella Durke?"

Shrug. "Can't say. She pissed off a lot of people, and the Left community around here is really a small world. It's entirely possible."

I closed the book and put it down.

"Okay, I guess that's all I need right now. And Frieda?"

"Yes?"

"Two things. First, don't sweat it yet. Second, the room looks perfect."

She smiled. I always said that while living with a neat freak may be hard, at least the place is always clean.

We went downstairs. I excused myself to make some phone calls before it got to be too late back east. "Back east" is what everyone calls it here, I discovered.

I wondered if I should call Sue again. I wanted her take on the Walter situation. What the hell?

"Sue, this is Lenny."

"Two days in a row? You miss me, or something?"

"From a distance of three thousand miles, I'd have to say yes."

"Ah, absence makes the heart grow fonder. If I lived in Ulan Bator you'd be my love slave. What's new?"

I filled her in on the Sophie development. She was aghast, natch.

"I can't believe that she's alive! How could her husband *do* that?"

"If you mean lie to her parents, I guess it seemed like a good idea at the time. He was physically and spiritually a wreck, and I suppose that he acted on the spur of the moment. Shit, he's just a kid himself, and she put him through the changes even before the accident. His whole life had just gone out the poop-shooter and he was not exactly in a philosophical frame of mind. Who knows? Maybe I'll ask him."

"What's he like?"

"Angry, hurt, depressed, frustrated, and that's just the appetizer. The main course is that he thinks he's washed-up and his life is over. He drinks two-buck-a-gallon sheep-dip and looks like he slept under a car. He's a friggin' mess, and the power of positive thinking won't cut it."

"*Oy, gevalt.* I cried because I had no shoes, and then I met a man who had no feet."

"Yeah, I cried because I lost my earring and then I met Van Gogh. By the way," I opened warily, "what would you think of my getting an ear pierced?"

"Lenny, you've been on the coast for too long. Why do you think you need to pierce your ear?"

"I'm tired of looking like a middle-aged businessman. I used to be a fairly hip guy, and now I could be, Lord knows, a Republican dentist with a Volvo."

"Don't be a schmuck."

"Sue, need I remind you that your associations over the years have been with several people whose piercings couldn't be mentioned during the family hour?"

"Yes, but I always seem to come back to you. Why do you think that is?"

I didn't like the turn this was taking. I ventured elsewhere. "Walter's in deep kimchee."

"I forget, kimchee is worse than yogurt, but not as bad as shit?"

"Something like that. Although he's not far from deep shit. Let's see if I can summarize the action to date. Walter has had bad blood with a woman named Bella Durke, a kind of man-hating professional lesbian. For some reason, she held special loathing for him."

"Did I detect a past tense?"

"Go to the head of the class. She was found dead the other night, stabbed, and I witnessed a major verbal brawl between them at a party. There must have been thirty people who witnessed it directly, and everyone heard about it within five minutes. It was pretty ugly. Well, a few hours later, Ms. Durke was done for. Now, she had more than her share of nonadmirers, but Walter . . ."

"Was the lastest with the mostest."

"God, you're good. So he's on the short list of possible croakers. Worse yet, he's a knife collector, and one of his prize displays has gone missing, a weird French bayonet. There is some possibility that she was stabbed with such a knife, although nothing was found at the scene."

"What's up with you guys and knives? Don't you collect them also?"

"Yeah, but not like him. He's got already a *collection*. I've got a few little things that are fun. I've always been fascinated with knives, though. My mother once accused me of getting into cooking so that I could collect a bunch of knives without looking like a psycho."

"Gee, I miss your mom. She even liked me. Funny that she didn't think you resembled a psycho."

"Yeah, well, I was always on my best behavior around her. You, of course, have a gift for bringing out the Ted Bundy in me. In any case, Walter's got an alibi, 'cause he was at the party when she got it, but he and Frieda are, like, *meshuggah*."

There was silence on the other end of the phone. I suspected that Sue was consulting her oracle.

"Lenny, it's not over. I get this terrible feeling that there's more to come."

"Christ, I hope not. It's getting hard to be around them. I'm positive that they'll ask me to get involved if it goes any further than routine questioning by the cops. And I *really* don't want any part of it."

"No shit. Well, I gotta go. My book club meeting is tonight."

"I didn't know you were in a book club. I want details."

"Look, it's no big deal. Just a bunch of us girls reading a book a month and meeting to discuss it."

"Cool. What are you reading?"

I sensed a hesitation. "Um, oh, you know . . ."

"If I knew, I wouldn't ask."

"Okay, we're reading *Adam Was a Rough Draft*."

"Let me guess: one of those books that reinforces the idea that men are subhuman morons whose grubby fingers are not fit to sully the hem of Womanhood's garment?"

"You've read it? Yeah, that about sums it up."

"Sue, the world's great literature is laid out before you like a sumptuous feast, and your group is reading the flavor-of-the-month man-basher?"

"Listen, I gotta go."

"Later."

"Bye. I miss you."

Ay, caramba! What was this sudden tenderness toward me? We have gotten along so much better since our divorce that I believed we had reached the ideal definition of our relationship. I didn't want to think about it. My brain hurt from its current load.

I decided to take a nap until dinner.

eleven

SOME TIME LATER, I WAS
awakened by loud voices from the kitchen above. I hauled
my ass out of bed, splashed water in my face, and brushed
my teeth. I went up to see what the hassle was.

Lois and Frieda were standing at opposite ends of the
kitchen table, each with one hand on a hip and the other on
the back of a chair, like an oddly mismatched mirror image.
Each had a similarly grim expression. Each was deep into
her own silence.

"Um," I opened boldly, "what's up, guys?"

"Ask *her*!" Frieda snarled.

Lois gestured in a pantomime of futility. "I don't have a
choice here. I didn't ask for this!"

"You shoulda quit!"

"Damn it, that's easy for you to say."

My head swiveled involuntarily to follow the volley. I
cleared my throat.

"Look," I said, "this really isn't any of my business—"

"No," Lois shot back, "and if you're smart, you won't
make it your business!"

"My mama didn't raise no stupid children. *Adios.*" I
turned to go.

"Wait a minute." Frieda froze me with a spear-point command.

"Um, yeah?" I stopped in mid-step.

"Listen, Lois, if this is gonna get worse from here, we're gonna need this guy. He's a detective, for God's sake."

"It's only gonna make it worse around here. It's not bad enough I'm living with a man I have to report on, and for a capital crime, but I also have to share my space with another investigator?" She stomped her foot. "This is getting too weird for me. I'm gonna check into a hotel until this whole thing is over."

I still wasn't part of the conversation. I was standing there like a bottle on ice until they were ready to put the corkscrew in me.

"You bitch! Do you mean to tell me that you think Walter's guilty?"

"Goddammit, Frieda, if I'm reporting on this I have to keep an open mind about it. I can't proceed from some preconceived assumption, no matter how hard I want to believe it."

"Excuse me?" I ventured. Two sets of gimlet eyes nailed me. "Can I ask a question, or am I just here to witness this for posterity?"

"What?" they both yelled.

"Lois, have you been assigned to this story? Is that what I'm hearing?"

She nodded. Frieda glowered at her.

"Is your editor crazy, or what?"

She waved her arms again in a show of frustration.

"Lenny, I told the bastard that this wasn't gonna work, that I was too close to the situation. I told him I have no objectivity, that I've already been tainted by association. He told me that I was uniquely positioned to report on this from the inside out, as well as the outside in. He said that this was potential Pulitzer stuff. His beady little eyes had stars in them. It was *not* a pretty sight."

"You should've quit!" Frieda bellowed.

"Wait a minute." I made calming hand gestures. "Lois, is this a done deal?" She nodded. "Maybe, Frieda, you could put yourself in Lois's position. She's stuck between this *thing* and her job. It's not a good thing. Give her a break."

"Get fucked. Some friend *you* are."

I was starting to get annoyed. "Yeah, well, listen. It's nice that you can be so high-minded and principled. I'm sure you'd give up your bike messenger job for a principle. Who wouldn't? This is Lois's *life*, newspaper work. Can't you understand this?"

Frieda lost it. "Why does everyone take her side? I can't help it if I'm not fucking gorgeous like her. Are you sleeping with her, or what? I want you out of my house, by tonight. This bitch pays rent, but you don't. Out!"

She turned and stormed up the stairs to her room. I turned to Lois, more embarrassed for Frieda than anything else.

"Well, glad I could help," I muttered.

Lois walked over to me and touched my arm. "Don't take it personally. She's always been wrapped a bit too tight, and this whole thing is obviously too much for her. Let's go get a beer."

"Music to my ears."

We walked out of the house into a pissing drizzle. Lois ran back into the house and copped a couple of umbrellas. We walked, mostly in silence, up to Hawthorne, and thence to the Barley Mill, which Walter and I had stopped in a day or so ago. It was certainly lively, with crowded tables full of typical Portlanders doing a typical Portland thing: drinking good beer and talking their heads off. We found a spot at the bar.

Lois ordered a pitcher of some kind of ale called Hammerhead. It was delicious. We had to lean in to each other to hear above the din.

"Listen, I'm sorry about yelling at you the other night."

"Oh, you mean before the party? Okay, then, I'm sorry about kissing you like that."

She blushed. "I was just surprised. It's not that I'm

encouraging you to hit on me or anything, but . . ." She strained for words. "I'm always being accused of trading on my looks. I'm always getting unsubtle suggestions from editors and executives that my career could be advancing more speedily."

"Like if you did the slippery willy with them?"

"Right. And not only from men. Women seem to like me pretty good, too."

"Okay, this is no bullshit. The truth is that you're very striking. Of course, you know this. You dress expensively and with taste. This place is revealing itself as way off-Broadway, you know what I mean? You just exist on a higher plane than most of the people here, so you're gonna attract attention even beyond what you'd normally get. Please believe that my flirting was innocent."

She held up a hand, as if to assure me.

"No, no. You have every right *not* to be hit on. It's not that I don't find you, ah, alluring. But it was just a flirtation."

She looked into my eyes. The *real* truth was that I could pop a chubby just from that.

"I'm really confused right now," she spoke as confidentially as possible in a slightly raised voice. "I came to Portland at least partially to escape a shitty end to a shitty relationship. I've been trying to figure out what I want from life, and whether that includes romantic entanglements. I may decide to be celibate."

I tried to prevent fat tears from forming in my eyes at the thought.

"I don't even know if I'm completely hetero anymore. Some of the women that have been approaching me have been surprisingly tempting. I know that you didn't mean to upset me, and that you're cool with this."

I was projecting sincerity like crazy. I turned away to drink my Hammerhead, and relax my face for a moment. The bartender caught this out of the corner of his eye, and gave me a peculiar look.

"Lois," I replied, "I want to thank you for understanding."

I had to change the subject. "What's going on with the case?"

She looked around to see if anyone was listening.

"Here's the latest. The Medical Examiner's report states that Durke's wound was likely from a sharp-pointed object without sharp edges. In fact, he's not willing to describe the weapon beyond that, because it doesn't necessarily fit a knife profile. When 'French bayonet' was mentioned, he shook his head. He was most likely thinking of the World War One type, which has a triangular shape, and makes a very distinctive hole. He said that it could almost be a fence picket. He's a bit baffled."

"Do the cops suspect Walter?"

"Only because of his well-known shouting match. But his alibi seems tight."

"How late did you stay at the party? I left pretty early."

Lois smirked. "You stayed long enough to chat Molly up."

"Hmmm. Nothing escapes the all-seeing eye. My guess is that a good reporter is at least fifty percent yenta."

"That's what my dad used to say. He called me that all the time."

"Only in New York would a full-blooded Indian call his daughter a yenta. What a place!"

She laughed, showing the beautiful curve of her throat as she tossed her head back.

"It *is* quite a place, isn't it? When people found out we were Indian, they would ask what tribe we were, and my father would say 'Schmo-hawk.'"

"Well, before we begin to get all soft and squishy about New York, let me get this covered. How late did you stay at the party?"

"You'd make a good reporter yourself. About one o'clock or so. The action was still going strong, and I saw Walter several times during the evening. Do you suspect something here?"

I rubbed my chin. "What I suspect is that I'm gonna be

sucked into this mess, and I want as much info up front as possible, especially from a trained observer, and especially while the memory is fresh."

Lois made an I-smell-shit face. "God, what a pair we are. It's not bad enough that we're involved peripherally, but I've just been sandbagged by my editor, and you'll have Walter begging you for help. Neither of us wants the duty, and neither of us can get out of it."

I smacked my forehead. "Speaking of getting out, I've got to find a place to stay tonight!"

She patted my shoulder. "Don't sweat it. Frieda is famous for saying things she doesn't mean, and then retracting them. I'll intercede for you. If she's still got a bug up her ass, you can stay with me. And," she added quickly, "I mean on the sofa bed, so don't get your hopes up."

I held up my hands and projected innocence. We finished the pitcher of beer, chatted about this and that, mostly Big Apple stories, and split back for the house.

When we arrived, Walter was there, in as sullen a mood as I've ever seen him. He was sitting at the kitchen table with a bottle of Jack Black in front of him, and a half-full water glass of the stuff.

"Walter," I asked, "what's up with, uh, the situation?"

"Lenny, ah, look, Frieda wants me to apologize to you. You, too, Lois." Lois nodded her acceptance. "She's totally wired over this shit, and she—you know. Anyway, you don't have to clear out. And Lois, we understand what a sorry-ass position you're in. So let's let it go."

"Thanks," I replied, "I appreciate it. So what can you tell us?"

"I don't want to talk about it. My only agenda right now is imbibing this Tennessee holy water. If you want some, you have to promise not to say a word. I might play some depressing music, if I get ambitious enough to put it on the stereo."

I looked at Lois, whose look back was somewhat inscrutable.

"Well, Jack Daniels and I have been through this together many times. I think I'll go to bed and let you two work it out. G'night, Lois, and thanks."

"Don't thank me, Sherlock. It was fun. Good night, Walter. I hope that you'll be all right."

She went upstairs; I went downstairs; Walter quietly went to hell with himself.

twelve

WHEN I AWOKE THE NEXT morning, I thought it was still the middle of the night. Not much sun got down to the basement to begin with, but there was none to be seen. The day was charcoal grey, and I could hear the sound of a steady, soaking rain. Ah, welcome to the Northwest.

I flipped on the NPR news, discovered a pledge drive in progress, and changed the station. I found KOOK, and got into the midst of a call-in talk show. The woman hosting was talking to a guy who wanted us to simplify our lives. Sounded good, until he suggested going back to a hunter-gatherer existence. I hoped that this wasn't happening soon, because my only loincloth was in the dry cleaners.

While I was listening to this benighted soul, Love came down the stairs and plumped himself down on the bed. He was wet, muddy, and yard debris clung to his fur at every possible point. What a mess. I found a dry spot under his chin to scratch for a while, and gingerly extricated myself from bed.

I found the jazz station, which was playing Art Blakey's "Moanin'," cranked it and headed into the shower.

When I got myself together, I went upstairs and found a mopey Frieda sitting at the table. She avoided looking at me when I wished her a good morning, but responded in kind. I poured myself some coffee.

"Thanks for making coffee. If I ever get up early enough before I leave, I'll fix breakfast for everyone."

She spun around to look at me and said vehemently, "I'm sorry I'm really sorry please forgive me?" It came out as one multisyllabic word, and took me by surprise.

"Ah, well, of course. Look, Frieda, I really do understand what you're going through, and you're entitled to get nuts every so often. It just happened to be me here at the time. Not to worry."

She nodded and smiled wanly, but hardly seemed comforted. I left it at that.

"Being that it's raining pretty solidly today, I think I'll rent a car. Not that the bike wasn't fun, mind you. Where's the nearest auto rental? Not the airport, I hope."

"Um, probably downtown at one of the fancy hotels. You can catch a bus on Hawthorne. Call them first, so you can be sure. The Yellow Pages is on the shelf under the phone."

"Thanks."

I let my fingers do the walking, and got it on the first try. The hotel clerk told me which bus stop to exit on, and where to walk after that. Then she wished me a nice day. I was getting used to the courtesy.

So I grabbed one of the house umbrellas and walked up to Hawthorne. The 14 bus came a few minutes later. I got on and faced the meter, not quite sure where to stick the dollar bill I held. The driver, a middle-aged black woman, was deep in conversation with a plump blonde in the seat right behind her. She looked over at me, I waved the bill futilely, and she pointed to the slot. I smiled gratefully, and took a bench seat opposite the blonde. They continued their conversation.

"So, like I said," the blonde woman continued, "the article said that this baby was born, and the minute she came out she said, 'My name is Penny.' Do you think it's true?

Somebody told me that those papers at the checkout make things up."

The driver mulled it over for a moment. "I don't think they would lie about something like this," she said, without a trace of irony, "folks could check up on it."

The blonde nodded, even though the driver couldn't see it. "Yeah. She must have been named Penny in a previous life."

I wondered if there was something in the water here, and how long I'd have to drink it before it affected me. A couple of stops later, two guys in German military uniforms, *circa* 1940, got on. I was about to panic, knowing about the neo-Nazis hereabouts, when I realized that the stuff was mostly U.S. Army surplus, and the helmets were plastic. They paid their fares, and told everyone on the bus as they walked toward the back to watch out that the Germans didn't get them. I began to think I was in one of those off-off-Broadway plays that used madness as an allegory for the modern condition. Art imitates life in southeast Portland.

When, as we passed the next stop, some young guy said, "Oh, shit, I missed my stop!" and wriggled out the window, I began to doubt my own grip on things.

Then, we crossed the river, and things calmed down. The driver and her friend were still deep in conversation about prenatal talking, but otherwise it was okay. Hans and Fritz had gotten off, and no one else made an unscheduled exit.

I noticed that the gutters were running water, and that several storm drains were backed up. I was glad I had the umbrella. When I came to my stop, I resisted the temptation to tell the driver and the blonde that I had been born clutching a long-distance phone bill, and hit the street.

I walked the few blocks to the hotel. It was a beautiful downtown hotel on a human scale. Everything in New York is so massive and overpowering. It was a pleasure to be in a place where you could see the sky, even in the middle of downtown. You could even see Mount Hood from some areas downtown. Something to be said for the small city.

I rented some bulbous American heap with an automatic transmission. The clerk gave me my paperwork and told me to wait out front for the car to be driven around. "You can bring it back here, or leave it at the airport. No extra charge. And you have a nice day."

I think I bowed. I waited under the hotel awning until the car came, studying a road map of the city and environs. Then I thought about what I had to do. I needed to tell Deak about Sophie. Since I couldn't come up with a decent subterfuge, I was going to have to fall back on the truth. I wanted to talk to Kimmel one more time before I called back east.

I ran into the lobby and called the number Kimmel had given me. It turned out to be a rooming house. They got him to the phone, and I convinced him, much against his will, to see me. I got directions from downtown. It was really only a few blocks away in the northwest section, but, what the hell, it was raining. One total immersion was enough. When I reemerged, the car had just come around. I tipped the kid who drove it, got in, adjusted the seat and mirrors, and took off. Ten minutes later, I was in front of a huge, sprawling, gabled-and-terraced Edwardian shit-heap. It must have been a mansion at one time. Now it was a run-down boarding-house, badly in need of paint and repair.

I went up to the front door and knocked. A frowzy bottle redhead answered, nearly dressed in a stained housecoat. Her nightgown was visible underneath. A roll-your-own cigarette dangled from the corner of her mouth, smoke trailing up into her kohl-smeared eye, which teared and did a Tammy Faye with her makeup. The door opened onto a dark and musty hallway, with a flight of stairs visible a few feet away. I asked for Kimmel.

Her head swiveled around frighteningly, like Linda Blair, and she bellowed, "D.K.!" The cigarette ash did a triple gainer to the floor. A moment later, Kimmel appeared at the foot of the stairs and came to the door. He was donning his raggedy coat over a Webfoot sweatshirt and a pair of patched jeans, his ruined shoulder still unsettling seen as part of an otherwise robust body.

"See ya later, Lainie," he said to the woman, who stepped aside to let him out and blew him a kiss. "I'll be home for dinner," he called to her as we descended the creaky stairs.

"She's been like a mom to me, since, you know . . ."

I looked at him. In all my deep analysis of the situation, this was the first time I stopped to consider him. He was a young man, not much out of his teens. In the past few months, he had lost a career for which he was gifted, a wife with whom he might still be in love, the use of his arm, and what he thought of as his life. If it had happened to me, I might drink a bit, and be a bit surly, even a prince among men like me.

"Where do you wanna go, kid?"

"Ah, let's go to the Blue Moon. It's only a few blocks away."

"Mind if we drive?"

"Are you kiddin'? Shit, no."

I let him into the rental and ran around to my side to get in. He had leaned over to open my door with his good arm, but was unable to figure out the trick by the time I got it open.

"Thanks for the effort. You didn't have to."

"I try to use my good arm for everything I can. I was right-handed, and now I'm a southpaw whether I like it or not."

I hesitated a second before asking, as I started the car, "How much can you actually do with that arm?"

"Not much," he answered with no hesitation. "They say that I might have some chance to get something back if I work on it in physical therapy, but . . ." His voice trailed off.

"But what?"

"I ain't done shit since the accident. I mostly stayed drunk. You saw."

"Look, man, I'm not gonna give you any free advice. You

gotta go through this the way you feel is best. I'm just wondering if you're convinced that this is the best way to do it."

"Make a left here." He gestured at the next street. He was quiet for a while. I didn't press. In a minute or two he said, "Park first place you find a spot. That's the bar on the next corner. And, no, this is *not* the best way to do it. It's been the easiest, and I'm into easy lately."

I found a parking place, and didn't embarrass myself parallel parking, for a change. We got out and jogged over to the bar. It was another McMenamin's, like the one on Hawthorne, but the whole atmosphere was different. Higher toned, eh, what? The walls were covered with movie memorabilia, rather than rock posters, and the crowd was a bit older and not quite so cutting-edge. The beers, thank heaven, were the same.

We found a booth. I asked Kimmel what he wanted to drink, and he got a funny look on his face. After a second, he said, "I'll have a Coke with lemon."

"I'll be happy to buy you a beer."

"Yeah, but I don't know how happy I'd be to drink it."

"Check." I waved over a waitron. "Pint of Terminator and a Coke with lemon." She nodded, and then got a look at Kimmel.

"Are you D.K.?"

He acknowledged that he was.

"Man, we used to go see you all the time. How are you since the, uh, you know . . . ?"

He smiled. "Gettin' better all the time."

"Great. I'll be right back with your drinks."

I looked over at him, as he wriggled out of his coat. The Webfoot duck wielding a baseball bat adorned his chest. "People still care about you . . . uh, what should I call you?"

"Everyone out here calls me D.K. That'll do."

"Where'd you get that?"

"Locker room. The guys, you know. I was always Donnie

before that. Lois Newsom picked it up from the guys, and once she printed it, it was me. It's okay."

"I know Lois. I'm staying in the house she lives in."

He brightened. "Say hello. She was always fair and smarter than the average sportswriter, besides being a babe. What's she doin' now?"

"Crime beat. She got bored talkin' to jocks, and dodging attempted feels, I guess."

He snickered. "Musta been the basketball team. We treated her decent. Basketball players can do no wrong in this town. Some town. More like a basketball team with a town attached.

"When the Webfoot owner wanted a few concessions from the city to keep the team here, they told him to go take a flyin' leap. They built a whole goddamn new arena for the basketball team when there wasn't hardly anything wrong with the old one, except the owner couldn't squeeze enough bucks out of it. And he's a fuckin' billionaire. Shit!"

I shook my head. "Well, round ball is king these days. People have the attention span of gnats. If they don't see constant motion, they get bored. So basketball gives them meaningless activity all the time. With baseball, you get a lot of quiet, important stuff which takes an actual IQ to appreciate. They don't have the patience anymore to dig the interior game between the pitcher and batter. A real baseball fan will feel thrilled to witness a double no-hitter. A basketball fan would fall asleep. And don't get me started on soccer!"

He grinned wryly. "Lemme guess. You a baseball fan?"

I laughed. "To a fault, I guess."

We spent the next hour talking baseball, players we had seen, our heroes (mine was Gil Hodges, his was Mike Schmidt), how much he hated artificial turf, and why the designated hitter was bullshit. I finished two stouts, he downed three Cokes. Then he made a request.

"Will you do something for me? You got some time?"

"I guess so. How much time will we need?"

"Hour and a half, maybe two."

I shrugged. "Sure. What's up?"

"Well, I wanna show you something, and it's a bit of a drive."

"Let's go." I paid for the drinks, and we walked out of the place. I helped him on with his coat. He stiffened at first, but decided to let me help him.

We got in the car, and he directed me back over to the east side, and Route 84. Route 84 runs east from Portland all the way to Pendleton, home of the famous woollen mills and an annual rodeo, then jogs southeast toward Boise, Idaho. D.K. and I rode east silently on the rainy, windswept road. I knew that this was the road he and Sophie had been on when they had had the accident. I was curious about where he was taking me.

We passed the airport exit. We passed the eastern environs of the sprawling city. There seemed to be an awful lot of room out here, but I'll bet that Portlanders are bitching about how crowded it's getting.

The view began to open out, and the Washington shore was visible across the Columbia River. We passed the paper mill that fouled the air every morning. The misty, rainy air made it seem darker than it was, and a spooky quality set in.

To the right were high cliffs, occasionally split by waterfalls. The tops were often obscured by mist. Everything was beautiful, and I vowed to myself that I'd see it someday when the sun shone on it. We rode on in silence.

"Take this exit," he said, his first words in twenty minutes. It was Multnomah Falls.

We pulled into a parking lot, surprisingly full for a late hour on a dank day. The falls, visible except for the very top, was hundreds of feet high, with a lodge and facilities visible. I hunched my shoulders into my inadequate jacket, and we walked to the falls through a tunnel and along a stream, which may have been the outlet for the falls to the river.

The roar of falling water got louder, and the cold and

damp increased as we neared the base of the falls. Mult-nomah Falls was beautiful and on at least two levels.

The high falls struck one level, forming a large pool, and spilled over to a smaller pool before heading toward the Columbia River. A stairway led down to the lower pool, and a paved path up to the upper pool. D.K. motioned that I should follow him up. The sound of the rushing water was loud but curiously calming. The air was damp and cold, with the cold increasing as we neared the falling water. We stopped to look at the water, practically a metaphor for the power of nature.

He turned to face me when we got to the edge of the pool, the water a roaring white noise.

"Sophie and me used to come here. We'd make a picnic, get a bottle of wine, munch out somewhere nearby, and sit and watch the falls. For some reason, this became our favorite place.

"When Sophie was in the hospital, and I didn't know if she was gonna live or die, I would come here. It made me feel better. I told myself that, if she died, I was gonna have her cremated and pour her ashes in the pool. She loved it so much, and she seemed happy when we came. Then, well, she took off with Goombah. I ain't been here since.

"I missed it."

I couldn't think of anything to say, and thankfully I shut up. He was quiet again for a while. The afternoon was well gone, and the evening near. I cleared my throat.

He turned around, and smiled. "Thanks for takin' me here. We can go now. Unless you want to stay longer?" he said, hopefulness in his tone.

"It's beautiful, D.K., and if it were earlier I might. But it's getting late, and I should get back."

He nodded, and headed for the path. He pointed up.

"The path goes all the way to the top of the falls. I used to run up to keep in shape. I don't think I could walk it in a week now."

We got back to the parking lot, and we were almost the

last car there. It was nearly dark, and the low, thick clouds and mist didn't help any. We made it back out to 84 and took the westbound entrance. I saw headlights in my rearview mirror, but I didn't think anything of it. Until we got out onto the road, and the car behind us came up at a ridiculous rate of speed. The headlights lit up the inside of our car. D.K. turned around to look.

"What the fuck's wrong with that guy? He's got the whole fuckin' road."

"I was just thinking on that very subject myself. He followed us out of the parking lot, but I thought he was just another nature lover."

I was in the right lane, but I moved over to the left to get out of his way. He swerved in behind me. Close behind me. It was very distracting, trying to watch the dark roadway while his headlights bounced off of the mirrors and into my eyes. I moved right; he moved right. He clicked on his high beams. D.K. turned around again.

"Jesus fuckin' Christ, Lenny. What's this asshole's story?"

"Ask me later."

"You know someone with a black BMW?"

"I don't know anyone with a BMW. Can you see a plate?"

"Not with this goddamn light in my eyes."

"Hold on."

I started evasive maneuvers. The rain had stopped, but the road was wet, and I was unfamiliar with it. The BMW stayed with me no matter what cute moves I made. His car was a bit superior to the rental heap I was driving, and, to be honest, he was probably a better driver. I don't drive that much, and even New York City driving isn't this dangerous.

I mentally crossed my fingers and swerved sharply to the right and then to the left. He was caught off-guard, I guess, because he almost lost control, and had to brake. I used the opportunity to step on it. The rental had the pickup of a truck horse, but I got it up to about eighty.

I took a quick look at D.K., and I could see that he was

pale even in the gloomy light. I wondered what I must look like. I already knew what my shorts looked like.

It didn't take long for the BMW to catch up. He pulled alongside of me. I snapped my head left, but his windows were tinted dark. He moved over toward me.

The son of a bitch was trying to run me off the road. I had to think quick.

I slammed on the brakes. The new tires and brakes grabbed pretty well, and I fought the wheel as the car wanted to skid. The antilock brakes took a lot off the potential skidding, and I was grateful. The BMW shot ahead of me by at least thirty yards, and I whipped the car into the left lane. I was going to try to pass the fucker on the left shoulder. It was a chance, because I could easily wind up on the other side of the freeway in oncoming traffic if he came after me.

I floored it, and the wheels took a few seconds to grab. Then we got launched. I ran up to within ten yards of the BMW and snapped the wheel left, taking the car onto the shoulder. I put all the pressure I could on that gas pedal. The engine was whining. We passed the BMW on the left, throwing a rooster tail of gravel behind us. I could hear the gravel pinging on the BMW.

Then I whipped the car right in front of the BMW, hoping that his driver's instinct would kick in, and he would slam on his own brakes. So he did, and the BMW careened all over the road. I kept the hammer down and started to open up some distance between us, focusing on the road for the first time in what seemed like hours.

Without warning, the car suddenly began a frightening skid. D.K. yelled, "Black ice!" and we did at least two 360s. The wheels weren't even touching the ground, as far as I could tell. No matter how I tried turning into the skid, there was no sensation of the car touching the road. We were headed for the right guardrail. Beyond the guardrail was a drop into the Columbia River.

"Fuck me hard," I said under my breath, "I'll be damned

if I'm gonna go out like this." I took my foot off the gas, made one final effort to turn the wheels into the skid, and slammed the shift lever into low.

The engine shrieked, the transmission sounded like somebody shaking a half pound of jingle bells in a gallon can, the wheels hit the gravel on the right shoulder, I braked and they grabbed. The car's momentum was stopped by the guardrail, and we came to rest with the sound of sheet metal being ripped off the car like a banana peel.

I looked over at D.K. He was practically catatonic. Just then, the BMW roared past us. All I could tell was that the car had an Oregon plate.

D.K. turned toward me. "I swear to Christ, my whole life flashed in front of me. I didn't think I was gonna make it this time." I'm not even sure he was talking to me.

"So, look," I said, "be sure and call me if you want to go for another ride tomorrow."

He turned toward me with a look of utter horror on his face, and then started to laugh. I picked it up and started laughing. Soon it became uncontrollable. I figured they'd find us like this in about an hour, and trundle us directly off to the local version of Bellevue.

Actually, it lasted just a few minutes more.

D.K. gestured up the road with a head movement. "Friend of yours?"

I shook my head emphatically. "I told you I don't know anyone with a BMW. But, if I find the motherfucker, I might have to pull his head off and shit down his neck."

Then we laughed some more.

The rental car made it to the airport at about twelve miles an hour. D.K. told me it was closer to get to than going back to town. The yokel kid running the rental return practically browned out in his coveralls when he saw it. There was almost no metal on the outside of the door. The rear quarter-panel looked like a sardine can with the top stripped off. When the car idled, it shook like it had the heebie-jeebies, black smoke came out of the exhaust, and it made a noise alarmingly like a death rattle.

I told the kid, "Good brakes, but she tends to fishtail when you turn quickly doing ninety-five."

He nodded, his lower jaw apparently permanently unhinged. He started to speak in tongues when I asked for a replacement. So I slipped him fifty bucks and promised not to do it again. He gave me another car, but he muttered constantly about his career in the auto rental business being toast.

I took D.K. back to the rooming house. He allowed as how dinner conversation that night would probably not lapse into aimless blathering about the NBA. I told him that I was going to call Deak Rowan and give him the whole story. He nodded. "I guess it's time."

I also told him to take it easy, and that he might want to treat himself to one beer, but only if it came in a container of less than forty ounces.

thirteen

I GOT BACK TO WALTER'S house and found a place to park the car. It was much easier than in my neighborhood. When I got in the house, Walter and Frieda were sitting in the living room. Each had a beer in front of them. I said howdy, and went and got a beer of my own.

Returning to the living room, I found both of them looking up at me like baby birds in the nest. Uh-oh.

"Lenny, sit down." I complied.

"We want you to help us with this Durke matter." Walter's face was a portrait of controlled agony. Frieda was crying quietly.

I cleared my throat. "Ahem! Well, uh, I don't know. My business here in Portland is about over. In fact, I'm about to call my client back east and give him what may be a final report. I could· be outta here by tomorrow afternoon."

"I could pay you. I *would* pay you."

"It's not the money . . ."

"Is it because I threw you out?" Frieda wailed.

"No. It's very important to have some kind of professional distance from my cases. I have zero on this one, and I have a bunch of preconceptions. This leads to shoddy work."

Frieda looked at Walter. "He's talking just like Lois. I knew it would be like this."

"Lenny, we're talking about my life here. This is not some traffic ticket. The cops called me in again. I was there for an hour playing verbal Ping-Pong before I asked them to arrest me or let me go. They want me for this one."

"Walter, do you have a lawyer?"

"Not yet."

"Okay, it's past time for you to lawyer up. If you get a lawyer, I'll work with him-slash-her." I could feel my better judgment kicking and screaming inside me.

Relief washed over both their faces. Big smiles lit up.

"Remember, I'm like a gefilte fish out of water here. My normal support network is gone, I have no snitches, no contacts on the force . . ." I ran my fingers through my hair obsessively. "If I'm any help at all, it'll be a miracle. And," I glanced significantly from one to the other, "whatever I turn up I tell the lawyer, so you've gotta be one hundred percent truthful all around."

Walter nodded furiously. Frieda hugged herself, grinning like a fool.

"Now, I've got a story for you."

They sat and drank beer while I told them about my day's events, already finding ways to embellish it. Just incidentally, I asked them if they knew anyone with a black BMW. They didn't.

We had a beer, or two, more. I had to call Deak. They decided to go to a movie at one of those local beer-hall-and-movie-houses. So we went our separate ways.

Even with a couple of beers in me, I wasn't possessed of the fortitude to tell Deak what I knew. It took an act of sheer will for me to make the call.

"Hope it's not too late, Deak."

"Nope. Just about ready for bed, but shoot."

I shot. "Sophie's grave is not in Oregon, because, as far as anyone knows, she's still alive."

"What!" Then a long silence.

I spoke only because I couldn't stand it anymore. I told the whole story: dope, Goombah, Harley-Davidson, and all. It came tumbling out beyond my will to stifle it.

"Kimmel's really a good kid. He's a mess since the accident. His whole life's in the dumper. There's some hope for him, though. What do you want me to do about Sophie?"

"Did Kimmel say some cop followed them to a truck stop?"

"Yeah, but the trail's cold from there. The only thing that seems to get noticed is that motorcycle. The truck stop itself is only a few hours east of Portland. They could literally have been going anywhere."

More silence. "Lenny, I'm comin' out there."

"What do you want me to do?"

"Stay there. I'll try to get a flight tomorrow."

"Check. This *is* good news, isn't it, Deak?"

"Shit, yeah. But, Jesus, I'm flipped out over this. Alive! And gone. No word to me, or her mother. Nothin'."

"If you can find any of her high-school buddies, you might call them and determine whether she called them recently."

"Yeah, good idea. I'll let you know what's goin' on."

I made sure that he had my phone number, and we hung up.

So there I was. Lenny Schneider, master detective. Three beers into the evening, unsure of my immediate future, stuck with one case I didn't want, deep into a mess I couldn't have anticipated before I got here, and I still had to tell Mickey I didn't know when I'd be back.

So I did what I could under the circumstances: I ran upstairs, rolled a joint of Walter's pot, came back down and watched cable TV.

The ringing phone woke me up. I saw a black-and-white George Sanders dressed in eighteenth-century costume, and oozing all over some woman with her bosom pushed up over the top of her dress. I looked at the clock; it was 1:15, too early for Deak to be calling, most likely.

Eventually, I got the idea to quit speculating on who it was and pick up the goddamn phone.

"Yo!"

"Lenny, it's Lois. I'm at the newspaper office listening on the scanner. Caliban Strunz has been found murdered in a porno shop on Sandy Boulevard. I'll meet you there."

She gave me quick directions. It was about a five-minute drive from the house. I was out of the house and on my way in thirty seconds.

I got there, and the cops hadn't responded yet. The Lady Faire Adult Emporium had blackened windows, and pink neon silhouettes of impossibly stacked females on the marquee. I walked into the porn palace. It was empty except for a hysterical clerk who was nearly in a faint.

The shop was set up with racks of videos and magazines, and showcases full of sex toys and other horny paraphernalia. I couldn't imagine what to do with half of them. They looked like vacuum cleaner attachments. The other half were intuitively obvious.

There were posters for porn flicks on the walls. A door at the back had a sign indicating "Mini-Movies." I walked toward it, and the frantic clerk did nothing to stop me.

The mini-movie setup was typical, and don't ask me how I know. There were several booths with doors, each featuring a large TV-type screen, and a coin box that took quarters. Opposite the screens were upholstered benches, with boxes of institutional facial tissues on the floor nearby. The floors would make a maggot retch, sticky and reeking of soured male essence. I had to fight nausea.

When I got to Strunz's booth, his corpse was sitting upright, nailed to the back of the bench by a long knife. The elaborate handle protruded from his chest. The blade consisted of a main shaft, with smaller shafts extending out at an angle from the handle. Strunz's pop-eyed face, instantly recognizable from the cable show the other night, was frozen in rage. This time, presumably, the rage was completely justified.

While Strunz was not a big person, it took some strength to pin him like a butterfly. Strength, or maybe a transcendent anger. He probably had died at once, since the only visible blood appeared to have drained from his upper body. The massive blow that pierced and pinned him could easily have destroyed his heart instantly.

As I ruminated on the crime scene, Lois came in.

"You didn't go inside, did you?" she asked anxiously.

"Uh-uh. Why do you ask?"

"Well, the cops are right behind me. If you walked into the crime scene area, they would tape you in, and you'd be here for hours while they took evidence, interrogated you, and generally busted your balls for fucking with their work."

"Whoa! Let's back off a few feet. I've seen enough."

We stood by like the picture of innocence while the cops came in. They established quickly whether we had trampled on the crime scene, and ignored us after we swore we hadn't.

I took Lois outside to talk. The rain had stopped, but a chilling dampness caused us both to shiver a bit.

"It's definitely Strunz. I recognize him from the cable show. Also, I'm sure that the knife is the bayonet that's missing from Walter's collection. I've never seen anything like it, and I'll bet there's not another one in Oregon.

"The thrust that killed Strunz was very forceful. It had to go through him completely and deep enough into the back of the bench to hold him almost upright. I don't know if Walter is that strong, frankly."

She made a face. "Hate is a powerful motivator."

"That had occurred to me."

A cop stepped outside to have a smoke. He was over six feet tall and thick around the middle. His suit and raincoat were rumpled and stained. His face was alky-red even in the unnatural pink light of the neon, and the broken blood vessels in his nose showed as black lines. Lois acknowledged him.

"Chauncy, over here."

He sidled over. "Hey, good-lookin'. Who's yer buddy?"

I extended my hand. "Lenny Schneider. I'm a PI from New York here for a client. Nothing to do with this." He ignored my proffered hand, so I jerked my thumb at the porn shop.

"So you were just in the neighborhood?" He squinted suspiciously.

I didn't want to let anything slip about Walter, so I said, "More or less. I recognized Lois, so I stopped."

Lois flashed me a look.

"Oh, yeah. Lois is from back there, ain't ya?"

"Yeah, I am. What's goin' on, Chaunce?"

"Medical Examiner's boys are doin' their thing. I gotta talk to the clerk some more. He's kinda hysterical. A little light in his loafers, if you know what I mean."

"Is he a suspect?"

"Everybody's a suspect. I became a cop because the nuns in school convinced me about original sin. Except you, honey. Easy to see that you're an angel."

"Jeez, Chauncy, my heart is all, like, pitty-pat."

Chauncy laughed a smoker's phlegmy laugh.

I couldn't resist. "Did the clerk tell you if he'd seen or heard anything?"

"What's it to you, peeper? Can't wait to read about it in Lois's rag?"

Cops are the same everywhere. If they find life in the ammonia swamps of Venus, the cops will be the same.

"Professional curiosity," I replied lamely.

Chauncy sucked deep on his cig and flicked it sparking into the street. He grabbed his crotch. "I got your curiosity right here. If you professionals'll both excuse me, I got work to do."

"What a sweetheart," I opined.

Lois waved her hand. "He's just squirting testosterone for you, big boy. He can be a source, but he'd rather play with me. I'll let you know what's goin' on."

I told her that Walter and Frieda had convinced me against my will to work the case. She nodded.

"They went to a movie. Should I wake them up and tell them about Strunz when I get home?"

She shook her head. "Nah. Walter hasn't been sleeping well as it is. Waiting 'til morning won't hurt. See you later."

I drove back to the house and fell into a troubled sleep.

The next morning, Love was there on the bed, sleeping peacefully between my legs. What a sweetheart. I didn't hear any rain, and took that for a good sign. The cat stirred when I did, and I took time to rub his belly before I arose. I got him to purr.

I didn't turn on the radio. I was surfeited with information, most of it unpleasant. I didn't want any more about Bosnia, or the Middle East, or the Religious Right. I took a long shower, letting the hot water pound my head in the vain hope of driving out the evil spirits.

I made it up to the kitchen to find Lois, Walter, and Frieda at the table, Lois wearing the same clothing I had seen her in a few hours before.

"Good morning, sunshine," Lois began, "I saved you from the horrible duty of informing them about Strunz. I got back from filing my story, and they came down shortly thereafter."

Walter looked up at me. "Is this like being in a good-news/bad-news joke, or what? The good news is that Strunz has died a horrible death; the bad news is that my ass will be in a sling over it."

I walked over to get some coffee, nodding as I went. "Yeah, I would call that a fair assessment of the situation. Lois, anything new to add?"

"The cops are being very close about this whole thing. My article benefited more from what you told me than from anything I got officially. Their mouthpiece mugged for the TV cameras, told us *bupkiss*, and then stonewalled questions. Aagh." She made a disgusted face.

"Are you planning to talk to the clerk who was on duty last night?" I asked.

"Sure, if we can get to him. I guess the place to start is back at the Lady Faire."

Walter smirked. "Forgive me for speaking ill of the dead," he tented his fingers in a pious charade, "but a porn palace strikes me as a fitting place for that asshole to have breathed his last foul breath."

"Couldn't have planned it better yourself," I observed, and got strange looks in return from both Walter and Frieda.

I looked over at Lois. "Do we have anything from the ME yet?"

"I could find out easily. The Medical Examiner's office is really good about giving information to the press. I could even get a copy of the report, if you need it."

I rubbed my chin. "No, all I need now is a time of death. I couldn't tell from looking how long Strunz had been dead, and I didn't want to trample the scene to check for rigor mortis. The light in there was so bad, I couldn't even tell how dried the blood was."

"I'll make a call," Lois said, and headed upstairs.

I called after her, "When are you going to get some sleep?"

"I'll get plenty of sleep when I'm dead," she yelled back.

"My mother always used to say that," I mused. "Walter, what did you tell the cops? Anything I don't know about?"

He shrugged. "They asked me about the bayonet. They asked how many people knew about it, et cetera. I told them several people had seen it, and that I'd bought it from Augie Stabile, and that Augie and I had, ah, a falling-out. I also told them that if someone wanted to pin the killing on me, the bayonet could've been stolen."

"They haven't called you in since Strunz got it?"

"Nope. I guess it's inevitable, especially since they've got the damn bayonet."

"Yeah, and a pretty thing it is, too. Nice carving on the handle, and the blade thing was interesting."

"You mean the way it springs out those other blades from the side? Nifty, huh?"

"Well, when the cops come to you again, don't volunteer any information, or anticipate a question like you just did with me. How did you know that the blade had been sprung?"

Panic twisted his features. "Uh, Lois told me!" Frieda's eyes got big.

"Relax, pal. If you're gonna break a sweat with me, you'll really lose it with the heat. You get a lawyer?"

"Yeah, some rad lawyer who works with local protestors. He works cheap."

I sighed. "Yeah, and he's probably worth every penny. Walter, a lawyer is like a motorcycle helmet, it's not something you want to try to chintz on. Why don't you get smart and get a good criminal defense lawyer?"

"He's right, honey," Frieda interjected. "You're better safe than sorry."

"Okay, okay. This guy's got a good rep, though."

"Rep, schmep. The criminal guys will twist and turn the cops and the court inside out. They just know what to do. You're not looking for some long-haired habeas corpus mechanic who'll spring you for chaining yourself to a bulldozer. This is a double murder, for crissakes. They got the death penalty in this state?"

They both nodded.

"Then get smart, and lose the hippie. You'll thank me."

Walter rubbed his face with both hands. "Yeah, okay," he sighed.

Lois came back into the kitchen. "ME says time of death was between ten and midnight. Hard to get it much closer, because there was no food in the stomach."

"Fuck flicks meant more than food to this guy. I don't think I would have liked him."

"Join the club," Walter and Frieda said in unison.

Lois and I decided to go down to the main cop house to try to get some more information. One of the day-shift guys working on the murder stiff-armed us, and even tried to pump us for what we knew. He was smaller and younger than Chauncy, but the attitude was the same. He didn't even tell us to have a nice day.

So we walked over to the Bijou Cafe for a late breakfast. I had some kind of omelette with local oysters. It was quite delicious, although the oysters weren't as sweet as the Blue Points I was used to, or even the Chesapeake Bay oysters, before they got ruined. A little too metallic. While we ate, we planned strategy.

"Let's go back to Lady Faire and see if we can get to the clerk," I opened.

"Yeah, my sentiments exactly. The cops are playing this one close. Maybe they want to turn this case into a TV ratings coup."

"Ah, so young and so cynical."

"Lenny, if you wanna rid yourself of cynicism, don't become a crime reporter. Between the cops and the crooks, well . . ."

I finished the coffee, which was excellent. "Let's get in the breeze."

She nodded, swallowed her coffee, and off we flew, back to the east side and up Sandy Boulevard to the Lady Faire. When we parked and walked up to the place, we saw the clerk and a guy in a cheap suit arguing on the street. I stopped Lois, gestured to be quiet, and hung back. They were too absorbed in yelling at each other to pay us any mind for a while, and I wanted to see if we could learn anything.

Cheap Suit was saying, loudly, "Do I need this crap? It ain't bad enough that the local goody-goodies are after us? Where's your fuckin' brains?" His hair was dyed some unreal shade of red-brown, and he gestured with each word, stabbing the air with a cigarette. His hot-pink shirt and electric-blue tie set off his pallor admirably. I was impressed that he was pale despite being angry. He probably never saw the light of day, if he could avoid it.

Clerk, still looking stricken from the night before, was waving his arms. "Did I *know* this guy was gonna get himself killed? What am I, a psychic? He comes in all the time, he's a goddamn regular. So I was supposed to tell him not to come in? Gimme a break here, Marty." He had on a fake fur coat, with green bell-bottoms and white plastic Beatle boots visible below the hem. Bad taste is timeless.

Cheap Suit Marty finally noticed us hovering. "Take a fuckin' picture, it lasts longer."

I wondered whether to tell him how devastated I was by his wit, but we needed his cooperation.

"Oh, yeah, sorry." I put on my most obsequious tone. "We were just wondering whether we could speak with you?"

Cheap Suit Marty gave us a nasty look. "You ain't fuckin' cops, or you wouldn't be kissin' my ass. What do you want?"

I took Lois by the arm, and we walked over.

Lois gently but firmly took her arm from my grip. "I'm Lois Newsom from *The Portlander*. I want to ask you some questions about last night."

"The fuckin' newspaper! Just what I needed. No comment."

Lois turned on the charm. "Hey, come on." Her voice dripped honey. "I'm not out to get you. This is your chance to get your side out. It won't take long. Promise."

"That shit won't work with me, sister. I got two topless clubs fulla willing bitches that are just out for my dough. They don't give a shit about me, and you don't either."

"Look," I tried, "the cops are controlling all the info on this. They're gonna make you look like the bad guy here, if it suits 'em. Why not take the opportunity to tell your side?"

Cheap Suit Marty looked over at the clerk. "Un-fuckin'-believable. What is this, double-teaming? Who the fuck are *you*, Tonto?"

I resisted the impulse to give him a shot in the snot-locker. "Listen, pal, we're doing a job. If you've got no respect for that, well, that's one thing. But if you're gonna act like king of the assholes, we may have to mix it up."

Lois stopped me. "Forget it, Lenny. His whole life is about being abusive. Why should he treat us differently?"

"This is fair treatment? Stick your fuckin' paper up your ass." He turned to the clerk. "Pinky, get scarce. I'll decide whether you got a job here anymore. Call me in a couple of days. I'll get Herman to fill in. He ain't as dumb as you."

Cheap Suit Marty looked back at us. "Take Tonto and buzz off. You're bad for business." He walked away, raving to himself.

"A prince among men," I said to Lois, as she stood shaking her head.

"Yeah? You should work for the bastard." Pinky was pissed.

Lois and I exchanged a glance, meaning: Pinky might want to talk.

We sidled over to him. He flashed us a look somewhere between apprehension and naked terror. "Pinky," I purred, "want a cup of coffee?"

Lois grabbed one arm, I grabbed the other.

"Uh, sure," he said unsurely.

We half-dragged him to a choke-and-puke luncheonette a few doors away. Finding a booth in the back, we sat him down, and we scrunched ourselves in opposite him. He stared down at the worn Formica.

"Um, Pinky. Can I call you Pinky?" Lois chirped.

Pinky nodded sullenly, still staring down. He looked like some kind of deranged teddy bear in his voluminous fake fur coat, and his pudgy pink face and wispy, dyed hair. The bulk of the coat took up most of his side of the booth.

"Can I get you some coffee, Pinky?"

He nodded.

"Cream and sugar?"

"Double cream, no sugar."

Lois looked over at me, and I got up to order the coffee. They still made it in those giant silver urns, but the insides of the urns were probably as neglected as the outsides. I prayed the stuff wouldn't cause brain damage. I brought it over, black for me and Lois, double cream for Pinky.

"Thanks," he muttered.

"So, Pinky, what went on there last night?" Lois inquired sweetly. We both knew he wanted to spill, partly from revenge on his boss, partly for attention.

He squirmed a bit. Lois and I showed forbearance while he struggled with his withered conscience. Soon, he looked up at us, his pink face a battlefield of conflicting pressures. He sighed deeply and gave in to one thing or another.

"I swear, I didn't hear or see anything. I just mind my own business behind the counter. The customers like it that way, and so does Marty." His voice was high-pitched and breathy.

"Pinky," I opened, "what's a typical night for you?"

Shrug. "I work the counter. Our customers are three quarters guys in suits, the rest some working guys, a few pervo types or weirdos, but not many. The ones that aren't regulars come in and do one of two things. They either run in and grab a specific video or book, pay, and run out; or, they look at every item in the store, including the dildos and blow-up dolls, and buy nothing." He gave us an arch, eyebrow-raised look. "I think those are the guys who come later and do the quick buy.

"The regulars come in, look around, maybe even shoot the shit with me. Can I say 'shit'?" he asked Lois.

"I've heard it before. Go on."

"The dead guy was a regular. Came in the same night every week, looked over the books and videos." Here he whispered. "He would ask about our 'special collection.'"

"What's that, Pinky?"

He rubbed his face, making it even pinker. "Oh, God, please don't tell Marty!"

"You afraid of what, violating his trust in you?" I asked.

"No, I'm afraid he'll kill me."

"Your secret is safe with us. Promise."

"Okay. We've got some stuff only a select clientele can get at. There's a catalog in a locked cabinet under the counter. It has books and videos in it, the worst! Kids, animals, sick bondage stuff. *Really* sick, not just dominatrix crap. Oh, God, we even have snuff movies from Mexico, Bangkok. The worst one I ever saw was made in Idaho, can you believe? Skinheads with a colored girl. I puked and couldn't sleep for a week."

Pinky shook his head. I ruminated on what could gross out a porn-store clerk. But not for long.

"The dead guy bought stuff with kids, and the most violent stuff with women. *He* bought the skinhead video. The next time he came in, he told me that it was the best thing he ever saw."

"What happened last night, Pinky?"

"It was typical. He came in about eight-thirty, looked around, asked for the catalog, and went into the mini-movie booth. He heard about a new video made at a nudist camp, one with a lot of kids in it. They're legal, 'cause the kids aren't having sex, or anything, but a smart photographer can get some hot stuff, if you like that kind of thing."

"Was he alone?"

"Yeah, yeah. He's always alone. Some guys come in in pairs, or even with women. But he's always alone. Was. Whatever."

"Did you hear anything unusual, noises coming out of the booth, anything like that?"

Pinky laughed explosively. "Hah! Are you kiddin'? There's always noises coming out of those booths, either from the movies or the customers."

Lois leaned in. "Was there anyone else in the store around this time?"

"There was at least six other guys around the same time. Marty does good business in these places."

"Did you see anything suspicious?"

"Look, we got those curved mirrors everywhere, but Marty's orders are not to look too close. It spooks the customers. We got electronic security on everything. If you try to get out with something you haven't paid for, a buzzer goes off, and the outer door locks. I don't pay much attention to what goes on on the floor."

"Did you see anyone new?"

"I see new ones every night."

"How did you find out he was dead?"

"Another customer wanted the catalog. I had to go knock on the door. When he didn't answer in a few minutes, I went in. That sword, or whatever, was sticking out of his chest. I thought I was gonna faint. I grabbed the catalog and ran out to call 911."

I looked stern. "So you tampered with the crime scene?"

"What?" He looked horrified.

"You removed the catalog, which was part of the crime scene," I said disapprovingly.

"Oh, sweet Christ. I couldn't leave it there! The cops see that, I'm in jail and Marty is out of business. Even Oregon isn't loose enough for snuff movies."

"Can you get us a name for any of the customers who were in the shop that night? Someone else we could talk to?"

"Are you serious? We do a ninety-nine-percent cash business. Guys don't want their wives to see a hundred bucks on a credit card slip from Lady Faire. Some jerk will occasionally pay with a check or card, but they're from out of town."

"Pinky, this is important. Try hard to remember if anyone else in the shop last night looked, I don't know, out of place, or seemed nervous."

"I swear to God that I didn't see nothing like that. Lots of guys are nervous in there, afraid to be recognized, or it's their first time, whatever. It was a normal night until I went in that fuckin' booth. Oh, sorry." He looked over at Lois, who nodded back.

"One last question. What time did you go into the booth?"

"No later than ten o'clock, maybe ten to."

"Thanks, Pinky. You've been a big help." I reached into my pocket and found two twenties to give him.

"Thank *you*. I may not have a job."

He smiled a sick, sad smile and made as if to leave. When neither of us said anything, he flew out as fast as his fun fur would let him.

I looked at Lois. "So, newsie, whadda we got?"

"I got some nice detail for my next piece, not much else. Unless I wanna do a snuff movie exposé. You?"

"I don't know. If Walter can establish his presence at the movies last night, he's home free. Not even in Portland can you be in two places at once. Let's go back to the house and see what's new."

When we got there, we found Frieda in a state.

"They came for Walter. They arrested him on suspicion of murder!"

"On what basis?"

"They found his prints on the bayonet."

"Where the hell did they get his prints? Did he let them take them when he was questioned?"

"No, it was an FBI match. He had to get fingerprinted to get a security clearance when he worked in D.C."

Lois sighed. "Well, that should put an end to the rumors that he's the Bureau's boy at KOOK."

"That's what I like about you, Lois," I remarked, "you always look for the silver lining."

Remember, for every silver lining, there's always a dark cloud.

fourteen

WALTER'S ARREST SEEMED
more for public relations than anything else. The cops were
under pressure to stop the killings, and they had a murder
weapon with Walter's prints on it. However, Walter had a
pretty solid alibi for the Durke killing, and a fair one for the
Strunz killing. The prints were explainable because the bayonet belonged to Walter, and it was quite possible that someone
who knew the weapon existed and had it in for Durke could
have made off with it from Walter's house the night of the
party. A first-year law student could create enough reasonable
doubt to get the case thrown out.

Once you got into the realm of who had it in for both
Durke *and* Strunz, the quarry became a bit rarer. But not
down to a class of one. Everything hinged on the alibis
holding up.

I took Lois aside.

"Listen, we've got to do a couple of things. First, we need
to talk to people who were at the party, to try to solidify
Walter's presence there. Then, we have to do the same for
the movie last night. Any other ideas?"

She scratched her head absently as she thought.

"The other people who had it in for Strunz are Augean
Stabile and B.B. Wolfe, most prominently. We should talk to

them, if they'll see us. We may get some insight into others who'd like to see both Bella and Strunz dead.

"Besides, it would give me satisfaction to get the real story here, and exonerate Walter in the process."

"Sounds good. I'll call Slim Reed. He knows who I am. Maybe he can help us get some input from the KOOK people."

"Yeah, okay. I'll get hold of Stabile and Wolfe. I'm still fairly harmless to them."

We made for our respective phones. Before I headed downstairs, I told Frieda to make sure that Walter's attorney was at the cop house ASAP, and to have that person call me. She made for her phone, too.

I found Reed's number in the book. His name was Louis.

"Hello, Slim? This is Lenny Schneider, Walter Egon's friend. I need a favor."

"Uh, yeah? What?"

"I need some names and phone numbers of people who were at the party the night Bella Durke was killed. I need to establish his whereabouts."

"Um, I don't think I can do that."

"Why not?"

"Well, I'm the station manager. I can't be seen to be helping an accused murderer."

My mind reeled. "Are you telling me that you're not going to give me names because you see this as a radio station political problem?"

"Look, everyone knows he hated Bella. I'll catch hell from the . . . um, from her supporters."

"Listen, you spineless snake, I won't tell anyone where I got their names from. What ever happened to the assumption of innocence? Isn't he supposed to be your friend?"

I could actually *hear* him writhing on the other end of the phone.

"Come on, Slim, I'm not asking you to stick your scrawny neck out here. You won't respond to doing the right thing, so at least do the minimum thing. I won't tell anyone where I got the names."

"Sorry, I just can't. I can't take the chance."

"You know, the worst part of Dante's hell was reserved for people who did nothing in times of crisis. Fuck you, worm boy!"

I slammed the phone on the cradle. Man, was I pissed. This asshole was so terrified of taking shit from people that he'd let a friend hang out to dry. So much for friendship. So much for justice.

On a wild hair, I called Molly. When she answered, I told her what the situation was, and begged her for help.

"So this is what it takes to get a phone call from you?"

"Okay, if you need to hold my feet to the fire on this, go for it. But my friend's life may be at stake here."

"I know, I just like giving you a hard time. I'll get my address book."

I thought vaguely about cruelties large and small while I waited for her to get back.

"By the way," she began, "I'll be willing to say I saw him there. I can't claim to have had my eyes on him the whole time."

"Thanks, Molly, you're wonderful. No, I understand. The party was at a big house with a lot of rooms. I'll be satisfied with getting enough people to say they saw him at various times to try to establish his presence for the evening. Give me some names."

She rattled off a list of names and phone numbers. She pointed out those who would be favorably disposed to helping Walter, which were more or less neutral, and which were not his friends. It gave me a list of thirty-five solid leads.

"This is great. Frieda didn't know everyone there, and certainly couldn't provide the insights. I'm very grateful."

"You could prove your gratitude by having dinner with me."

"I know you're not gonna believe this, but I'm more than happy to do it, never mind the help you've given me."

"I believe you. When?"

"Tomorrow night?"

"Can do. Sevenish?"

"Yeah. Think of a place you like. Shall I pick you up?"

"Actually, it would be better if I met you. I live in a place that newcomers can't find easily. Meet me at Yen Ha. You like Vietnamese?"

I told her I did. She gave me directions, and we rang off.

I hung up to put the list of people she gave me in some kind of priority order. The phone rang, startling me.

"Hello."

"Lenny? This is Deak. I'll be in Portland tomorrow."

This was sudden. "Do I need to pick you up at the airport?"

"Nope. I'll rent a car and stay at a downtown hotel. Can you get hold of Kimmel?"

"Sure. What do you have in mind?"

"Just a meeting. I want as much on Sophie as I can get. I'm workin' on Goombah from this end."

"Jeez, Deak, I don't feel like I earned my money here."

"You did great, son. I know that my girl's alive . . . I feel like . . . I don't have the words. Like possibilities."

"Yeah, I understand. When will you be in?"

"Say four o'clock, or thereabouts."

We made some plans. I called D.K. Lainie answered the boardinghouse phone, and bellowed for him.

"Yeah?"

"D.K., this is Lenny. Deak Rowan is coming to town tomorrow, and he wants to see you."

"No way, Jose."

"Hey, think about this. He's not coming to give you grief. He's gonna be looking for Sophie, and you're one of the last with any real information. Don't sweat it."

"Oh, shit, man. We've never had much to say to each other."

"Quit whining, for crissakes. I'll be there to grease the wheels."

"Okay." His voice oozed reluctance.

We set up a meet, and hung up.

I started calling the list of party-goers. Out of thirty-five, I got six. Most copped out on a kind of paranoia about the police talking to them about anything. Some didn't give a shit, and the rest of the "nos" had already made up their minds that Walter was guilty.

But six people were good enough to put themselves out, six plus Molly. As I compiled their pieces of the puzzle on a sheet of paper, I found a disturbing softness ("Yeah, well, I *think* I saw him.") for about a half hour dangerously close to the time of death. I needed to talk with Frieda about the party, and the movies the night Strunz got it. She was the mucilage that held his alibi together.

As I was gathering my sheets of names and statements together, Love came down and plopped onto the bed, right in the middle of everything, natch. Luckily, he wasn't wet or muddy. I tried to move him, and got a nasty scratch for my trouble. I had to remember that he was just playing, or I would have given him a flying lesson.

He jumped off the bed. I quickly threw everything together, and he began rubbing against my legs. Since I was on my way upstairs anyway, I figured I'd feed him.

When we got to the kitchen, I rummaged around in the cupboard for a can of cat food, grabbed a plate, and dumped the nasty stuff onto it. I put it in his little corner.

He walked over to it, and sniffed at it tentatively. Then, he tried to cover it up, like he had just taken a dump.

Boy, I thought, what a restaurant critic he would make.

Frieda came in at that moment.

"Thanks for feeding Love. I guess that's not exactly what he wants. He's really spoiled."

She busied herself replacing the food in the can. "He might eat it another time," she said, as she put it in the fridge.

"Won't he eat it if you just leave it there? He did it for me the other night."

She looked at me with some surprise. "That would be truly unprecedented. If he rejects it, you can either throw it out, or try it again another time. It's definitely off the menu for the moment."

Just then, Lois came in. We all compared notes. Frieda had spoken to the attorney, recommended to them by their hippie lawyer. He was in the process of trying to spring Walter, although it would have to wait until after the arraignment. The lawyer was judge-shopping for a softie. So far, so good.

Lois had spoken to both Stabile and Wolfe, and both had agreed to talk. She had arranged to meet Wolfe at a coffee shop in an hour. Stabile wanted an open public place, so they chose Pioneer Courthouse Square in downtown. That was two hours later.

We threw together some sandwiches, munched them quickly, washed down with some good beer, and headed to the Common Grounds Coffee Shop on Hawthorne, which prided itself on using organic beans grown in nonexploitive situations, like co-op plantations. Ah, Portland.

When we got there, Lois looked around and pointed to a table over by the back wall, half in shadow. We walked over. Seated there was Yosemite Sam, or someone who looked a lot like him. Short, pugnacious, florid, extravagantly mustachioed, all he was missing was the twenty-gallon hat and the shootin' irons. At least there weren't any visible. He had an attaché case on the table. He was dressed in jeans, beat-up cowboy boots, and a flannel shirt. There was a buckskin jacket over the back of his chair.

"Who's this?" he said, pointing at me.

"Hello, B.B.," said Lois, "nice to see you again."

"Who's this?" Amenities were lost on this guy.

"My name is Lenny Schneider. I'm trying to help Walter."

He snorted. "If that fucker did it, it's the only good thing he ever did."

"Now, now," cooed Lois. "We're trying to find out who else might have had both Bella Durke and Strunz on their shit list."

Wolfe twirled his mustaches. "Could be a lot of people. Not me. I didn't give two shits for Durke, loudmouth twat, but I really had nothing to do with her. Strunz, now he's another story. Son of a bitch could piss off Saint Francis."

"I heard you two used to be buddies," I said.

"Buddies? No fuckin' way. We worked together for a short while. He was such a miserable motherfucker, though. He shit all over his cute little wife, too. I don't know why she stayed. Maybe *she* killed him."

Lois seemed to consider this for a second, then looked him in the eye. "B.B., do you have any *real* idea who might have killed these people?"

He shook his head. His expression seemed genuine. I believe he would have lost his shirt playing poker. Whatever else B.B. Wolfe was, he was no liar.

"What happened to drive you two apart, you and Strunz?"

"Well, the only thing that we had in common was hating that bunch of losers at KOOK. Other than that . . . Look, I'm a serious researcher. Strunz was supposed to be a journalist. I figured we could work together, him developing local stuff, me doing background on national and international stuff. But let's just say that, no matter how we tried to work something out, it wasn't good enough for him.

"I run these lectures on The Present Danger, bring my audience up to date on what's happening. I figured he could share the mike, give us a local perspective. Forget it! He wasn't playing second fiddle to me, is the way he put it. Had a real exaggerated idea of his abilities. Down deep, he was a fuckin' moron. He had no idea of how to do research, or analyze information. All he could do was to exploit a situation, and he didn't care if he had to screw around with the facts.

"One night, we were trying like hell to put together a lecture that he could participate in on some level. Well, he wanted to run the goddamn thing! He accused me of bein' an egomaniac who wouldn't take him seriously. We got into a fight, a screaming match, but it was ready to come to blows. Augie Stabile was there, and he tried to break it up. That just pissed Strunz off more. He accused Augie of bein' a traitor, sneakin' around behind his back, any fuckin' thing.

"I finally told Strunz to get the fuck outta my house. He started to break things up, screamin' like a lunatic, eyes poppin', face red. . . ." He twirled his mustaches to fine points.

"Well, I hadda call the cops. Me! I didn't know what else to do. He was a maniac. My girlfriend was hysterical. It was either call the fuzz or shoot the fucker. It was a tough choice."

Wolfe sat back in his chair. He got briefly thoughtful.

"As far as someone who *really* hated Strunz, you gotta talk to Augie Stabile. They actually lived in the same house for a while." He laughed, a kind of grunt. "You sure didn't have to be Dr. Joyce Brothers to see that it wouldn't work. Those're two of the angriest guys I ever met."

"What kind of car does Stabile drive?" I asked on a sudden inspiration.

"He's got a beat-up van that he hauls his video equipment around in, but he usually has one other one, a nicer one. He likes to cruise the roads in a good car. He had a Lexus recently, but I heard he was lookin' for something else."

"A BMW?"

"Maybe." He shrugged. "He's not hurtin' for money."

"Where's his money coming from?"

Wolfe's eyes narrowed. "What's this got to do with Egon? I didn't volunteer for you to pump me for dirt."

I held up my hands. "Okay, question withdrawn. Can you think of anything else that might be useful?"

"You got enough. I gotta go." Quite abruptly, he got up, put on his coat, and left.

Lois and I sat there and looked at each other for a bit.

"Well, did we learn anything?" she asked.

"We learned that Strunz was maybe worse than we thought, and had enemies we may not know about. What we don't know is whether any of these enemies was also capable of killing Durke. What about his wife?"

"Nah. Why would she also kill Bella? Maybe I should work it from the other side, talk to Bella's friends." She chewed her lip in contemplation.

"Maybe we're making a mistake assuming that just because Durke was stabbed, she was stabbed with the same bayonet they found in Strunz. Or even by the same person. *Oy, gevalt*. My brain hurts. What time do we have to meet Stabile?"

She checked her watch. "About an hour and a half, but it's downtown. Let's take a leisurely drive down there, and maybe have a beer before we see him."

"I like the way you think."

We left, and took the car through the misty streets. It had been raining on and off all day, and it was currently off. I turned to Lois and asked, "Where *does* Stabile get his money from?"

"I can give you the rumor I've heard. Not much more."

"Shoot."

"It is alleged that Augean Stabile is the son of wealthy industrialists in Austria. It's also rumored that he doesn't come into a private inheritance, independent of his parents, until he's forty years old. The story goes that, as a teenager and a young man, he was so vile to his mother and father, and such a hell-raiser, that they've been supporting him to live anywhere in the world, other than Austria. They supposedly send him checks, if he'll stay away from them. Once he inherits, I guess he can go plague them again. Anyway, that's what I heard."

"Do you believe it?"

She thought for a moment. "It's conceivable. He never seems to be broke, and has no visible means of support. He may not be getting a fortune, but he makes a point—flaunts, really—that he lives like a poor person. *If* you don't count the cars he has a fetish for. He gets a new one every now and then. The old van *is* for public consumption. The Lexus was for private use."

"A remittance man. Far out."

"Huh?"

"A remittance man. Robert W. Service used the term in a poem. It pops up in Brit colonial literature, too. Evelyn Waugh, that sort of thing. It's a guy who lives on the largesse of others, often at the price of physical absence from his benefactors. Like the story about Stabile, that his parents are buying distance for money. In Service's poem, the remittance man has given up the high life in London to sit in a cabin in Alaska and live a natural life. He lives by others putting 'a little in his purse.'"

"Nice term. I'll have to work it into a story sometime."

"Well, after we meet Stabile, you may work it into a story about who murdered Durke and Strunz."

Lois drove directly to a parking garage to save time. Amazing how cheap parking is in Portland.

We popped into a sports bar a couple of blocks from where we were to meet Stabile. Lois told me about the Portland Mavericks, a minor-league team of flakes and castoffs, which featured the actor Kurt Russell at second base, and Jim Bouton and Luis Tiant on the mound, and the weird stuff they used to pull. Like hiring a sound truck when they were on the road, which they would use to insult the local town, its denizens, and their baseball team. This would guarantee a large and vocal attendance at the games. Somebody really ought to do a book on them.

We drank a local beer, noshed a few French fries. It was all quite pleasant. Certainly in comparison to what followed.

Pioneer Courthouse Square, according to Lois, is sort of the living room of downtown Portland. Brick floor, sweeping stairs set into it. In the summer, they have concerts and festivals, and free lunchtime music. In the winter, they set up the city Christmas tree and menorah here. It's a hangout for skateboarders and street kids. It has a Starbuck's, of course.

Now, in the evening damp, it was almost deserted, except for the hard-core street people, and a lanky presence stalking the place like Hamlet on depressants. That would be Augean Stabile.

We approached him, and he raised a video camera.

"Do you mind if I videotape this?" he asked, his breath steaming.

"Do you mind if I ask why?" I asked back.

"It's for personal reasons."

I looked at Lois and shrugged. She shrugged back.

"Okay. We've got nothing to hide."

"Now, what do you want? I'm busy."

Lois stepped in. "Let's cut to the chase, then. You may know that Walter Egon is suspected of killing Bella Durke and Caliban Strunz."

The camera hid most of his face. The vapor of his breath obscured much of the rest. It was disconcerting, and made it hard to read him. I noticed a knife, another, larger knife than before hanging in an elaborate sheath from his belt. Scary.

"I didn't know he had it in him. Two more vile specimens are hard to imagine. Eliminating them improves the human race."

His glee was unconcealed. No trouble reading that.

"Very Teutonic of you, Augie," I said, as wryly as possible.

"Actually, we are Italian. My family has been in Austria for many years, but we are not krauts. So, who is stereo-typing?"

"Touché. By the way, what kind of car do you drive?"

I could see the sneer. "A 1975 Dodge van. Almost 200,000 miles on it. Want to buy it?"

"No, Augie, the *other* one. Not a black BMW, is it?"

"Are we here to discuss my transportation, or is there something else before I leave?"

"Just a minute, Augie," Lois interjected. "We think that

there may be someone else responsible for those deaths. Walter was not around to commit them. It looks bad for him because one of his knives was used, and his fingerprints are on it."

"Yeah," I added, "and it's one that you have some knowledge of yourself. It's that three-bladed French bayonet you sold him."

"Ah, the plug bayonet. A nice piece, I was sorry to let it go."

"So we're interested to know if you can think of anybody who had reason to kill both Durke and Strunz."

"Maybe lots of people. They were both vile, as I said before. Durke was a foulmouthed pervert. Not really a capital offense, I grant you, but who knows? I didn't care enough about her. We didn't move in the same social set, you might say.

"But Strunz . . . I assume you already know we were housemates at one time. In truth, I could easily have killed the stinking wretch with my bare hands. He was a nasty and arrogant big-mouth with poor personal habits. He did not respect my property." Stabile began to show some emotion here.

"He used my things without permission, and for inappropriate purposes. Once, he took a rare samurai *tanto* and used it to open cartons. The blade was stained with glue from shipping tape. After he used it, he left it lying around the house like a letter opener. It is one of the prizes in my collection of edged weapons, and he used it like a cheap tool. I could have killed him for that alone."

He was really getting hot now and raising his voice. Even the street people were beginning to notice. The video camera was shaking in his hands, the little red light making ephemeral lines in the misty gloom.

"Egon is another waste of human flesh, as far as I am concerned, but I will send him a bottle of wine for killing Strunz!"

The little red light on the camera went off, and he lowered

it. His face was contorted. "Good night!" he snapped, and stalked off.

"Well," I said to Lois, "that was no help at all. I'm beginning to think that we're not going to find an alternative suspect to Walter so easily. Stabile's so, um, blamable, though. Have you noticed the endless variety of knives he carries? Only we can't begin to prove that he uses them on anyone."

"Yeah, maybe we need to go to Plan B. By the way, what's all this about a black BMW?"

I realized I had never told her about the car that had chased Kimmel and me on Route 84. I covered it quickly, with her emitting low whistles every so often.

"And you suspect Stabile?" she asked.

"Hey, I don't know who to suspect. Stabile just strikes me as the type who's capable of it. Because I suspect him of that, I kind of like him for the killings, also."

"Yeah, but he and Durke weren't enemies."

"Everybody is Stabile's enemy. We need for you to work Bella's friends to find out for sure. I'm sure Wolfe wasn't involved. And, even though I shudder to think about it, if we eliminate Stabile, we'd better come up with another suspect pretty quick. Or make Walter's alibis ironclad, which, at the moment, they ain't."

We walked back to the garage without much talking. I was thinking that I might be in Portland longer than I wanted to be. Although going back to New York wasn't that tempting right now, either.

fifteen

WHEN WE GOT BACK TO the house, a grim-faced Walter and Frieda were sitting at the kitchen table. Frieda had the dregs of a beer in front of her, and Walter was having another session with Jack Daniels, the oracle of Lynchburg.

Lois and I wondered what was happening.

"Well," Walter began, "I guess you were right about getting a lawyer who knows what he's doing. I'm out on bail, and the guy has presented several petitions on my behalf, including a couple to suppress evidence, the bayonet in particular. I don't even understand everything he's doing, but what the fuck? I'm out, and on a low bail, 25K."

"That's why I wanted you to lose the bargain-basement shyster. You look hopeful for the first time in days. And more good news: Augie Stabile is sending you a bottle of wine for killing Durke and Strunz. He considers it a civic improvement," I said brightly.

"Oh, great!" Walter laughed. Even Frieda cracked a smile. "I can always count on my old friends."

"Yeah, but you may want to talk to Slim Reed sometime, and ask him why he wouldn't cooperate."

"What?"

I related my conversation with Reed, and how I eventually got the names I needed.

Walter shook his head. "That guy has nothing in the way of intestinal fortitude. If he'd been a real manager, we'd all have been better off at the station, but this . . . I guess I should have expected it. It still hurts." Walter's expression was properly pained. "Thank heaven for Molly, though. She's got her head screwed on right."

I nodded in agreement. "Yeah, and I have to pay a terrible price for her information. I have to have dinner with her tomorrow night, some place called Yen Ha."

Walter laughed again. It was good to see him relaxing.

"Whoa, some terrible price! You have to spend the evening with a smart, funny, and attractive woman eating the best Vietnamese food in Portland. You poor devil!"

"You see what I go through for you. By the way, when is the lawyer gonna call me?"

"Good question. Sooner rather than later. He needs to get your witness list, and whatever else you know. I think he might want to use his own detective. Any problem with that?"

I felt a sudden lightness. "No, no. Far from it. I'll be happy to give it over. My other case will probably wind down in the next day or two. And I can go back to New York in time to hate east-coast winter anew."

"I want to pay you for your time."

"Not necessary. I'm on the clock for the other thing, and I haven't neglected it, much. So, well, don't worry about it." I was a little embarrassed.

Lois said, "Walter, I'll want to talk to your lawyer as well. I'll need something from him for the story. I won't ask you anything, because he probably wouldn't want me to. Okay?"

He shrugged. "Solid. Let me get you his card." He hiked up on his chair and fished around in his pocket, coming up with a slightly bent card. "Here ya go."

I read over her shoulder, Hampton Freer, Attorney-at-Law, Criminal Defense, etc.

"So," I offered, "is anyone hungry besides me?"

Three hands shot up.

"Okay, let me pick up a few things, and I'll cook dinner." I quickly ascertained the state of the larder, which provided good quality pasta, olive oil, canned tomatoes, and a good array of spices, herbs, and condiments. There was a nice selection of pots, pans, and utensils, all properly broken in. A well-stocked house, as I would have suspected.

Lois and I ran out to an overpriced but convenient market, which featured free-range chicken, organic produce, and the like. I bought some dreadfully expensive scallops, fresh organic collard greens, some Parmigiana Reggiano, a couple of bottles of a cheap Verdicchio I was taking a chance on, whipping cream, a large loaf of sourdough bread, lemons, and salad greens.

When we got back, I set tasks for people: washing the greens, making the salad, grating the cheese, boiling water for pasta. While they were occupied, I chopped and boiled the collards with some garlic, chopped onion, lemon juice, and vegetable broth from a bouillon cube.

Then, I sautéed the scallops in olive oil, garlic, and fresh-ground pepper until they were done, removed them from the pan to a bowl, and reduced the juices, adding some chopped tomato. I deglazed the pan with some of the Verdicchio, which we were already drinking, and added cream until there was enough for a sauce. I re-added the scallops for just a minute to warm them.

The linguine, cooked and drained, went into the bowl, and the scallop sauce on top. I tossed the pasta with the sauce. I hate getting naked noodles on my plate that I have to add sauce to.

The collards were served with the cooking juice, not real pot-liquor, but on short notice, well . . . I added lemon juice and dill weed to the salad greens, tossed them, and drizzled on some olive oil. The bread was sliced, more wine poured, and we chowed down.

After dinner, my mind drifted back to Walter's case. I was

wondering about his movie alibi. I didn't want to break the mood, but I had to.

"Walter, forgive me for asking, but what movie did you see the night Strunz got killed?"

Frieda sat up angrily. "Do you have to? We told you the lawyer is going to use his own detective."

Walter waved her down. "Take it easy, it's okay. Now, we saw an old English movie, *Colonel Blimp* I think it was called. It was playing at the Mt. Tabor Theater, one of those cheapie places that serves beer. It was pretty good, actually." ·

"And you were there from when to when?"

"Oh, from about nine to about eleven, give or take a few minutes."

"Anybody see you?"

"Several people, I guess."

"Anyone you know? You know, that can ID you?"

He shrugged. "No one I know by name, some neighborhood characters who might know me by sight."

"Walter, this is the weakest part of your alibi. I'd get working on firming it up. Have the lawyer's guy find out who was working at the theater that night, and . . ."

"Look, you're not the only competent detective in the world!" Frieda got up in my face. I got pissed.

"Listen, Frieda, it wasn't so long ago that you were begging me to help. I'm still trying to make sure that my old friend gets the most he can from what he has to work with. What's your problem, here?" I wasn't shouting, exactly, but Walter felt he had to step in and calm things. It was good that he did. I was beginning to get tired of the vindictive neurotic he had hooked up with.

"Take it easy, Frieda. Lenny's right. We need all the help we can get. Sorry, Lenny. We're just cranked up a few too many notches here, lately."

"No problem." I didn't look at Frieda for the rest of the meal, and the banter never got loose again. What the hey? I was out of here in a day or two.

They absolved me from scullery duty because I had bought and cooked the meal, and I didn't argue. I begged off watching the tube with the group and headed for bed. I had a feeling that tomorrow was going to be a long day.

sixteen

THE NEXT DAY, I LAY LATE abed. Sometime after a grey dawn, but before I got out of bed, Love came down to sleep between my legs. I wondered if he liked me, or if I was just a kind of furniture to him.

I turned on the radio, and the news fell out in fetid dollops, each chunk less welcome than the previous one. Maybe I'd move to Australia. Kangaroos, koalas, aborigines, the outback, the Great Barrier Reef, gruff and hearty beer drinkers who loved Americans, or so I had been told. All I had to worry about was skin cancer, Vegemite, and colonial English cuisine. And maybe everyone was really named "Bruce."

I was beginning to get homesick for New York, the cold weather notwithstanding. I was tired of the mellowness, the smug eccentricity. I hated the smell of the paper mill in the morning. A-pulp-alypse Now! I missed Bruno and Uncle Sol, and even Sue.

Was there a decent kosher deli in Sydney?

I got up to shower, careful not to disturb Love's sleep. My mind was an utter blank. I didn't want to think about anything, if I could avoid it. I wanted coffee and the comics, and no conversation for a while.

When I got up to the kitchen, it was blissfully empty.

There were two notes waiting for me on the table. One was from Frieda apologizing to me, yet again. Even the punctuation looked insincere.

The other was from Lois, asking me to call her when I got a chance. I would, right after coffee and Zippy the Pinhead. Imagine my shock at not finding Zippy in *The Portlander*. There was a strip about some nuclear family and their wild imaginations. The drawing style irritated me, the content was saccharine, and the worst thing was that it was probably offered up as a replacement for Calvin and Hobbes. Gross.

So I rummaged for food. I found a bagel in the freezer, threw it in the toaster, and raided the fridge for cream cheese. There was this "Lite" stuff, and no other.

When the bagel came out of the toaster, I lathered it with the ersatz cream cheese, and had a bite. It was soft and squishy and the cheese was thin. Pseudo-bagel, pseudo-cheese, pseudo-comics. God, what a crab I was. Maybe the whole Walter thing, and the Sophie-is-alive thing had gotten to me. Thank heaven the coffee was good.

I heard the phone ringing downstairs and leaped up to go after it. "Hello!" I yelled breathlessly.

"Hey, boy, it's Deak. I'm here in Portland. Can you get me with Kimmel?"

I took down the hotel name, and called D.K.'s rooming house. He was at the stadium. I called the stadium, and spoke to Mr. Smiley.

"Yes, he's here, and this is the first week he's been here when he didn't have alcohol on his breath. What did you say to him?"

"I told him that if he straightened out, you would replace the artificial turf with real grass. What's up with that stuff, anyway? I thought Oregon was known for growing sod."

"Yes, Mr. Schneider, but this facility is used for college football this time of year. When we had real grass, the rain and the player's cleats would turn the field into a most unpleasant condition. It was never back in shape by spring."

"Maybe it's just cheaper not to have to pay a grounds crew to care for the grass?"

"Maybe. Did you want D.K.?" he asked testily. I think I hit a raw nerve.

"Yes, please."

A few moments later, I heard, "If you want me to meet Rowan, the answer's no."

"Hello to you, too. Come on, don't be a schmuck. If you can't stand it, I promise to get you out of there the minute you ask."

It went back and forth like that for a few minutes, and then he caved in. I told him to be in front of the stadium in a half hour.

I called Lois.

"Lenny, I'm a bit concerned about something."

"Shoot."

"After you went to bed last night, I went down to the Mt. Tabor Theater and checked on the movie. *Colonel Blimp* was playing, and at the times Walter said. The guy selling tickets, and one of the people behind the bar were both working that night, but they couldn't say for sure whether they saw Walter or not. One of the little snots said, 'You seen one fat old hippie, you seen 'em all.' They were also no help on giving me any names of others who were there that night. I couldn't tell if they just didn't know, or didn't want to tell me."

"Yeah, people are a bit reluctant to get caught up in anything like this. I always try to use misdirection, to come at it from an oblique direction."

"Gimme a break, Lenny. I didn't just fall off the ice wagon."

"You're too young to remember ice wagons. So, unless we can come up with another way of establishing his attendance there, it's only Frieda's word."

"Shaky, huh?"

"Well, if it were me, I'd want something a bit more substantial. But no one can put him at the Lady Faire, either.

Pinky sure won't be much help to them." I got a mental image of Pinky in his plush-toy coat on the witness stand, and suppressed a chuckle.

"Maybe it's just to make me feel better."

"I know what you're talking about. Something doesn't feel right about this whole thing, and I can't nail what it is."

"Okay, see you later." She hung up, and I scurried out to the car to pick D.K. up. The dank air stank. It was raining slightly.

I bitched out loud to an empty car about Portland drivers, too timid to pull into the right lane to go around a car making a left turn. Or not getting out into the intersection when they turn left, or stopping in traffic when they get confused. By the time I got to City Stadium, I had to perform an act of will not to be pissed off. I wanted to deal with this whole thing with a level head.

"Hey, buddy, jump in." I reached across the car to open the door lock.

Kimmel got in, looking morose. He pouted all the way to the hotel, while I made inane chatter trying to rouse him. There were no spots on the street, so I put the car in a nearby lot.

"I don't wanna do this," he grumbled as we walked into the lobby.

"C'mon, D.K., this is a good thing." He flashed me a look, but went silent again.

It was a nice old hotel, with a comfortable lobby. I went over to the desk to get Deak's room number, and the clerk asked me if she should announce us. She called up, and Deak asked her to send us up.

The elevator ride was like the steps to the gallows for Kimmel, who sunk deeper into his coat with each floor. If we had been in the Empire State Building, he would have wound up six inches tall.

Deak let us into his room. He was casual, in jeans and a Mets sweatshirt.

"I was gonna introduce you two, but I guess you've already met," I said lamely.

"Hello, Donnie. Been a long time." Deak extended his hand, and was slightly taken aback when Kimmel reached out his left hand to shake. But he composed himself and shook it gingerly.

"Come on in." Deak gestured to a couch along the right-hand wall of the room, which was nice without being fancy, and cozier than I'd expected. "I called room service, and they'll be sendin' up some coffee and pastry."

"Thanks, Deak," I replied, as I shucked off my coat.

Deak looked at Kimmel when he removed his coat, wincing slightly at the peculiar gesture Kimmel used to shrug the thing off his wrecked shoulder. We sat down.

"Lenny tells me you got a job down at the stadium?"

Kimmel nodded silently, like a shy seven-year-old.

"How much do you like it?"

"It pays the rent, and leaves enough for, uh . . ."

"For a few beers?"

"Yup."

Just then, there was a knock on the door. It was room service, with a huge tray of coffee, sweet rolls, donuts, and other assorted baked goods of the tooth-rotting variety. Deak tipped the kid, and poured us cups. Kimmel seemed interested in the pastries. He had a sweet tooth, apparently.

It was Deak who broke the slurping-and-munching session to speak again.

"So here's what I've found out back in Jersey. Goombah called to tell one of his friends that he was in Montana, hangin' out with some bunch of fuckups, but that he wasn't gonna stay long. That was about a week ago. I figure I can go out there and check the story. Maybe he ain't gone yet. So that's the reason I ask if you like your job, Donnie."

"D.K. People call me D.K. now."

"Sure. I'm askin' if you want to go with me. You and me can track that little monkey down, and get her ass straightened out."

Kimmel looked up at Deak, donut crumbs on his lips, and burst into tears. He tried to talk, but the sobs made his words unintelligible.

Deak walked over to the bed and fished a couple of tissues out of a box. He handed the tissues to Kimmel, who blew his nose loudly and wiped his streaming face.

"D.K., do you still love Sophie?"

The kid just nodded.

"Yeah," Deak went on, "me, too. Whatever she's got into, and how, we gotta rescue her. Look, I found out a lot about her I didn't know when I went lookin' for Goombah's rat-bastard friends. I'm sorry for what I believed about you, and I'm sorry that my little girl fucked up your life. I know that you did the best you could, and I wasn't no help. Whether or not we find Sophie, and whether or not we can save her dumb ass I don't know. But as far as I'm concerned, you're family."

At this point, I was crying myself. I got up and brought the tissues over.

I leaned over and put my hand on D.K.'s back. "I told you this guy was a class act. If you've got an ounce of brains, you'll hook up with this man."

"I ain't as stupid as I look. Thanks, Mr. Rowan. I can drive, if it ain't a stick shift."

"Automatic it is. Let's go shopping. You're gonna need a few things."

"I don't have any money."

"Well, if you're willing, come back to Jersey with me. I'll get you into my business."

"A one-armed refrigeration mechanic?"

"Hey, I got one guy now with a hook, and a blind lady who does my computer stuff. Just as long as your brain works, we're in business. Besides, we got a box at Shea for Met games, and I go down to spring training every year in Vero Beach. You'll be talkin' baseball until you turn blue. We had a football fan workin' for us once, but I fired his ass 'cause he was so boring."

I was beginning to feel like an intruder. I got up.

"Deak, I guess I'll go. Doesn't seem to be much else I can do."

Deak got up and threw his long arms around me. "Thanks, Lenny. I'm real grateful to you. You got me back my family."

I stammered, tried to protest.

"Don't give me no shit. If you're havin' fun here in Portland, stick around for a while. Have a couple of good meals on me. I appreciate you not loadin' up the expense account."

"Thanks, Deak. I hope everything else works out this well."

"There *is* one thing about a destroyed rental car."

I looked at D.K., and we both started to laugh. He looked at Deak and said, "Whatever you do, don't go for a drive with this clown. I'll tell you all about it."

"I'm outta here." I headed for the door, grabbing a chocolate donut on the way out.

seventeen

WITH THE DEAK ROWAN matter seemingly well settled, I bombed around Portland for a while, trying to ignore the boneheads they let drive out there. Okay, so New York drivers are aggressive and nasty. They know how to merge a couple of lanes of traffic, and they don't sit like zombies waiting for something to happen. Okay, so in making something happen the result could be gunplay or vehicular manslaughter, at least it's not boring.

I decided to visit the bookstore everyone I'd met told me they liked better than Powell's, Great Northwest Books. It was on Stark Street, just about where it runs into Burnside at an acute angle. Whoever laid out the streets here had a serious problem. I marveled at the human ability to take a simple task like laying out streets and complicating it beyond use. You ever been in downtown Boston? Maybe those Midwesterners with their square grids really had the idea.

I parked the car and went into Great Northwest. The first thing that greeted me, besides the comfortable disorder, was a large shelf of baseball books, mostly used. The invention of the used bookstore ranks with the discovery of penicillin in its importance to the human race.

I browsed. I picked up a fair copy of Jim Bouton's *Ball*

Four in hardback, with an autograph yet, in much better shape than the paperback I'd owned for years. I found a bio of Gil Hodges I hadn't read. Next, I took a Bob Feller bio. I was trying to decide on a novel entitled *If I Never Get Back* when I felt someone's eyes on me.

I looked up, and there was a thickset guy in a flasher's raincoat and a baseball cap lurking around the edges of the store, and checking me out. He was chipmunk-cheeked, and had a droopy mustache. He looked at me from the corner of his eye.

"Can I help you?" I asked, not wanting to tell him to get lost right away.

He sidled over, and in a flat, breathy voice said, "You a private eye?"

I was stunned. "Uh, yeah. How did you know?"

He looked at me enigmatically. "It's my business to know." He dug the Feller book. "You a Cleveland Indians fan?"

"Uh, no. Brooklyn Dodgers."

His eyebrows shot up. "Isn't that like being a St. Louis Browns fan?"

"A little, but the Dodgers still exist in one form or another. The Browns are invisible within the Baltimore Orioles."

"Where are you from?"

"New York. Why?"

"Just asking. You read detective novels?"

"Not much anymore. I used to love Sherlock Holmes and Dashiell Hammett, but my all-time fave is Raymond Chandler."

His face lit up. "'Down these mean streets a man must go who is not himself mean; who is neither tarnished nor afraid.'"

"Ah, from *The Simple Art of Murder*. How about, 'When in doubt, have a man come through a door with a gun in his hand.'"

"'It was about eleven o'clock in the morning, mid-

October, with the sun not shining and a look of hard, wet rain in the clearness of the foothills.'"

"*The Big Sleep*. Okay, 'He was a big man, but not over six feet five inches tall, and not wider than a beer truck.'"

"*Farewell My Lovely*. How about . . ."

I held up my hand to stop him. "Enough. We'll do this all day. You say it's your business to know. What's your business?"

"That's *my* business." And he did a take, and split.

Another Portland eccentric, but he knew his Raymond Chandler. The truth is, I was about out of remembered quotes. Time to read the master once again.

I went up to the desk, manned by a tall guy with a Captain Ahab beard and two sets of glasses on strings around his neck. Maybe he needed one pair to see the other one.

"I see you met Gordon," he said.

"Huh?"

"Gordon. That was him you were talking to."

"Odd duck."

He waved his hands in a semaphore of disagreement. "Not once you get to know him. You new?"

I nodded. "Yup. I was here on business, and I've heard from some local people that this is a good bookstore."

His face opened into a radiant smile. "Wow, not Powell's?"

"I've been there." His face fell slightly. "This place seemed better right away." Smile, again. "Mind if I look around?"

"Take your time. Want me to hold those for you?"

I gave him the two bios and the novel, which I had decided to buy. He stored them behind the counter.

I wandered around through the funky, crowded shelves, thinking about Walter and browsing the odd book. I was definitely heading home tomorrow or the next day, and I wanted to make sure that he was in good hands. I felt uneasy that his alibi, which was his only defense, was porous. I needed to talk with him, and his lawyer, maybe.

I walked past a fifties/sixties shelf, with Hunter Thompson, John Clellon Holmes, and *A Child's Garden of Grass*, a marijuana cookbook. I wondered yet again what the world saw in Richard Brautigan, or Charles Reich.

Time to go. I had a hot date with Molly, and I wanted to relax a bit beforehand.

I walked back to the counter. The guy was on the phone, and gestured for me to wait. A moment later, he hung up.

"That was Gordon. He wanted to know if you were still here."

"Just barely. I've got to split. Wish him my best. By the way, are you Phil or John?"

"Phil, why?"

"Lois Newsom told me to ask for either one when I got here. I just remembered. I'm staying in Lois's house while I'm here."

"Wow, are you doing something about Walter Egon?"

"How do you know about that?"

"Well, it's on the news. Walter's a friend, but I haven't spoken to him since, uh, all this."

"I really shouldn't talk about it." I really didn't want to talk about it. "What's your take on it, if any?"

"I think he could have done it, but I know a few people who could. That whole KOOK situation is a mess."

"Can we count on you to come up with names if we need to? We've been having a hell of a time developing a list of alternate possibilities."

He looked pained.

"I know it's not easy. Call Lois if you think you can help."

He nodded, and rang up my sale. "I'll give you another ten percent off, since you're Lois's friend."

"Thanks."

"Want a sack for that?"

"Sack? Oh, a bag. Yeah, it's raining on and off."

"Thanks for coming in. Have a nice evening."

"Yeah, you, too."

As I walked back to the car, I had a brainstorm in the rainstorm. Was it really possible that someone had broken in and taken the bayonet? Could some kind of reasonable doubt be created with that possibility at its core? I wanted to talk to Walter even more now. We might get the charges dropped.

eighteen

WHEN I GOT BACK TO
Walter's, I was greeted with an astonishing sight: about
twenty women carrying signs and yelling at his front steps.
One sign read DYKE DEFENDERS DEMAND JUSTICE FOR BELLA
DURKE! Another said, STRAIGHT WHITE MALES = HOMOPHOBIC
VIOLENCE. Like that.

I tried to enter, but got braced by three women.

"Where do you think you're goin'?"

"Um, into the house."

"Who're you?"

"Who's askin'?" This was getting on my nerves.

"You another killer?"

"You ever heard of 'innocent until proven guilty'?"

"He's guilty. He's a homophobe!"

"Do any of you actually know him?"

"We know his type."

"What type is that?"

"Homophobe!"

"Killer!"

I could see that this was getting nowhere. I tried to move,
but the women surrounded me and stopped me on the stairs.

"Hey, come on. I'm staying at this house, I'm from out of
town, and I have nothing to do with this," I lied.

They didn't budge. Just then, Lois opened the door.

"Hey," she called out, "he's okay. Let him come in."

They didn't budge. Lois took an umbrella from inside the door and came down.

"Let him go. You can't do this kind of thing."

"Justice for Bella!" one of them yelled.

"That's what we're working on. He's trying to find her killer."

"The killer lives here. He should be rotting in fuckin' jail!"

"Just because someone is accused doesn't mean they're guilty. Now back off!"

She grabbed me and hauled me bodily out from their encirclement, up the stairs, and into the house. The crowd outside took up a new round of yells.

"God, thanks. You may have saved my life."

"You don't know how close to true that is. I have no idea how much they're capable of. They're vigilantes in Doc Martens and overalls, and they scare me."

"Do they do this thing all the time?"

"Whenever they feel like it's necessary, and more frequently with time. Someday they're gonna do something they'll regret, and their target will turn out to be innocent."

We went into the kitchen.

"Lois, I think we need to investigate the possibility that someone stole the bayonet to implicate Walter. It's really possible."

She cocked her head and thought about it. "Yeah, okay, but it's hard to prove. There's been a lot of rain, and activity outside the windows could have been washed away. With that crowd outside now, they could be trampling on something important."

"Who's got keys to this place?" I asked.

"Ah, that's another problem. This has been a group house for years. I can't even imagine how many keys are out there. You know, old housemates who've never given up their keys, assorted boy- and girlfriends, people in the neighborhood who fed pets, on and on. We've been meaning to change the locks, but, well, you know how that goes."

"Well, that might be to Walter's ultimate advantage. It helps create doubt that he was the only one with access to the bayonet. By the way, what time is it?"

She consulted her watch. "About 6:30, why?"

"Shoot! I've got a date with Molly at Yen Ha at seven, and I haven't cleaned up yet."

"Nice lady. Besides, this is Portland. If you don't actively reek of B.O. you're ahead of the game."

"An Oregon fashion tip? Thanks, but I want at least to wash my face and brush my teeth. See you later."

I dashed downstairs, did a quick ablution, and changed my shirt. If I stayed in Portland much longer, I was going to have to do a laundry. I ran out of the house, catching the Dyke Defenders by surprise. They were getting cold and wet, and the fun seemed to be out of the event. Still, they managed a perfunctory round of insults to my Y chromosome as I ran through their ranks.

Yen Ha was only about a ten-minute drive, so I got there in time, and found a place to park. I entered the place, which was crowded and full of good smells, to find Molly waiting for me just inside the entrance.

It was a large, bustling restaurant full of noisy chatter and scrambling waitrons. Molly greeted me.

"Hey, Dick Tracy, you're punctual. I like that in a man."

"Hi. Yeah, I consider lateness to be a form of rudeness, so I try to be on time. What's the story with a table?"

"They assure me that we have only a few minutes to wait. Someone is finishing up now."

"Interesting decor. It looks like they painted over some ugly Chinese reliefs with gold paint. And what's with the walls?"

"I like the walls. They look like they were painted with fudge ripple ice cream."

A hostess came over and ushered us to a table. The menu

was huge, not always a good sign. I'd rather have a small, well-done menu than a large one that's out of control.

"What's good?"

"I'm a vegetarian, so I get some kind of veggie thing. I'm told that the curries are good, and the seafood stuff."

To my amazement, I found several dishes featuring frogs legs. I went for it, frogs legs with curry and lemon grass. Molly ordered stir-fried tofu and mushrooms with egg noodles.

We ordered a couple of Singha beers, and chatted while we waited for the meal. She was vivacious and droll, and beautiful. She told me dirty jokes, and funny stories about being a single mom with two young teenage boys, many of which revolved around feminine hygiene. The blood mysteries are a vexation to men, and terrifying to adolescent boys. If women knew how much this freaks men out, they might be less inclined to hate it.

The food came. Molly wouldn't try mine, but hers was nicely spiced, with a tart and slightly sweet sauce. The frogs legs were perfection, cooked in a well-balanced curry, aromatic with lemongrass. Good food.

Molly wrinkled her nose at the little pile of bones accumulating on my plate as I ate the legs. I had to laugh.

"The first time I ate frogs legs, I felt like the giant in Jack and the beanstalk. They are disconcertingly similar to tiny human bones."

"Yeah, and to a vegetarian it's even worse."

I looked cross. "Are you saying that meat-eaters are the equivalent of cannibals?"

"Hey, pal, if the shoe fits. I am content to synthesize my own protein from the plant kingdom."

"Don't come running to me when the next Ice Age hits, and all the broccoli dies, and you have to eat little furry things that skitter across the tundra."

"If the reindeer in Lapland can survive on lichens and moss, so can I," she said with ironic pride.

"The difference between mere survival, and a good

venison roast, with sautéed moss and lichens on the side, will always elude the vegetarian. It's simply a matter of living well."

"How would you like to come home with me tonight? The kids are with my mother."

"I'm not going to be here much longer, maybe a day or two. I don't want to . . ."

"Bullshit. I'm a big girl. Besides, you may want a reason to come back. The summers are what this place is about. Think of it: summer in the Northwest, and me."

"What if there's a man in the picture?"

"Well, you'll have to get rid of him."

"Let's get a check."

We packed up the remains of our dinner, paid the check, and I followed her to her home. I would definitely need a map to get back. It was a tiny house set back from a street that seemed on the verge of becoming busy. New construction was everywhere.

The place was warm and cozy inside. Books overflowed a set-in wall shelf, and stacks of records and CDs engulfed a small stereo on a cinder-block-and-board shelf. There were theater posters on the wall.

"This place used to be in the boonies," she said, as she offered me a glass of wine, "but they say that 50,000 people a year are moving to Oregon, and they're putting up housing everywhere. I'll be an island in the ocean, soon."

"An oasis. Cheers."

We clinked glasses, drank a bit, and then she put down her glass and gave me a deep and powerful kiss. Her body was warm and yielding, her lips soft. Her tongue entered my mouth and caressed every corner. The heat escalated quickly.

We skipped the couch and went directly to her disheveled bedroom.

"Sorry about the mess," she apologized.

"Just like home," I replied, trying to take off my shirt, kiss her, and speak at the same time.

We got naked and hit the bed. It was like I had known her for years. Comfortable, yet arousing. Familiar, yet exciting.

I caressed her ample body, running my hands over her curves, and squeezing or stroking as I was moved to do. She went right for Mr. Schwanz, greeting him like an old friend, cupping him and running her fingers around his twin companions.

I redirected my mouth from her lips down her neck and to her large breasts; her breath caught and she gasped as I licked and nipped lightly.

My arousal was so complete that I was afraid of finishing before we started. My hand moved down between her legs, and I began to softly manipulate her, wanting to give her a climax, in case I couldn't last inside her.

She said something I couldn't hear.

"Hmmm?" I purred.

"Rubber," she said. Welcome to the nineties.

She reached over to her bedside drawer and got out a foil packet. Not my brand, but what the hell?

I took it, stashed it nearby, and continued to stroke her. Soon, she quivered and moaned, and we clutched each other. She reached behind me and took the packet. She opened it, extended the thing, and reached down for my woody. She teased and tickled it with her fingers until it throbbed, and I was afraid I was going to give her an eyewash.

She pulled the rubber over me, lay down, and directed me to her. When I entered, we both shuddered a bit. Her flesh was so warm and soft, her mouth so adept on my ears and neck, her body so in harmony with mine I was actually lost in the act, for the first time in maybe twenty years.

I guess I was inspired, because the danger of a quick finish receded as we entwined and moved on the bed. Rolling to this side and that, gasps and moans added to the soft fleshy sounds.

When at last I finished, we both cried out in exquisite release. Unbelievable.

I lay down by her side, and removed the raincoat.

"Let me get that for you. Do you need to use the bathroom?"

"Uh-uh." I couldn't have gotten up, anyway.

She was back in a moment, the sound of a flushing toilet off somewhere, and cuddling with me.

"Still leaving soon?"

"Ouch. You know where to grab a guy, don't you?"

"It was just, uh, very nice."

"Yeah, it was. I can only attribute it to the inspiration provided by my partner."

"My, you *are* a gentleman, aren't you?"

"No, I'm serious. I didn't think I was capable of that kind of thing anymore. My compliments."

"Will you be able to see me before you go back east?"

"I'll surely try. I have to tell you, though, that I have a disturbing tendency to fall in love with women who do this to me."

"Well, ain't you some shit? Would you take my kids to ball games?"

"Are we making plans? Not a good idea."

"Agreed. Can we do this again?"

So we did.

Later, she said, "Look, don't take this the wrong way, but I would rather you weren't here when my kids come back in the morning. If we had dated for a while it would be different, but I don't want them to think . . ."

"Say no more. No offense taken, although the idea of sleeping in your arms is wonderful. There *is* my snoring, however."

"Screw the snoring. It's the price I have to pay."

"Want to move to New York?"

"Not even a little."

"Check. I'll get dressed."

We exchanged a few deep and soulful kisses before I left. She told me how to get home, and it seemed easier than I thought. I got lost, anyway. It's the price I had to pay.

nineteen

I GOT BACK TO WALTER'S about eleven-thirty. The Dyke Defenders had gone to wherever the righteous go to celebrate. I let myself in.

Walter, Frieda, and Lois were arrayed around the table, drinking beer. I joined them.

Lois was looking at me with a peculiar, amused smile.

"What?" I inquired.

"So, is Molly a real blonde?"

I looked offended. "A gentleman never tells."

"But we can safely assume that Mr. Schneider has had his ashes hauled? You have that look."

All three were peering at me now. "What the fuck is this, high school? I feel like I'm back in the old locker room."

Lois laughed. "Okay, just busting your hump a little. Molly's a terrific person, and I like you with her."

"Hey, wait a minute. I'm going to be here a matter of hours, and then it's back to The Apple. There is no hope for anything unless she moves back to New York."

"Don't tell me that you won't ever come back to Portland." Walter leaned into the conversation. "We were just getting used to having you around. And the summers . . ."

"Yeah, I know: the summers are to die for."

"You spend a summer here, and you may never get back to the east," said Frieda, with a malicious glint in her eye.

"Don't we, mature adults all, have anything to discuss besides my sex life and future travel plans?"

"Yes," said a voice from another room, "we can talk about giving my name to the police."

We all spun around in the direction of the voice, the entrance to the dining room. Stepping out of the shadows into the lighted doorway was Augie Stabile.

"How the hell did you get in here?" Walter shouted.

"Easily. None of your windows are locked. There isn't the slightest trouble."

"So," I turned toward him, "is this how you got in to steal the bayonet and do in Durke and Strunz?"

"I didn't do that. I have been harassed by the police for days now, because one of you gave them my name. How *dare* you give them my name! They are fascist thugs, Gestapo. They have searched my house, disrupted my life. They were glad to have a reason to mess with me, and someone here gave it to them."

He reached behind his back and pulled out an enormous knife with a black blade. Frieda let out a shriek, and Lois gasped.

"Which was it? You, Egon, you fucking worm? You, Schneider, you hired snoop?"

"Put the knife away, Augie," I said as calmly as I could, "you're only making it worse for yourself. If you hurt anyone here, the cops won't even bother looking for anyone else for the murders. You'll be dog meat, especially if you use a knife."

"Shut up! I missed my chance on the freeway, and I'm going to take it now." He moved closer, and we all tensed.

"That *was* you, you cocksucker. I should break your fuckin' neck just for that." I grabbed for a beer bottle.

"Don't touch that!" He began to inch forward and wave the knife in front of him. The blade must have been a foot long.

Love appeared out of nowhere, and began to rub against Stabile's leg. It distracted him momentarily, and I stood up, beer bottle in hand.

"Sit down!" he bellowed. "Get away, animal!" He kicked at the cat and sent him sailing a few feet. He began to advance on us, and Love launched himself, grabbing Stabile by his long, skinny leg like a pole climber, and sinking his teeth deep into Stabile's flesh.

Augie shrieked like a scalded castrato, and tried to bring the knife down on the cat without stabbing himself. I cocked my arm and threw a perfect pitch, high and inside. The bottle caught Stabile on the side of the head and dazed him. Lois and I jumped at the same time, like we had it planned. She grabbed Love and pulled him off of Stabile's leg, taking some of the galoot's pants and a lot of his meat with her. Stabile swiped at her and missed by not much just as I slammed into him.

We both hit the floor, and I barely avoided his blade as I attempted a move Bruno had shown me. I slammed the heel of my hand, just so, into his nose. He yowled in agony, and tried to grab his nose. In doing so, he hit it with the hilt of the knife, causing himself even more pain. I rolled off him, and kicked his nuts into next week, then grabbed the wrist of his knife hand and broke it over my knee like a twig. He dropped the knife. I chucked it onto the kitchen floor.

"Don't get up, motherfucker, or I'll ruin you!" I stood panting, just far enough away from him to be out of his reach.

I looked over my shoulder for a split second and yelled, "Somebody call 911, goddammit!"

Augie used that split second to try to get up. He was fast, like a snake, but hurt bad enough not to be at full speed. That gave me the chance to stop him by kicking his legs out from under him. He went down like a sack of potatoes, and lay there groaning.

I bent over him and forced him onto his stomach, pinning his arms behind him. He screamed as I manhandled his broken wing. I knelt down, resting my knees on his arms, smashing his face into the floor. I hissed at him through clenched teeth.

"Augie, I swear to God, if you try anything I'll fuckin' kill you, and I have three witnesses here who'll swear you deserved it. Which you probably do."

I called out, "Lois, bring me something to tie this fucker up with!"

A second later, she was there with an extension cord. "How's this?"

"Perfect." I took the cord and wound it tightly around his wrists, knotted it, and bent his legs at the knees, tying his ankles together. He was trussed up pretty well, and groaning very satisfyingly. I stood back and admired the chunk Love had taken out of Stabile's leg. This cat was the Bruno of the feline world.

Walter came over. "I called the cops. I already told them that he might be the guy they were looking for. Maybe this will ice it."

"Looks good to me. Is everyone okay? The cat?"

Walter let out a huge laugh, at least partly from sheer relief. "Are *we* okay? Damn, man, are *you* okay? We didn't do shit. Remind me never to get you mad at me." He laughed some more.

Then he bent over Stabile's knife.

"Don't pick that fucking thing up!" I yelled. "That's all you need is your goddamn fingerprints on it."

He considered the weapon dispassionately. "Nice knife. Military fighting knife, custom design. You can cut through metal with that blade, then shave with it. Good thing he never got near us with it. You still got a good arm."

"Yeah, but it was a terrible waste of beer. You got another bottle for me?"

The cops came and did their thing. They collected evidence, took statements, carted Stabile off, and generally had a good time doing it. Stabile was well known by the cops, and not loved. Too many of them had had his video camera shoved in their faces over the years, and been asked if they were fascists. Walter assured me that a lot of what he charged about the police was true, and all that did was add to the animosity. I wondered what he would look like by the time he was let out of the police van.

It was four in the morning by the time we got to bed, but I slept the sleep of the righteous for the first time in days.

I had to remember to give Love a treat.

twenty

THE PHONE WOKE ME
about eleven o'clock. It was D.K.

"Thanks for everything, dude. I'm gettin' to think I might
have a life again."

"Good luck, my friend," I said, half in a doze. "I hope you
find Sophie in reasonable shape. Keep in touch. I'll do
anything I can to help you two. And give my best to Deak."

"Will do. See ya."

I leaped out of bed before I had a chance to fall back to
sleep, showered quickly, and made a plane reservation for
the next day. I headed upstairs, hoping to find some coffee.

There was a full pot of coffee, and a note from Lois:

Dear Lenny:
I am in the office. Didn't get much sleep, but I've got
a nifty exclusive. Eyewitness, first-person journalism.
Pulitzer committee, please copy. Maybe my editor isn't
such an asshole after all. Nah. Call me.

Lois had signed it with a huge letter "L," replete with
flourishes. Who said that it's an ill wind that blows no good?
For that matter, who said that an oboe is an ill wind that no
one blows good?

I must be relaxing, I thought, I'm getting stupid again.

I rummaged for breakfast food and found some awful and healthy cereal. It tasted like leaf mulch, so it must have been healthy.

After feeding the machine, I called Lois.

"Yo, Lo, whaddaya know?"

"My, aren't you chipper this morning?"

"Well, a little life-threatening exercise before bed does wonders for me. I presume that Augean Stabile has moved up to suspect number one with a bullet? No pun intended."

"None taken. Yeah, it seems that he has no—I repeat, no—alibi for either killing. The result of a lifetime of pissing people off. He's alone and virtually friendless."

"Unless you count a pal like B.B. Wolfe."

"Like I said."

"Listen, Lois, I made a plane reservation for tomorrow morning. It's time for me to ride off into the sunrise."

"Want me to drive you to the airport?"

"I couldn't think of anything nicer."

"So what do you think of Portland, other than murder and mayhem?"

"Ah, food is fair, except for the deli stuff; people are mellow to a fault; getting behind the wheel of a car seems to cause a trance-like stupor in the local drivers; weather is not as bad as expected; good to see the counterculture hanging on like grim death. I'm happier knowing that the old hippies have come to a nice place to die."

"Yow! Is it that bad?"

"Hey, it's not bad, so much as not *there* enough. New York is the only place in America where evolution is still going on, based on survival of the fittest. It's too easy here. You may remember, in New York, 'Blow me!' is considered civilized conversation."

"And you still like that?"

"I don't know anything else. If I'm ever ready to give it up, now doesn't feel like the time."

"You need to come back here in the summer."

"Yeah," I sighed, "that's what Molly told me. Maybe I will."

"You'll always have a place to stay."

"Thanks, Lois. I love you. I wish I had someone like you back home."

"You mean a gender-confused neurotic with no life outside the office and a clotheshorse habit?"

"Who could ask for anything more?"

"See you later."

We said aloha and rang off. I called Molly.

"I was just on my way out," she said breathlessly. "What's up?"

"Uh, well, I'm leaving tomorrow for home. If we get together again, it'll have to be today or tonight."

"Oh, God, Lenny, real life has intruded on our blissful pairing. My ex is giving me a hard time about the kids, and I'm trying to squeeze more child support out of the shithead. I'm off to see my lawyer now, and I have to see the ex tonight. I'm really sorry."

I sighed, for real. "I'm sorry, too. But I'd just fall in love with you, and then where would I be?"

"Come back in the summer. Can I call you?"

I gave her my number, and kissed the phone. Most unsatisfying. I called Bruno and arranged to have him pick me up at the airport.

So, said I to myself, what to do? I have another day in Portland, it will not be spent doing the juicy with Molly, and all the loose ends seem to be nearly caught up.

I got my coat and went out into the early-afternoon damp. The paper mill smell lingered in the air, trapped by the wetness.

I got in the car and went up Hawthorne Boulevard. I parked and killed time in the string of used book and record stores, and the odd antique store. I found a couple of gems.

I got a used CD of Shorty Rogers's big band, including all the tunes on a scratched, old 10″ LP I'd had for years. And a used CD of The Incredible String Band's second LP, a relic of the psychedelic era that got me through more than one scary acid trip. Amazing what's on CD these days.

I got hungry, went into an Irish pub, and had a very creditable fish-and-chips and a pint of Guinness. I was at odds here in Portland, with no one to show me around, no tasks needing doing, and I was mentally halfway back to New York in any case.

So I ordered another pint and took stock.

Walter was probably in the clear, although I was still uncomfortable with his alibis. I guessed that it didn't matter much anymore. Stabile knew about the bayonet, knew Walter had it, had gotten into the house when he wanted to, hated Strunz, and had a history with him, to boot. Bella Durke didn't exactly fit in, but she had pissed off so many people in her time, who knew what could have gone on between Stabile and her?

So case closed. Right? It was all circumstantial, true, but so was the case against Walter, and this had more substance.

I finished the second pint and went straight back to the house. No sense doing any more driving with two pints of stout under my belt. When I got back, I put on the Shorty Rogers stuff and stretched out on the couch. I must have dozed off, because I was snapped back by a wet and muddy fifteen-pound cat jumping on my belly. I could push him off, or I could deal with it. Since I owed him one, I dealt with it. He made a big warm spot on me, which I liked, and stank of wet fur, which I liked less. He purred and nuzzled me. It occurred to me that no one seemed to pay much attention to him except when he was being fed. He just wanted some loving.

We fell asleep.

Some time later, we were awakened by Lois's voice saying, "My, isn't this the picture of bliss? Just a boy and his cat, and nothing to come between them but some mud."

I opened my eyes, yawned, smiled, and stretched.

"Hey, hi there. What time is it?"

"About four. I split early. My editor was thrilled with

developments, ecstatic about my story, and clearing space
for the Pulitzer. Jerk. Anyway, I got us some steaks, and
some salmon for Frieda, and a couple bottles of California
pinot noir. Celebration time!"

I moved slightly, causing Love to wake up, yawn, stretch,
and head off for parts unknown. I got up.

"Need any help, Lois?"

"Nope, it's all on me, and I'm happy to do it. Relax, open
the wine if you want to."

So I sat down with a glass of wine and watched Lois
move around the kitchen with liquid grace. I wondered if
she ever looked bad doing anything. When I was fourteen or
so, I would worship my adolescent goddesses from afar, as
they seemed completely unattainable to me. I couldn't
imagine the really beautiful ones doing anything like, say,
sitting on the crapper. Presumably, angels came with golden
buckets and removed the offending matter to spare these
girls the indignity of a bowel movement.

Needless to say, I know better now. Yet someone like
Lois would revive these feelings in me. I hoped that
whoever was lucky enough to get close to her, of whatever
sex, appreciated her like I did.

Frieda came in, rain gear dripping.

"I can't believe you actually went to work today," I
exclaimed.

She laughed. "Someone's gotta bring in the money.
Walter's let his work go to hell lately, and it'll be a while
before he gets rolling again. We don't need much, but even
we can't live on nothing."

"Well," Lois interjected, "I bought some steaks for us red
meat eaters, some nice salmon for you, and we're celebrat-
ing tonight."

"Yes, Frieda," I said archly, "and you have something to
celebrate. I'll be gone tomorrow morning."

She gave me a completely unreadable look. "I'm going
upstairs to change." She turned and went.

"Odd one, she is," I mused.

"Tell me about it," Lois responded. "I'm seriously thinking that it's time for me to get my own place. Frankly, she's a big part of it."

"It's none of my business, of course, but I'm glad you're thinking of it. I hope that the thought is father to the deed. She's like Lady Macbeth on a bicycle."

We both had an evil laugh over that one, and I poured us some more wine. Shortly thereafter, Walter came down, looking more himself than I'd seen in some time.

Dinner was easy. We didn't even speak of the recent unpleasantness. Lois went up early, I volunteered to do the dishes, and Walter and Frieda remained while I worked.

When I finished, I said, "Walter, I'm gone tomorrow. Thanks for everything. I'm very glad that things are working out, and I'm happy that you've found someone like Frieda who'll stand by you when the game gets rough. I'm going back to New York City, I do believe I've had enough." Frieda pulled that same face she gave me before.

"Lenny, I'll always be grateful to you. We haven't talked money. How much for your time and effort?"

"Consider it a no-charge, for old times' sake."

"You're all right."

He got up, and we hugged.

"Good-bye, Frieda. You may be gone when I leave tomorrow, so now's my chance to say good-bye."

Frieda stood up and gave me a cold fish handshake. "Have a good trip home."

"Thanks." I went downstairs, got into bed, soon to be joined by the cat. I fell asleep scratching his ears.

twenty-one

I AWOKE BEFORE DAWN, nervous as usual on a travel day. Love was off somewhere. I turned on the NPR news and caught a few amusing stories of Republican machinations in the Congress. They were apparently frustrated by the President's outmaneuvering them using their own tactics, and stealing their agenda. I laughed, until I realized that they were getting big chunks of their agenda enacted, only with no credit to them. The bottom line was no comfort to me: a Republican agenda. I thought I had voted for a Democrat. Silly me.

I showered, and put on absolutely my last clean clothes. I had a whole suitcase full of dirty laundry. I also had something in the pit of my belly I couldn't get rid of, a kind of unease.

Not like from bad seafood, or anything like that. Rather a feeling that not all was right somehow. I couldn't quite get my brain around it. I decided to ignore it.

I packed up my dirty clothes and stripped the bed. I like being a good guest. I went upstairs, suitcase in hand, and found Lois making coffee.

"Ah, what an angel you are."

"Fuckin'-A," she said, as she poured the water through the

cone and filter, and the brown nectar began streaming into the pot.

"What time is your flight?"

"Nine-something, 9:45 I think."

"We need to be there about—what? Forty-five minutes ahead of time?"

"Are you kidding? Is that all?"

"Yeah. It's still a nice little airport here."

"Cool. Can we go out for breakfast?"

She looked hurt. "You mean you don't want my famous jalapeno-and-onion omelette?"

"No, no. *Au contraire*. I wasn't aware that it was an option."

"Good. Spicy, or mild?"

"Spicy."

"Excellent choice. Whole wheat toast, toasted bagel, or English muffin?"

"Jeez, uh, toasted bagel?"

"Good. Sit down and I'll get you a cup of coffee."

"If I'd known that I was gonna get this kind of treatment, I would have left a couple of times."

"Now, now, mustn't be a piggy. This is special because it's special, you dig?"

"Twenty-three skiddoo, hepcat." In the morning when the sun comes up, she brings me coffee in my favorite cup.

I sipped the hot java and watched her work. In a few minutes, she placed before me a royal repast: a steaming omelette, cheese running out the sides, topped with salsa, and accompanied by a perfectly toasted onion bagel and fried potatoes. Take me now, Lord, right after breakfast. I tucked in. It was really good.

"It's nice to see you enjoying that. Love rejected what I gave him this morning. It sits there on his plate, uneaten. I might as well chuck it out."

"Believe me, you won't have two uneaten offerings this morning."

She whipped up an omelette for herself, no potatoes,

whole wheat toast. We made chitchat and started to get ourselves together for the trip to the airport. We jumped in her car and set out.

On the way, we made deeply felt promises to stay in touch. I meant to keep them. If she decided she was straight, someday, I wanted to be there.

We pulled up to the Departures area of the terminal, and I got out. She opened the trunk where I had stashed my bag. I removed it, and we stood facing each other.

"Lois, I honest-to-God will miss you. You're gutsy and smart, and you ain't bad on the eyes. No matter what, I'll never forget you."

"Lenny, I feel the same. You're a good man, and there's not much in the way of bullshit about you. I'll remember you, too."

She reached for me, put her arms around my neck, and hugged me tight, putting a warm, sweet kiss on my lips. I hugged her back, feeling that lithe body fit against mine. We broke just in time, as Mr. Schwanz was beginning to rear his head.

"Gee," she said, "I must be losing my touch. I expected you to get a woody."

I laughed so loud that everyone for twenty feet around looked at me. "Have no fear," I finally managed, "woody's here."

"So long, Lenny. Call me."

Another quick kiss, and she was gone.

I went to check in, and that thing started gnawing at me again. I tried to put it out of my mind. I got a seat assignment, and my bag got loaded on the conveyer. I walked toward my gate.

I thought about Molly, and how I never asked her her last name. I thought about the fact that my life may have been saved by a cat. I thought about Love, and how I really wanted to change his name. Weird cat, a lot of quirks. None of my cats were ever so finicky about what they ate, and I only fed them twice a day. I would never indulge them by feeding them different things until they were satisfied. If they left it, they went hungry, and . . . suddenly that thing that was rolling in the pit of my stomach, that thing that was bothering me, it slid into place like Jackie Robinson stealing home.

I turned and ran out of the terminal, and hailed the first cab I could find. I gave him Walter's address, and fidgeted all the way back into town. When we got to the house, I tipped the guy too much, and ran to the front door. I realized that I had never returned the key, and that made it all the more easy.

I let myself in. Frieda's bike was gone. Good. I quietly went up the stairs to Walter's room. I could hear music playing, Walter singing vaguely along, like you do when you're distracted and no one's around. It was "Something in the Air," by Thunderclap Newman.

Walter was polishing his knife collection. He had a stiletto in his hand, rubbing it with a cloth soaked in some kind of pink liquid polish. He was oblivious, and I was able to get right up to his door.

". . . and you know that it's right," he was singing, "and you know that it's right."

"I know what's right, pal." He jumped straight up, almost throwing the knife away. "I know that you killed Bella Durke, and I'm guessing that you did Strunz in also, because the weapon was the same."

"Lenny! What the fuck? Aren't you supposed to be on a plane?"

"Yeah, but something occurred to me. The night of the party, the night Durke got killed, I came back early, and I fed Love. He rejected it, and I left it, thinking that he would eat it later. Sure enough, it was gone later, but not because he ate it, because someone gave him something else to eat more to his liking, and *that's* what he ate."

"What are you talking about? Are you crazy?"

"No, Walter, just a bit slow. You—or Frieda, but I'm betting it was you—came back and got the bayonet, went

over to the station, killed Durke, and got back to the party
before anyone really missed you. Only, when you got here,
the cat demanded to be fed, and you had to do it. You knew
I was here, and you didn't want the cat to bring me upstairs.

"The party was a great cover. It was a big house, lots of
rooms, people moving in and out, going for beer. Your alibi
was a little light for about half an hour, but in a party like
that I felt it was normal for someone not to be seen for a
while, especially when so few witnesses would cooperate
with me.

"The reason I think it was you, Frieda is just too small to
kill Bella Durke with that bayonet. She's wiry, but Bella was
awful big. And Strunz was nailed to that bench with the
bayonet. She couldn't do it. You have the physical strength
to do it, and you had the rage. Right so far?"

"You're Sam Spade, all right. You got me, shamus. Yeah,
it was me who got the bayonet, and who fed the cat. I killed
Durke, stashed the weapon, and went back to the party. I
caught her by surprise, so she wasn't able to grab me. She
was pretty slow, anyhow. No one missed me at the party. No
one gave a shit. Frieda told them I went to get a beer, or to
take a leak, or whatever."

"How did you work the movie?"

"We went to the movie house, bought beers to establish
our presence, and watched the flick. I went to the john, and
slipped out the back door. I just never came back. I waited
outside in the car until the movie was over, and joined
Frieda on the street talking about the movie. It wasn't
perfect, but it could have come off."

"What about Stabile?"

"Lucky break. I did rat him out to the cops, and they
hated him, so they went and leaned on him a bit. I just
wanted to bust his balls, give the cops someone else to
bother. I didn't realize that it would work out as well as it
did."

"It worked out so well that he could have killed you."

"Yeah, but he didn't. Thanks to the cat. And you, of course."

"Why? What for?"

"Why did I kill those miserable shits? It was as much Frieda's idea as mine. Look at it this way: I came out here trying to escape all the bad things in my life. When I got out here, I discovered KOOK. It satisfied a lot of needs, as a creative outlet, as a source for friends of similar point of view, as ego jollies, and it allowed me to think that I was back in the struggle, the one I had abandoned in the early seventies, because of the shallow, brainless dorks that got into the movement late.

"When I got into station politics, I discovered that most of the people there were head cases who were working out their loony tunes by making them into politics. They were a bunch of losers who were mad at the world, never did anything right, never had a good job, never will. So they blame the system, capitalism, or the banks, or the polluters, or Christ knows what all, anything except themselves, 'cause if they blame themselves they'll have to acknowledge that they're pathetic fuckups. And, if they did that, they'd have to blow their brains out."

"Ouch, Walter, aren't there any serious, dedicated progressives there? They can't all be like that."

"Yeah, okay, a few. But the worst cases, the man-haters like that fat dyke, or the psychos like Strunz, for some reason they had to jump in my shit specially. You know, I've spent a lot of my life trying to be a good person, and these scumbags called me things . . ."

"Come on, Walter. Being harassed by a couple of people you really had no use or respect for is no excuse for cold-blooded murder. When we were kids in New York we endured worse insults from ten-year-olds. Shit, we *gave* worse than we got. When did you become so sensitive?"

He seemed to think about it. "Maybe since I got here. I don't know, it's something in the air, like the paper mill, or the rain, or the bullshit we dispense at KOOK. I just brooded about it; Frieda's the one who made me really crazy. She's really the one who planned this. Don't get me wrong, I'm not trying to shift the blame. I could have said no at any time, but, once the decision was made, Frieda became the general."

"Did you have anything to do with the attempted slashing at the radio station?"

"You mean Carl Gibbon?"

"Yeah, I guess that's the name."

He smiled. "Well, that was actually Frieda. She made such a mess of it, she decided to stay on the planning side. If you hadn't got us, Gibbon might have been next. The son of a bitch has it coming. I lied about Stabile's van, of course."

"'Lady Macbeth on a bicycle,'" I said to myself.

"What?"

"Nothing. Look, Walter, I'm gonna have to call the heat. As bad as Stabile is, he's innocent."

Walter looked down at the knife, and I got nervous, so nervous that my leg jerked and kicked Walter hard enough in the kneecap that he almost fainted. He dropped the knife and slid to the floor in agony.

"Sorry about that. I didn't want to trouble Frieda to come up with another bullshit story."

After a few minutes, he regained himself.

"Lenny, do me a favor?"

"Walter, do I owe you a favor?"

"No, but do it anyway. Take Love. He likes you, and Frieda and I aren't gonna be around to feed him. I don't want him gassed at the pound."

"Oh, man, I don't know," I whined.

"Take him, goddammit! There's a cat carrier in the next room. I'll pay for a seat on the plane so he doesn't have to go in the baggage compartment."

"Oh, fuck it. Okay."

"Thanks, man."

"Can I change his name?"

"What's the matter with his name?"

"It sucks desperately. It doesn't fit him. He should be Spike, or Killer. No offense."

"Change his name. I don't give a shit."

I apologized to Walter, and tied him up. I didn't want the son of a bitch sneaking up on me with an assegai, or some other cutlery.

I called Lois, and after a moment of shocked silence, she thanked me, and gave me the number of her cop friend Chauncy. I called Chauncy and told him the story. He swore interestingly for a while, thanked me in his fashion, and hung up. I called Bruno and told him not to go to the airport until I called him back with a new flight time. I called the airline and told them to hold my luggage.

I found the cat carrier, cleaned it up, threw a bunch of cat food in a gym bag, and looked for Love in all the wrong places. When he actually showed up, curious about the cop cars, I picked him up and told him that I was his new daddy, so he bit me. I stuffed him in the cat carrier and called a cab.

twenty-two

THE FLIGHT HOME WAS uneventful, except for the growling and other disturbing noises emanating from Love's carrier. One of the flight attendants actually came over to ask me if I was carrying a dangerous animal in violation of airline rules. I told her it was a house cat, for Pete's sake, and he was dangerous only if you were a chickadee or a rodent. I didn't mention the knife-wielding loony part. She insisted on looking in the thing anyway.

"My, he's a big one." She was impressed.

"Yeah, and he's being moved from Portland to New York, so he's not happy."

"I've got some shrimp in the cooler left over from the last flight. Think he might like it?"

"It might ease the pain of transition. At least it'll keep him quiet while he eats it."

She returned in a minute with a big plate of nice-sized shrimp, covered with a towel. "Here. Don't let the other passengers see if you can help it. We've got fettuccine for lunch."

I slipped the shrimp in one at a time, with an interval of a few minutes between each one. The cat scarfed them, with nice little satisfied noises, and took the bargain. He curled up and slept for the rest of the flight.

It would take me a while to process what had happened in Portland. Not so much with Sophie Kimmel, although that was rather amazing itself. I thought more about Walter, his disillusionment, and its consequences. For good or not, I wasn't that angry anymore. Maybe it was because he hung out with political types. I associated with petty crooks, small-time grifters, lowlifes, and hoodlums; it appeared to have worked out to my advantage.

My own Leftie sympathies weren't what they used to be, perhaps as a consequence of getting older, or a drifting from the Left community. I do remember growing tired of the constant, "purer than thou" arguments, the factionalization even within factions.

When I was young, I was fascinated by Leon Trotsky, more for his romantic image, and his literary gifts, and that he was Jewish, than anything else. I knew that Stalin was bad, and that he had Trotsky assassinated, which only added to Trotsky's mystique for me. When I got involved in New Left causes, I was encouraged that the old factionalism that destroyed the Left seemed to be absent. It was supposed to be the best time since the United Front, but it proved to be just as illusory. My wearing a button that said "Trotsky" got me in trouble with the purists, who never go away. And times had not improved. Walter, who became the thing he hated most, the ultimate purger of his adversaries, may only have been acting out what others felt. The only difference between him and Stalin was one of scale.

Granted, that's a big difference, but I wonder if he and Frieda would have stopped at two. Thankfully, we'll never know.

I ordered a Bloody Mary from the flight attendant. She sat with me and talked for a while, while Love lay sleeping.

twenty-three

BRUNO WAS WAITING FOR me when I arrived, a clear spot six feet in radius around him even in the crowded waiting area. He looked askance at the animal carrier.

"What's in dere?"

"Cat. It belonged to my friend, but they don't allow cats in Oregon State Penitentiary."

Bruno smiled. "You got da same kind of friends everywhere."

"Not really. I'll fill you in on the drive home. Anything on my luggage?"

"Airline says your bag is enjoying da weather in Puerto Rico right now. Don't expect no postcard."

"Good thing there's nothing in it but dirty laundry."

"Dat's why nobody stoled it."

We drove into Manhattan, and I told Bruno the whole grim story. I thanked him for the heel of the hand into the nose maneuver.

"Yeah, always go for da nose first. It hurts like hell and bleeds a lot. Takes da starch outta most guys right off."

"Have you heard from Weezil?"

Bruno's face fell. "It ain't good. I seen him yesterday. He

got dem blotches on his face, purply things, whaddaya call
'em?"

"Kaposi's sarcoma?"

"Yeah, dat's it. He's in da hospital for some tests now, but
Lam ain't takin' it so good. It's enough to make you cry. I
used to bitch about a dose of clap."

"Yeah, I know what you mean."

Bruno parked illegally on Sixth Avenue and left a police
courtesy card prominently in view on his dashboard. It said
he was a clergyman on a visit. The First Church of the
Bruiser, Rev. Bruno, pastor. I asked Bruno what was up, but
he wouldn't say.

"Hey, Bruno, what's your last name? I've known you for
years, and I have no idea what your last name is."

"How 'bout that?"

We walked through the evening chill to Yvonne and
Arletta's apartment. When we got in, Uncle Sol and the two
women were playing pinochle, drinking wine, and generally
having hysterics.

"*Boychik!*" yelled Sol. "Welcome back."

"So, you solved the world's problems in Seattle?" Yvonne
asked as I kissed her on the cheek.

"Portland," I replied as I kissed Arletta.

"Seattle, Portland—west of the Hudson River it's all
Iowa to me."

"You used to pay attention when Woody Guthrie told us
about the Columbia River. You must be getting senile,"
Arletta snapped. She was probably still pissed off about
something.

"So, what's new?" I tried to change the subject.

Sol gave me a look. "Mickey's new beau is going back
with the wife. Her salsa musician dumped her for a chickie,
so she called the husband. A real soap opera, no?"

I groaned. Lord knows what kind of mood she'd be in. I
just hoped that she wouldn't exact revenge on me.

Bruno was talking quietly to someone on the phone. He

hung up and came over. "Let's go. You can see dese old farts anytime. I got places to be."

Yvonne piped up, "Hey, keep that little snip off our cases!"

"You mean Sue?" I asked.

"Who else, Eva Perón? She's makin' us all nuts with her health food. Take her out and force-feed her a cheeseburger."

"I thought you and Arletta were into this kind of stuff. What's the problem?"

"The problem is that she's not just into it, she's the fuckin' Billy Graham of natural food! She wants to save your soul with herbs and bee pollen. We've been eating this shit for fifty years, and we ain't up to her standards. She brings us baskets of goodies, like we're Little Red Riding Hood's dyke grannies. Send *her* out to fuckin' Seattle!"

I was beginning to feel like I'd never left. I said my good-byes, and Bruno drove me home. Standing in front of my building was Sue, with a basket on her arm.

"Bruno, you bastard, did you call her just now?"

"Hey, just wanna welcome you back." He grinned.

"Up yours. I'm takin' my cat and leaving."

"What's his name?"

"I don't know. Any suggestions?"

"How about Jack da Bear, like da Ellington tune?"

"Not bad. He's big enough. Maybe Moose the Mooche, like the Charlie Parker tune."

"Dat'll work. Later."

I got the carrier, and the gym bag of food, and stepped away from the car. Bruno waved to Sue, and took off.

"Lenny, hello!" She gave me a big hug and kiss. It was nice. Then, she looked at the carrier. "What the hell do you have there?"

"Walter's cat. Let's go in, it's cold out here."

My apartment was warm, one of its few saving graces. I dumped everything and opened the carrier. A very wary cat emerged. He was not thrilled with the surroundings.

"Jeez, I gotta get a litter box. I'm not letting this cat out on the Lower East Side, he'll get killed. Take a walk with me."

We left the apartment, and Love began howling almost immediately. The pet store a few blocks away on Avenue A was closed, but I begged to be let in. I got a litter box, some litter, and a couple of cat bowls.

"Hey," I said to the clerk as we left, "how come you didn't tell me to have a nice day?"

"It's printed on the fuckin' receipt. Whaddaya want, blood?"

Ah, it was good to be home.

We raced back to the apartment, and set up the litter box. Love took one look at it and ran to the window, indicating that he wanted out.

"Not on your life, pal. You're an indoor cat from now on."

His face registered pure loathing. He jumped off the windowsill, ran over to my bed, and peed on my pillow.

"Holy shit, have it your way!" I opened the window, and he streaked out.

I sighed. "I'll never see him again. I don't think a Portland cat will last five minutes out there."

"Lenny, let's talk about your health," Sue said brightly.

"Can't this wait until tomorrow? I'm bushed. I'll tell you all about your former boyfriend, the murderer."

Her eyes got real big. "I always knew that little putz was capable of anything. Yeah, okay. I'll be here for breakfast, and I'll cook."

"I can't wait. See you then."

She split, and I had a beer, savoring each mouthful, because I wasn't sure it was on Sue's natural diet plan. I was rolling a skinny joint, when I heard a meow. The cat was on the window, asking to be let in.

I was amazed, and grateful. I let him in, opened a can of food, and he ate it up with no complaints. He must have been starving.

"Whatever your name is, I think we're gonna do just fine."

Just then, I heard the outside door buzzer. I went to the intercom. "Yeah?"

"You got a big orange cat?"

"Yeah, why?"

"He just killed my dog!"

It was good to be home.